Start Me Up

Start Me Up

Nicole Michaels

St. Martin's Paperbacks

This is a work of fiction. All of the characters, organizations, and events portrayed in this novel are either products of the author's imagination or are used fictitiously.

START ME UP

Copyright © 2015 by Nicole Michaels.

For information address St. Martin's Press, 175 Fifth Avenue, New York, NY 10010.

ISBN: 978-1-250-05815-7

Printed in the United States of America

St. Martin's Paperbacks edition / March 2015

St. Martin's Paperbacks are published by St. Martin's Press, 175 Fifth Avenue, New York, NY 10010.

10 9 8 7 6 5 4 3 2 1

To Michael, our love story will always be my favorite.

Acknowledgments

How exciting to finally have the opportunity to thank all the people who have helped get me to this point. First, my amazing agent Sarah E. Younger. Your unwavering support and dedication make me a very lucky writer. The entire NYLA team, you're all wonderful. My fabulous editor Lizzie Poteet, thank you for loving this story and making my dream a reality. Everyone at St. Martin's Press who had a hand in bringing this book to fruition, you're all fantastic.

Tracy McLaughlin, there are no words adequate enough to thank you for all of your constant encouragement, help, and reading. Love you to pieces.

Marsha Lytle, thank you for judging my horrible contest entry and inviting me to First Tuesdays. It changed everything. Natasha Hanova, Dawn Allen, and Leatrice McKinney: thank you for helping me take my writing to the next level. Your talents taught me so much, thank you.

Jennifer Kuhn for keeping me sane, laughing, and well caffeinated. *insert BFF and coffee cup emojis*

Dana Elmendorf, my OLBFF, it's so nice to have someone who understands the wonderful yet traumatic process of publication. Meredith Lockard, thank you for the impromptu Target celebration, I'll never forget that moment. Sabrina Ball, your encouragement and fabulous party skills inspired this book. Christina Holland, my early partner in romance reading . . . loved all those texts and book recommendations. All of my friends and photo clients who have been excited with me through this journey, I appreciate all of you more than you know!

To Naomi Shihab Nye, *whose amazing words will travel with me.* Your encouragement about my writing made me realize that I might have a real talent for stringing words together. You unknowingly changed my life.

My mom Denise and my sister Lauren for so many things I couldn't mention them all. I love you both. Linda for all the support and love, and all of my extended family for being wonderful.

Finally, Sean, Branden, and Blake, your patience with all the computer time is appreciated—you're the best kids ever and I'm so proud of each of you. I love you. Lastly, my own personal "Mike," literally. Thank you for making my dreams your own, and for loving me so much. You're my perfect.

One

The only way to improve a Saturday full of coffee, naps, and mindless television was to end it with a beer and a beautiful woman. Fortunately, for Mike Everett that was the plan. Right now the coffee was French roast and hot, and tonight the woman was blond and even hotter. The past few weeks had been filled with plenty of innocent, and not-so-innocent, flirting with his attractive neighbor. Last Saturday, however, at the dive bar near his auto shop and makeshift apartment, she'd hinted that getting laid was almost a foregone conclusion. And thank God because it had been a while.

Unfortunately, one sip into his second cup of coffee and the lounging part of the equation was derailed by a frantic call from his sister, Erin. Her husband was called out of town on business, and as usual she needed a favor. Despite years of trying, Mike had never been good at telling her no, which explained why thirty minutes later he was walking up to a small yellow bungalow hand in hand with his six-year-old niece Bailey.

The exterior was meticulously groomed with natural

stone pavers leading to the porch, and small pink flowers lining the path. Everything about the quaint house screamed *fairytale perfection*. Not really unusual for a small boutique town like Preston, Missouri, but still intimidating for a guy who currently resided in a space that was more than likely an extra-large storage room at one time. It was certainly convenient to live on site at his shop, but this did have the whole homey thing going for it.

A multicolored pennant banner was draped along the white porch railing while gigantic bouquets of pink and blue balloons bracketed the entryway. There was no way anyone would doubt this was where the party was.

"It's so pretty!" Bailey bounced beside him as they stepped up to the front door. "Don't you think, Uncle Mike?"

"Sure is, Boo." Truthfully, it seemed a little much for a kiddie birthday party, but what the hell did he know.

Beside the front door was an easel with a fancy hand-made chalkboard sign, again all pink and blue. Bailey read it out loud, slowly sounding out the words.

"The . . . parrrrty is . . . under . . . wwway, chhhoose your cost . . ." There was a long pause and Mike shifted the wrapped purple gift package to rest under his other arm and decided that his sister really needed to define what a "small" favor meant in her world. Lucky for her, Mike loved his niece more than anything else on earth, so he tried to ignore his agitation, and the ruin of his plans to squeeze a nap in before his date with Katie.

"Choose your costu—" He tried to help, thinking about the worn couch in his office that was calling his name.

"Don't help me, Uncle Mike. Mommy always lets me read." A tiny fist rested on her hip. She was so like her mother with that quick temper.

He couldn't help but smile. "Sorry, Boo, you were doing great."

"Chooose your costume . . . so you . . . can stay." Bailey turned and grinned up at Mike. He returned her enthusiasm, allowing his pride to show on his face. She was his favorite person these days, and that sweet face could make him do nearly anything. Apparently that included digging through a trunk under the chalkboard that was filled with pink, pink, and glittery pink accessories. Glasses, tiaras, feathers, and tutus spilled onto the welcome mat as he helped her make a dress-up selection.

Just as he put the finishing touch on Bailey—a ridiculously large pink beaded necklace—the front door swung open and a mixture of screams and giggles flowed from around the back of the house.

"Bailey!" Another tiny female launched herself into his niece's arms, her blond hair twisted into tiny knots on each side of her head. She pulled back and snatched the gift from Mike's fingers. "Ooh, my present."

Kids.

"I'm so sorry. She's a little overexcited," a smooth female voice said as his niece was dragged inside.

Mike looked up and froze, his eyes widening as he took in the gorgeous blonde in the doorway. It hadn't occurred to him there might be an attractive female at this birthday party, but he certainly wasn't going to complain. Her welcoming smile faltered a little, her eyes darting around awkwardly near his feet. It was then that he realized he was standing there staring like an idiot with a pink boa draped around his ankle. He leaned down to grab it and toss it in the trunk as she spoke again.

"Would you like to come in?" she asked. He could tell she held back a laugh by the way she bit at her lip.

He hesitated. What would happen if he did? His sister had just asked him to drop Bailey off. In fact, he recalled her specifically saying there was no need to stay. But suddenly he *wanted* to stay just a little longer. Just for a minute. He had to admit the incredibly pink atmosphere and tiny feminine squeals coming from the back of the house were a powerful man repellent, but *she* most certainly was not.

"I mean, you don't have to. You can just come back at three." She obviously sensed his hesitation and began to step back into the house. His arm reached out instinctively to the wooden frame, signaling her not to close the door.

"Maybe, just for a second. Make sure Bailey's okay," he said. Her expression called bullshit. You only had to be around Bailey for half a second to know she'd never met a stranger or been in a situation she couldn't manage, much to her overprotective uncle's chagrin.

"Okay, well, come on in. You're very brave. A couple of other dads practically ran." She laughed, and the sound was so genuine and sexy. He couldn't recall being so turned on by just a laugh, but hers was—simply *perfect*.

He entered the house and was instantly met with a familiar floral smell. He wasn't sure if it was a candle or just the natural scent of her home. Two plush couches were loaded with enough brightly colored blue and red pillows to stack all the way to the ceiling. Shit, he wouldn't mind taking a nap right here, but no, the beautiful woman in the room was more appealing, and as she led him through the house he admired every inch of her.

She was curvy—her hips were full and her ass round. A body that most women would stupidly think needed improvement, but guys thought was just right. She turned to face him in the kitchen as she said something about what the dads who'd left would be missing and he nodded in agreement while he tried not to be too obvious about checking her out.

Her pink dress was snug around her shapely chest, with a white flower pinned over her left breast. Was it a corsage, like you'd wear to a prom? Or just a piece of jewelry? He didn't understand, but he also didn't care because it drew his eyes right to her cleavage. Her legs were endless and bronzy, and her pink sandals were once again adorned with flowers. Good God, what was with the flowers and why did he suddenly find them so hot? She grabbed something off the table and he spotted yet another bloom on the smooth ponytail at the back of her head, nothing out of place, no detail forgotten. And then suddenly it occurred to him what she'd just said and what she must be assuming.

"Oh, I'm not Bailey's father. I'm Uncle Mike." And he was officially an idiot. *Uncle Mike?* Oh well, he was no doubt two seconds away from being introduced to her Ken doll husband who probably drove a foreign car, liked sushi, and was the ideal father. Did he look like he'd just been imagining her wearing nothing but flowers? He needed to pull his thoughts out of the gutter.

"I'm sorry. I just assumed. Well, it's nice to meet you. I'm Anne Edmond, Claire's mother, obviously." She opened the screen door that led to the backyard then stopped to look over her shoulder. Her lips quirked and her eyes were a sparkly blue this close up. His gaze dropped to her lips as she spoke, her words leaving parts of his body in a state that just might cause a problem. Then her voice dropped into a conspiratorial whisper that he was sure she hadn't intended to be hot as hell, yet it was. "You better brace yourself for this, *Uncle Mike*."

He stepped onto the patio and into a little girl's dream come true, which thankfully proved an instant cure for the rising problem in his jeans. He now knew exactly why the other dads ran. The backyard was meticulously landscaped, which he could appreciate, but the party decor was so over the top he didn't know where to start. Every direction he turned he encountered an explosion of crafty shit; his eyes had trouble focusing on one thing.

Giant pink and blue paper flowers hung down from the wooden pergola above the patio. An antique wagon was painted white and held all the gifts, the trees in the yard were strung with tiny pink lights, and even the grass was dotted with striped pinwheels. Everything coordinated and looked like it was handmade just for this day.

Pink and blue cupcakes stood on various cake stands on the food table, colorful candies filled bowls, and little zigzag-painted bags that were decorated with all the guests' names sat off to the side in an oversized tin bucket. Seriously? He'd been to weddings that weren't this over the top.

The little girls were taking turns batting with a stick at a flower piñata in the yard, and a loud *whack* pulled him from his fog. He stopped gawking long enough to notice the group of four women staring at him from the grass near the patio. They were obviously the other moms. Shit. Why had he chosen to stay again? Everything about this situation was out of his element. Was it too late to run?

A finger tapped him on the shoulder. "Here ya go, you can have a *grown-up* drink."

Anne said it with a wink, which made him think a lot of *grown-up* thoughts until he glanced down at her outstretched hand and the . . . jar drink? The kind of jar that his grandmother would have filled with pickles, okra, or tomato sauce, but this one was filled with a bright-pink beverage and a blue-and-white-striped straw. Jesus, what the hell was he doing here?

Apparently he was going to drink pink lemonade from a jar, because she was waiting. He gently pushed the straw to the side. "Not really a straw guy."

"Oh . . . of course."

He lifted the jar to his lips, his eyes on her, her eyes on his mouth, which made him wish he'd picked up a razor this morning. The drink tasted decent, a little sweet for his taste, but standing here with her was worth sipping a girlie beverage. He smiled. "It's good. Thank you."

"There's just a touch of champagne in there. It is a children's party, of course, but I like the parents to enjoy themselves, too."

"I'm impressed. You think of everything." He meant it: This was quite a party.

She looked pleased with herself and placed a hand on his biceps. The innocent yet forward gesture surprised

him. Glancing down, he noticed her nails were also manicured pink with blue tips—the same shades as all the
decorations—and her hand was warm on his exposed
skin. He instinctively flexed and then felt like the biggest douchebag. She began to pull him toward the group
of women. Talking to the mommies wasn't exactly what
he wished to do, but as long as her hand was on him he
was following. He needed to think of something to say,
a distraction.

"Your nails are pink and blue. They match. Nice
touch."

"Oh, actually everything is raspberry and aqua,
but—" She stopped and removed her hand from his arm.
"Oh gosh, I'm sure you think I'm ridiculous, but this is
kind of . . . I don't know, *my thing*."

She shrugged and tilted her head with a brilliant smile.
The kind of smile that would make a man take up an
interest in whatever hobby she was into. He grinned at
her, glancing again at her amazing full lips. "No, you're
not ridiculous. I kind of like . . . *your thing*."

God, he was a total asshole. He was hitting on a
mother and wife in her expertly decorated backyard at
her daughter's birthday party, and the heat he saw in her
eyes verified that she wasn't completely uninterested. He
should leave, but the look on her face made his body
respond, tensing from head to toe. She didn't seem to be
offended at all. Mike had done a lot of things he wasn't
proud of in his life, but home wrecking wasn't on the
list. He needed to down this fruity drink, get the hell
out of here, and not return until the clock hit three like
Erin originally suggested. He'd heard enough stories

about bored suburban housewives, and becoming someone's piece on the side was not his style.

"I'll introduce you to everybody." She didn't give him
a chance to decline the offer so he walked with her over
to the group of women, who were obviously very curious about the conversation they'd just tried to appear not
to notice. If he knew anything about females, they hadn't
missed a thing.

Anne introduced him to the four women and pointed
out what child belonged to whom. There was no way he
would remember the information and he honestly didn't
care. He couldn't stop staring at Anne as she spoke and
laughed with the other women, her large blue eyes sparkling.

She was gorgeous; everything about her seemed so
effortless and graceful. She made mother and wife look
like something he wanted to have in his life. An interesting epiphany for a twenty-nine-year old bachelor
who'd planned on getting married *someday*, but as of
yet hadn't given it any serious thought. Usually his next
beer, next restoration job, and next lay were the only
items on his immediate agenda. But she made the whole
white-picket-fence thing seem like it was what made life
worth living.

How nice would it be to lie on a couch with matching pillows instead of ones that smelled like spilled beer?
Anne's house was warm and cozy, made for napping and
all sorts of feel-good activities. He had married friends,
and they seemed happy enough—but until now he'd
never envied them. Anne was Betty Crocker, Martha
Stewart, and *Playboy* Playmate wrapped up in striped

aqua paper with a raspberry flower pinned on top. What man wouldn't find that appealing?

All these thoughts floated through his mind as he absently watched an overwhelming number of girlie toys opened, games played, and pink and blue cupcakes eaten. He even managed to avoid several awkward conversations with the nosy moms. He tried to shut out their voices as they gossiped about teachers, PTO, and how beautiful Anne's "tablescape" was. What the hell did that even mean? Were they talking about the table or the landscaping?

It wasn't until he checked his watch and it was two fifteen that he realized it didn't make sense to leave and come back. Plus watching Bailey laugh and have fun made him happy, although hearing the "awwws" from the women every time she called for "Uncle Mike" was getting a little annoying.

It also ticked him off that when Anne escaped to the kitchen to get a trash bag for the pile of wrapping paper and paper plates, the other women began to talk—about her.

"I swear to God, I don't know how she does it. I mean, she stenciled chevron onto the goodie bags. I'm lucky if I get a cake ordered from the grocery store." The offending woman took a long drink from her grown-up jar as nods of agreement erupted from the other ladies.

"If Ellen thinks she's getting a party like this, she's crazy," said another woman. "Have you seen some of the pictures on Anne's website? It's ridiculous what people are willing to pay her for."

"Right?" the first mom said again. "I mean, I pin

things like this all day long, but I know I'll never actually *do* any of it."

As far as Mike was concerned, these women were speaking a foreign language, and he was getting more than a little annoyed at their tone regarding Anne. Why? He had no clue, but they were just jealous bitches as far as he was concerned. He felt only respect and amazement when he looked around at what she'd done for her daughter, but he also wasn't a woman, and as every man knew, women could be a little crazy. One of the comments made him curious, probably too curious for his own good, but he wanted to know more. He found himself leaning into the woman closest to him. She must have sensed his presence and tilted her head toward him, a wide smile on her face.

"So Anne has a website?" he asked.

"Oh yeah." She turned fully, her eyes lighting up. "She has this amazing blog with two of her friends. *My Perfect Little Life*, where she highlights all these parties she does, and the other ladies post other stuff, too. I mean it's crazy creative stuff that the average person wants to do, but doesn't really have time for, you know what I mean?"

He didn't really know, but he nodded in agreement and fake enthusiasm. "That sounds interesting."

"Oh my gosh, it's totally interesting, you should . . . well, I don't know if a guy like you would like it, but you could find something cool for Bailey to do on there I'm sure."

He was trying to figure out what she meant by a guy like him, although he was pretty sure he knew, when

Anne came back outside with another woman, a cute little blonde wearing jeans and a pink T-shirt. She had her curly hair in a messy bun and her front was covered with flour and what he hoped was chocolate. When she walked closer he read her T-shirt. CALLIE'S CONFECTIONS. He was pretty sure he recognized the name from an awning down on Main Street.

The other moms immediately began singing praises about the cupcakes and cake pops to the woman, as if most of them hadn't been on the verge of real shit talk just moments before. Even the tone of their voices changed. Were all women capable of this complete 180? He'd heard of this kind of behavior, but witnessing it was nuts.

Suddenly something occurred to him as he glanced at Anne. Her left hand was lifted, her fingers lightly fidgeting with a beaded necklace that rested on her golden skin. Anne wasn't wearing a wedding ring. *Huh.* Now, that was interesting. The thought of her being . . . *available* made everything around him look different. The world shifted and all the pink and . . . no, all the *raspberry* and *aqua* seemed a lot more vibrant and interesting. Not to mention the guilt of potentially becoming a home wrecker lifting off his shoulders and bringing a lot of possibilities. She caught him staring and gave him a small smile before looking away. When was the last time just a woman's smile threatened to give him a hard-on?

He spotted a grill tucked away behind the party and he instantly pictured himself there and making Anne dinner, sitting outside on a beautiful evening in this backyard, a cold . . . *jar* in his hand. Shit, he needed to stop thinking. This woman and her *Better Homes and Gardens* lifestyle were really fucking with his brain. She was gorgeous, stylish, and instead of thinking about how sexy she'd look out of that dress, covered only in him, she had him considering a life that included more than a cold beer and a hot date, but a house that felt like a home, family. The way Anne made everything and everyone feel special—damn, it was hot as hell, and crazy appealing.

That thought sobered him and brought his fantasizing back into focus. He wasn't polished or fancy. He was dirty cars, facial hair, and longneck bottles. He was definitely not meant for little kids and parties with handcrafted goody bags. Hell, he was wearing one of his better T-shirts and nice jeans, yet he still felt out of place. This woman was a catch—that much was obvious—but she wasn't for someone like him.

As the party wrapped up, Mike excused himself from the table, on a mission to grab Bailey and leave, when all the little girls ran inside. He followed, just in time to catch sight of them running up the stairs. Well, he certainly wasn't going to follow her up into the personal living space. He walked back toward the kitchen and straight into Anne. They stopped in the narrow hallway between the living room and the kitchen, their bodies close. A light sheen of perspiration had built up on her cleavage and on her temples. He realized the floral smell wasn't only the home, it was also her.

"Hey, this was a really nice party, Anne. Bailey seemed to have a great time," he said.

"Thank you for bringing her. Bailey and Claire have become best friends this year at school. I think the party turned out well, too." She looked genuinely happy about his comment, which made him think of a few inappropriate things he'd like to thank her for. He took a deep breath and tried to resist his baser urges, the ones telling him to get closer . . . ask her out, say something to let her know he was into her.

No, he'd already decided that was not going to happen. Never mind the fact that his sister would kill him if while doing her a favor he ended up trying to hook up with one of the school moms. As if Anne was even the hookup type. No, she was definitely the making-love kind of woman. He expected her to rotate any second, put some space between them, but she shocked him by stepping slightly closer as she spoke.

"So, I . . . um, put some stuff in a box." He glanced down, and she was holding a pink pastry box with the Callie's Confection's logo on it. He raised an eyebrow, and she instantly looked embarrassed. "I mean, there were just *so many* cupcakes left . . . and Lord knows the last thing I need is more sweets in the house."

She bit her bottom lip and scrunched up her nose in the most adorable nervous tic he'd ever seen. He was pretty sure she was trying to flirt with him by giving him take-home treats. She wasn't offering any of the moms boxes to take home. At least he didn't think she was. In that moment he wanted to take the awkwardness away, assure her that flirting with him was not only welcome, but a complete turn-on.

"You're perfect. I think you should eat all the sweets you want." He edged closer, placing his fingers over hers on the box. The sharp hitch of her breath made him feel a little bolder and a lot like ignoring the part of his brain telling him this was not a good idea. She chewed again lightly at her lower lip, the sight of it sending inappropriate signals throughout his body. *Well, fuck it.* "And thank you, I'm sure what you're offering is . . . delicious," he murmured.

Her lips parted on a tiny gasp and he worried he had gone too far, misunderstood the gesture. Some women liked to feed the dude in the room. But then her expression softened. Her mouth slid into a little smile, relaxing his nerves along with it. She was so out of his league, and he didn't exactly fit the mold of ready-made stepdad. At least he hoped he didn't. So what really *was* her motivation? Maybe she was interested in a little fun.

"You know." Her head tipped to the side and her voice had gotten soft. "Claire and I were going to head to Settlers Park in about an hour . . . you are more than welcome to bring Bailey and meet us there. I mean since they're best friends . . ."

"Oh, Anne, I'd love to, but—" Shit, there was nothing more he would like to do than go to the park with Anne, which surprised him almost as much as her asking him to do it. But he had a date with Katie. He couldn't even bring himself to say it out loud. "I can't."

"Oh my gosh, I mean, of course. God, I'm so sorry, I don't even know why I asked . . ." She made the cute little scrunched face again, and it was killing him to see her uncomfortable. He didn't want Anne to regret being forward with him, hell it was amazing, but why did she have to suggest today of all days? "It's Saturday, you probably have . . . oh gosh, you would never want to go to the park. Never mind, the girls will see each other at school, and gymnastics class or . . . something."

"Uncle Mike has a hot date tonight. He told me." Bailey was jumping down the stairs above them, and each thud of her feet hitting the squeaky old wood matched the pounding of his heart as he watched the expression of understanding and then embarrassment on Anne's face.

"Well . . . good for you. How fun, it's such a beautiful day. It should be, umm, perfect for a date." Anne's words were excited and over-the-top happy, making this even harder and more uncomfortable.

"I'm sorry—" he started.

"Oh goodness, stop." She held a hand up to shush him and smiled. "No need for all that, let me just, um. Let me get Bailey's goodie bag and you guys can get outta here."

She walked away, her pink dress swishing around her legs. He caught her rubbing her temple, a gesture that implied she was upset or embarrassed, and it pissed him off that the situation had gone from flirty to awkward in a matter of seconds. It was only a hunch, but he would bet that Anne Edmond didn't make the first move often. She likely wouldn't be repeating it anytime soon after this.

Then again, maybe it didn't really bother her. Hell, it wasn't like she could possibly be looking for something serious, not with some random blue-collar guy that showed up at her daughter's birthday party. She probably felt safe flirting with him, testing the waters before she worked up to someone who was her equal, someone she would want to build a family with in this cute little house. It was really for the best. He had no business considering spending any more time with Anne because they were complete opposites and she needed the sushi-loving man who wore a tie. Mike was not that guy. No, he was the man that would get grease stains on her matching pillows. It wasn't a natural fit, not by a long shot, and he'd known it from the moment he laid eyes on her.

He had done his job, covered for Erin, played the parent for the day, and now it was time to go back to his very unpink, uncluttered, and unhomemade life. He had a date with Katie and he was pretty damn sure her hobbies were more of the carnal variety. Which was exactly what he needed in order to forget Anne Edmond.

Two

The last guest had finally left. Claire was upstairs going through her new loot, and Anne headed into the kitchen to find her best friend, Callie, at the giant farmhouse sink gently washing the vintage cake stands she'd used for the desserts. Thank goodness for friends who helped you clean up messes without having to be asked. Anne didn't know what she'd do without Callie and their other close friend Lindsey. Not only were those two women the creative geniuses who helped make their blog the success that it was, but they'd become critical to Anne's happiness. They were truly the best friends she'd ever had, and always willing to talk her off the edge if need be. Like now.

"Callie, I think I'm gonna throw up," Anne said, holding a hand to her stomach before plopping into a kitchen chair. It was time for the Spanx to come off and the yoga pants to go on. But first she needed to wallow in the embarrassment and humiliation she'd just endured due to her own stupidity.

"What's wrong?" Callie patted a milk-glass cake

stand with a towel. "Everything looked amazing, and holy shit that dad and his muscles were a hot addition to the festivities. Did you see his ass in those jeans? If you could include him in birthday packages, you'd be booked until the next millennium."

Anne held back a groan. Why did he stay? If he had just left, like every other normal guy, everything would have been fine. But he *had* stayed, even when she was pretty sure he hadn't planned on it, and that made her think that—that maybe he was interested. Interested in *her*. He'd made those comments about *her thing*—was she really so old and disconnected that she'd confused a harmless comment for innuendo? Surely she hadn't misunderstood the tone of his voice, because she could have sworn he was throwing out vibes. But that was crazy. She was thirty-two, a single mom, and on the wrong side of curvy.

"I did something really stupid. I don't even want to tell you about it." Anne dropped her head into her hands.

"Please tell me you finally told Kelly Hobbs that skinny jeans are not her friend," Callie said. Anne looked up with a start.

"Oh my gosh, right? No woman who's had five children should be wearing skinny jeans, especially yellow ones. I think she buys them in every color of the rainbow. But no, no, no, no." Anne waved her hands in front of her face. "It's worse, so much worse, and it has to do with the hot guy. And he's not Bailey's dad, he's Uncle Mike."

She sneaked a glance at Callie, who had gone utterly still, her eyes wide and a smile playing at her lips.

"*Uncle Mike*, huh? That's kind of hot." Callie came

around the small island and joined Anne at the kitchen table. "What did you do?"

"I gave him food." Anne moaned, nearly in agony. She shifted on the chair, reached up under her dress, struggled for a moment, then much to her relief pulled off her Spanx—all of which Callie ignored because they were that kind of friends—and tossed them into the chair next to her before sagging back down in relief.

"Well, sweetie, you fed everyone here. That was like . . . a herd feeding," Callie said.

"No, I gave him one of your fancy little boxes with extra cake pops and a cupcake. In addition to the herd feeding, to take home."

"Oh wow, so it was a direct feeding. I mean, not direct as in you held a cupcake up for him to take a bite. But exclusive. Like, I want you to lick-this-buttercream-at-home-tonight-and-think-of-me kind of offering. And my buttercream is the shit, by the way, so good move."

"Ugh, yes! God, I'm so stupid. And he used that same word, *offering.*"

"Seriously? What did he say?"

Anne made a pained face as she recited back his words. "He said, 'I'm sure what you're offering is delicious.'"

Callie's eyes bulged and her mouth dropped open. "No freaking way. Wait, how did he say it? Was it 'I'm sure what you're offering is delicious.' Or was it 'I'm sure what you're offering is . . . *delicious.*' There's a subtle but very important difference."

"Hell, I don't know, there was a pause, and a—"

"Was there a smolder?" Callie was nearly on the edge of her seat doing her best smolder imitation. Too bad she didn't know yet how this had all ended, because it had all gone so very wrong.

"Maybe, I mean, I thought it was something, but you don't know the worst part. I asked him . . . to go to the park with us tonight." Anne threw her hands up in the air in exasperation. Her idiotic behavior with Uncle Mike was inexcusable, and so incredibly embarrassing. She didn't ask guys to do anything except write checks for their kids' fancy birthday parties. And he'd said no, with a look of pity on his super-hot, chiseled, scruffy face. Who knew not shaving could be so sexy? She'd wanted to feel it against her skin more than anything. But that was never going to happen. Ugh.

"Oh sweetie, what the hell were you thinking?" Callie's incredulous and pity-filled tone was the final straw. "The park? That is so not hot."

Anne leaned forward before getting hysterical. "Yes, the park! I'm an idiot, I know. A hot, muscly, young— too young I'm sure—totally sexy guy came to my party and I asked him to go to the fucking park . . . with me and my *child*. What the hell is wrong with me?"

She had whispered the last bit since she didn't want Claire to hear her cursing. Anne rarely cursed—usually only after speaking to her ex or in very drastic or traumatizing situations. This was one of the latter. She was trying hard not to picture him, disheveled dark hair and hard biceps. The way his jeans had ridden low on his hips like he'd just rolled out of a big manly bed and thrown them on. He was celebrity-level hot, built as solid as an athlete, and the deep blue of his eyes had made her a little crazy. Why she had ever thought he would say yes to such an outrageous offering was beyond reason.

"He didn't look *that* young, but I'm gonna assume he said no since we're having this conversation."

"Of course he said no, Cal. Look at me! I'm a chubby mommy who corrected his colors. 'No, Mr. Hottest Guy Who Has Ever Stepped Into My Home, that is not *pink*, it's *raspberry* thank you very much, and here's your grown-up drink with a goddamn straw. By the way, how does a playdate sound?'" Anne was completely exasperated and furious with herself. She should have known just by looking at him that there was no way he was interested. "He was probably thinking I was the most ridiculous woman he'd ever encountered. Why Callie, why?"

"Good grief, Anne, don't be so hard on yourself. I'm proud of you for putting yourself out there. It was good practice, don't be discouraged. Next time just . . . don't mention parks and invite small children. Right?" Callie stood up and grabbed the towel to dry the rest of the dishes.

"Thanks for the encouragement, but that was scarring. I don't ask guys out, and this is why. I don't even meet guys. I plan parties for people under the age of eighteen, which usually only involves married men or grandfathers."

"Hey, don't knock it," Callie said with a laugh. Anne shot her a dirty look. Callie continued, "You know I'm teasing. Listen, it's Saturday night, which means I have really big plans, but I think *Downton Abbey* and my newest bottle of Moscato will forgive me if I'm a little late."

Callie grabbed the leftover bottle of sparkling wine, a glass, and a cupcake. She set them down on the table in front of Anne. "Why don't you take these, draw a bubble bath, and drink your worries away while I take Claire to the park to burn off the excitement of receiving eight new Barbies."

Anne slumped into the chair again. "I love you."

"And I love you. We may stop by Tomatillos for some unhealthy dinner. If I'm gonna cheat on *Downton*, I'm goin' all-out. I'll bring you some of those chicken tacos you like."

"Extra cheese and guacamole?" Anne said quietly, feeling marginally better.

"You got it. This level of self-pity calls for extra everything."

Anne gave a weak smile as Callie gathered her purse and some of the supplies she'd delivered that morning with the baked goods. Callie was the owner of Callie's Confections on the little Main Street in Preston, a trendy strip of boutique shops, restaurants, and antiques stores. She also was part of the *My Perfect Little Life* team. *MPLL*—as the three women affectionately referred to it—was a blog that Anne had started on a whim four years ago after creating a dream two-year-old party for Claire.

At the time her marriage had begun to show signs of unraveling, and instead of confronting the problem Anne started to focus on the things around her she could control. No one had to know that she and Scott were miserable, especially when she could make everything appear to be okay. She'd hoped that putting all of her energy into creating a great life for them might actually make it come true. Anne had grown up in a home where people were celebrated and felt loved. She'd wanted nothing more than to give her own daughter the same experience no matter what was happening between her parents. That included fantastic birthday parties. Memorable, beautiful days that made you feel like a princess.

That first big party that Anne had thrown for Claire had been a total success. All of her and Scott's friends had been blown away by her creativity and style, and she'd wanted to showcase it. That evening she'd loaded all the photos onto the internet, giving a few how-to details, and *My Perfect Little Life* blog was born.

She continued to share ideas for parties, crafts, and repurposing found items, and within four months she had reached a thousand followers. Shortly thereafter it really took off like wildfire. Companies began contacting her to try their products out for free if she blogged about them, and even paying her for advertising space. Two months later a reporter for the *Kansas City Star* interviewed her for the Home and Hobby section, which had turned into a recurring Sunday column about home and entertaining. The more time she put into her new career, the more resentful her husband became.

He tried to blame it on her newfound attachment to her imaginary Internet friends, also known as her commenters or followers. But they both knew better; their marriage had been suffering long before Anne had taken to the web for companionship. He often accused her of not being happy with who he was, said she wanted things to be perfect and that she wasn't fun anymore. It had shocked her.

The irony was that while the blog made to showcase

her happiness wasn't the cause of their divide, it had pushed them farther and farther apart. What may have started as a way to try to save her family had turned into her escape. Those online relationships gave her something she wasn't getting in her "real" life. The women who visited her site were kind and encouraging, told her how creative and special she was, made her feel valuable as a human and a mother.

The day Anne walked in her bedroom to find Scott cheating on her, it had been hard to muster any emotion at all except anger . . . and relief. The divorce had come quickly thereafter, and the thing she'd hated most was that she'd failed.

Unknowingly, her faithful blog readers had supported her through her divorce, a move, and the start of her local party planning business. Those same women from all over the world had also embraced the addition of each contributor as Anne one by one added the two other women. Each brought her own creative strength. First came Callie with her baking, and then Lindsey and her upcycling and repurposing design expertise. The thing Anne had in common with these women was that they all just wanted to make their lives a little more lovely and meaningful, and she had thrived post-divorce with their friendship and support. She didn't regret any of it. Not the blog, not the separation, not the hard work.

Sadly, she sometimes still longed for a man in her life, a man who would appreciate her desire to make things special, a man who wanted *her*, a man who would make her feel beautiful and—dare she ask—*sexy*. She'd started to feel a little bit sexy today when Mike looked at her across the patio. But now she wasn't sure. She was prim and proper Anne; why couldn't she just loosen up and be the kind of woman a guy desired?

Callie came inside after taking out several bags of trash, bless her. "Okay, I'll send Claire down to say bye. I'll text you when we're on the way home so you can put your vibrator away." Callie grinned and ran out of the kitchen before Anne could vocalize her disgust.

After giving Claire a quick kiss good-bye, Anne pulled herself together, and decided to use the alone time to get a few things done. She downloaded some photos from her camera, put up a teaser blog post about the party—good publicity for her growing business—and considered the full post she would do tomorrow. Her readers would pin the photos for ideas, and that would draw in even more unique hits. The beauty of a web-based businesses was the way it all happened so organically—if you did it right—as each post and bit of metadata drove up the reader base, therefore increasing the revenue from advertisers. She loved the process and the freedom it afforded her to work from home so she could be available for Claire.

Within another hour Anne emptied the champagne bottle, ate the cupcake, and allowed herself to become a prune in her old claw-foot tub, an indulgence she didn't partake of often enough. She was making some tea to take out on the patio with a good book—and probably another cupcake—when her phone dinged. Okay, so they were on their way home early. She could barely blame Callie; Claire's constant talking was only charming for so long. She picked up her phone and read Callie's message.

CALLIE: You'll NEVER believe who just drove by the park as we were leaving.
CALLIE: Uncle Mike.

Three

Mike was pretty damn certain the cupcake chick had seen him, which really pissed him off because now he looked like a stalker. He had no clue why he'd decided to drive by Settlers Park. In his defense, it was on his way home from his sister's . . . it didn't matter that he'd chosen to take a few side roads. But still, shit, what was he thinking? He didn't even have Bailey with him, so stopping would have been weird. He was acting like a lovestruck teenager.

He had a date tonight, one that almost assuredly would include a happy ending. That was what he needed to focus on, not Anne. She had a kid, she planned frilly parties for a living, and everything about her said *looking for a husband*—which meant "run" to a guy with no intention of starting a long-term relationship anytime soon. But damn if he hadn't wanted to get another look at her. Would she have worn that dress to the park? What did she look like not all fancied up? In other words, what did she look like naked? Naked with him, in her bed, hair down, face flushed, and completely undone.

After pulling into the alley behind his shop, he put his car in park, leaned back, and banged his head against the seat. This day had started out so easy and now he couldn't even collect his thoughts. His mind was full of images of Anne, Anne's dress, Anne's hair, and Anne's lips wrapped around a pink cake pop. *Shit.*

He got out of the car quickly and headed to the door with his pink box of treats. It was nearly five and he needed to shower before meeting up with Katie at six. She was just going to walk over, since she and her room-mate lived in a duplex just beyond the alley that ran behind his shop. Katie was what he should be thinking about. She was a nice, super-sexy girl. Once he saw her, this issue would resolve itself. But as he stuck his key into the lock, he had the most brilliant idea. Okay, maybe it was a horrible idea, but he figured it might be best if he just got this out of his system.

He tossed the keys onto his cluttered desk, gently laid the pastry box down, and wiggled the mouse to bring the computer monitor to life. Pulling up a search engine, he typed in . . . what was it? Pretty Little Life? A few suggestions down he spotted it. My *Perfect Little Life.*

Click, and there he was, staring at sweet, beautiful little Anne's website. The top of the screen where the title showed was all vintage looking, muted colors, polka dots, and girlie swirly shit, welcoming him to their life-style blog. What the hell did *lifestyle blog* even mean? He used the Internet for total guy stuff: scouring for old cars on Craigslist, downloading music, and watching stupid YouTube videos. For his own business he had a one-page site that was basically his name and contact info. This whole blog thing was beyond him.

The front page already showcased photos of Claire's party. He scanned the images, reliving the explosion of pink and blue. She had close-ups of the cupcakes, decorations, and his favorite: the grown-up jar drinks. A shot of the girls in their dress-up outfits, and Mike smiled when he saw the grin on Bailey's face. Her arm was wrapped around Claire's neck, and Mike realized how much Claire was a mini-Anne. She was a really beautiful little girl, a little chatty, but sweet.

The whole thing had only happened a couple of hours ago; he couldn't believe she'd already put it on the Internet. Obviously Anne took it very seriously, but why shouldn't she? This was her business. It made him consider that maybe he should beef his site up a little more, include some before-and-after photos. Then again, did his clientele look at stuff like that? He doubted it would make a huge difference—and he was doing just fine— but it was something to consider. He scrolled down a little farther and saw something else that surprised him . . . sixty-three comments. Jesus, were that many people interested in a stranger's birthday party? It was a Saturday night, for God's sake, and these photos could only have been up for a short time.

He kept perusing the site and found a tutorial on painting an old chair (why bother?), making curls out of chocolate (what for?), and another themed birthday party. This time it was *Star Wars*, which Mike thought was pretty cool. There were even full-on characters, men dressed as real-life Darth Vader and Boba Fett. What the hell? Who had that kind of money? Another one showed the "tablescape"—he now knew the correct term—with cake, lightsabers, and green drinks. The final image was of all the boys attending the party decked out in Padawan costumes. This was crazy. When he was a kid, going to Mickey D's was a killer birthday party. He scanned the barrage of photos, advertisements, and clickable buttons until he saw the one that said MEET THE GIRLS. *Yes—click.*

A professional photo popped up of three women standing in tall grass. Smiles graced all of their faces. It was a very good-looking group of females, that was for sure, but his eyes immediately settled on Anne. Her hair was down, waving around her bare shoulders, and good God, she was gorgeous in a white strapless dress that molded her breasts. He scrolled down, and the next photo was just her, same spot, but close up. Her grin was so big and happy that a little dimple showed on her cheek next to her white teeth. He stared at it for what felt like five whole minutes.

A short bio was off to the side, telling how she started the blog after creating a princess-and-castle-themed birthday party for her daughter, blah, blah, blah. She was passionate about family and making everyday moments memorable—yeah, he'd had some memorable moments in her presence, that was for sure. Despite the family comment, he'd caught the words *single mom*, so her availability was officially confirmed. He hated to think she might have experienced a bad marriage, or worse, but was relieved to know she was not a kinky housewife who ditched her ring and came on to men at her kid's birthday party. Maybe she had genuinely been interested.

No, no, *hell* no. Mike ran his hands through his hair. No way was he giving this another thought. He stood up and stalked toward the bathroom before cranking the shower on. He needed to stand under the stream and burn her memory away, steam it out of his pores.

Thirty minutes later he was dressed in his nicest jeans and a button-up shirt, hair combed. He felt better, ready for Katie. She was a hairdresser at a little shop on Main Street, and living so close together meant that they'd seen each other often at Smokey's, the bar nearby. He'd become good friends with the bartender there, Aiden. Mike had spent several evenings over the last few weeks flirting with Katie, and she seemed to have the same goal in mind. Easy, fun, and nothing serious.

At ten till six his cell phone rang. He answered only to regret it the minute he heard the voice on the other end. It was his oldest, most demanding—yet wealthiest—customer, Dan Monser. Mike had just started on a complete overhaul of a 1965 Mustang Fastback for Dan's almost sixteen-year-old daughter, Jessica. He had no qualms about taking the man's money, but it did make him a little sick to his stomach knowing that this amazing and somewhat rare piece of American automotive history would be gifted to a teenage girl who would probably run it through an automatic car wash, set her designer purse on the hood, and text while she drove.

"Dan, what can I do you for on this Saturday evening?" Mike answered, emphasis on *Saturday evening* when his shop was technically closed.

"Just need an ETA on the car, Mike. Jill had it all planned to unveil on the ballroom floor at the country club the weekend of July Fourth, but they had a sewer line back up and flood the first floor and kitchen. All events through the summer are canceled." The man sounded livid. "Apparently not even the hundreds of thousands of dollars I pump into that place every fucking year have any sway on how fast this is fixed. So we're moving the party up. Can I count on you?"

Well, shit. Mike had two jobs due to be completed before the Monser car. It was a tight schedule already, removing the interior and trim was as far as he'd gotten on the Mustang. "How early we talkin', Dan?"

"Maybe mid-June. Depends on Jill and what she can figure out for the party. We'd had everything going through the club from the music to the food, and since we're in Hawaii right after the Fourth until nearly August, it has to happen before."

What a tough life. They *must* figure out how to throw together a five-figure party for their daughter so they can fly to the beach for month. "Well, Dan, I'll see what I can do. It was tight, but you know I wanna take care of you."

"I need you to have it done, Mike. I send a lot of business your way."

It was a less-than-subtle threat, but the man wasn't lying. He'd helped get Mike's business off the ground when the '65 Shelby Cobra that Mike restored for him appeared in *Muscle Car Magazine* several years back. No surprise that Dan Monser had turned out to have rich friends, and that meant expensive toys. Mike wanted, no needed, to do right by Dan, despite the fact that it was for a teenage girl.

"All right, I got you, but this is gonna hurt."

"I'll make it up to you, Mike. I knew I could count on you to take care of my end. The party shit is up to Jill now. I'll keep you posted."

An idea hit Mike in that moment. "Hey, Dan. If you're

interested, I know of a party planner—she may have some connections if you're in a bind. Not sure if she does large parties, but it's worth a shot."

"Really, they reputable?"

Mike could have laughed. Anne was cherry-pie wholesome. She was more than reputable. Mike leaned over and clicked on the CONTACT button. "Anne is absolutely reputable." *And sexy as hell.*

He looked to his computer screen and rattled off Anne's contact number—how convenient, all women should have a website—and email address before hanging up with Dan. He clicked back to Anne's picture and stood there looking at her. He hoped she could help the Monsers out. It would be good money. Not that she appeared to need money, but hell, who couldn't use a good paycheck?

He jumped when arms wrapped his waist from behind.

"Surprise, hot stuff," Katie said in a purry seductive voice. Mike turned and found her in a tight black dress, revealing and sexy. He glanced over her shoulder to the open door that he should have had locked and quickly plastered a smile on his face before he frowned. So much for everything being right when he saw her.

"Hey you." He said as he gently pulled himself from her arms. Her face fell, clearly disappointed at her greeting, or lack thereof. He stepped away and grabbed his keys. "Ready to go? I thought we could drive into the city. Find a new scene for dinner."

"Sure. Whatcha lookin' at?" she asked. He glanced over his shoulder. Katie leaned on his desk, looking at the website with Anne's photo just the way he had been when she came in. "She's pretty—a little old, though. Says she's a single mom. Do you know her?"

Her tone came off as jealous, *great*. They hadn't even gone on one date. However, what really bothered him was the way he instantly wanted to come to Anne's defense. He wasn't making much progress in his plan to stop thinking about her.

"Nah, not really. She planned an over-the-top birthday party I took my niece to this afternoon. There were just some photos of it." He shrugged while Katie laughed, making him feel like a total jackass. Now he had put down Anne's *thing*, and after he'd told her he liked it. He hadn't been lying then, so why was he now lying to Katie?

"I can't believe you went to a kiddie party. That doesn't seem like you at all." She ran her hands up his arms, her grin wide. "There are much more fun things to do in an afternoon. Wouldn't you say?"

Truth was, Katie really didn't know much of anything about him. Spending time with Bailey was one of his favorite pastimes. The woman standing in front of him couldn't have been more of Anne's opposite if she tried. Mike closed his eyes and sighed as they left the building before locking the door behind him. His evening was not shaping up to what he imagined: The hot blonde on his arm wasn't the one he was thinking about.

Four

Anne stretched out in her king-sized bed, pointing her toes and shoving an arm under the pillow to feel the coolness on her skin. She didn't really need such a big bed, but it was one of the few things she'd requested from her and Scott's house during the divorce. The funny thing was that it had been in the guest room. Who knew what he'd done in the bed they shared. *Gross.* However, she was quite pleased with her request. Despite the fact that it now took up 80 percent of the floor space in her little master bedroom, it was the most comfortable bed she'd ever slept in.

Anne glanced over at the vacated spot beside her. She could have sworn Claire had joined her at some point early that morning. She leaned up on her forearms and glanced at the clock. Oh gosh, she'd slept until nine. That was like noon in her world, even for a Sunday. Something caught her senses, and she sniffed at the air. Was something burning?

"Mommmmyyyy, your Pop-Tart's ready!" Claire called from downstairs.

"Oh crap." Anne stumbled out of bed, grabbed her robe off the footboard, and ran down the stairs and then into the kitchen. "Claire, next time wait for Mommy before you cook, please."

Claire stood on her helper stool at the small island. A burnt strawberry pastry was peeking from the top of the toaster, and another one—also charred—was on a plate at the small kitchen table. It had a fork resting beside it.

"That one is yours, okay? I'm making me a new one because this one is all burned up," Claire said matter-of-factly as she pulled open another foil packet. "I gave you that one because I know you don't like to waste."

"Oh, well, thank you so much for your thoughtfulness." Anne sat down and picked the blackened edges from the pastry then took a bite. It was edible.

After a couple more nibbles she stood up and made her way to the coffeepot, which had filled on an auto-timer nearly two hours ago. Luckily the heating element hadn't shut off; still, it was bordering on bitter sludge and scalding hot, though nothing a liberal amount of creamer wouldn't fix. She would need at least two mugs to recover from her champagne-and-mortification hangover from yesterday. She wasn't positive, but she was pretty sure she'd had an X-rated dream featuring her special party guest and his well-fitted jeans.

She couldn't stop thinking about him driving by the park. Had he meant to see her? Was it his normal route? Surely not, Settlers Park was in a neighborhood, not really near anything. Then again, she didn't know where he lived. The whole thing had been making Anne crazy, but she needed to let it go. If he'd been interested, he would have said so. But no, instead last night he was on a hot date. Shit, he might be waking up with that hot date right now . . . or sneaking out of her place. Good grief, it was like Anne had never interacted with a handsome man before.

Ironically, she used to be married to a handsome man. Scott Edmond had made her heart pound and body quiver once upon a time. She worked at the local community college in the humanities and social sciences office when she first laid eyes on the cute guy in khaki cargoes and plaid flannel shirt. He looked like a rock climber or a model from an L.L. Bean catalog. His tanned legs had caught her eye immediately when he walked into the office, then he proceeded to unabashedly flirt with her while she transferred him to a different public speaking class. He asked her out before he left the office that day.

It was a romantic courtship. He took her to fancy parties hosted by his well-to-do parents and friends, basically treated her like the most special person in the world. Even Anne's mother had been won over by his boyish charm. When he finally proposed she thought she knew exactly what he wanted from a marriage—someone to make his life effortless and his home comfortable, plan nice parties, look good on his arm. It never really occurred to her that she would be wrong, or that one or both of them would grow to be unhappy, because at the time it had all seemed so right.

Sadly, she'd allowed her Prince Charming to talk her out of finishing college. A stupid mistake, because she had worked so hard to get there, not starting until she was twenty and applying for financial aid to pay her way since her father's final years of cancer had squelched her family's savings. Quitting left her undereducated and without a career to fall back on when she found Scott screwing his cousin's wife in the bed Anne shared with him. Thank goodness she had started to make money off her blog by then, or she didn't know what she would have done.

After the initial dust settled, the most painful part was feeling like she'd let Claire down. Anne wanted Claire to have the same happy childhood she'd had when her parents had adopted her out of foster care when she was four. And after her divorce, she had felt like the worst mom ever. Thank God when she told her mother about the divorce her reply had been, "You can do better than him anyway." She supported Anne without question, emotionally and financially when the need arose for a short time.

Anne took another long sip of coffee, the scent of vanilla filling her nose. She hadn't thought about her divorce in a while, tried not to in fact, but here she was two years later still processing the failure. Obviously her recent dealings with this handsome man were bringing up repressed thoughts. It was a sign she just needed to live like a nun.

No, she was not going to let those depressing thoughts control her. She missed being touched, and the affection that came with a partner. Not that she'd gotten all that much from Scott toward the end, but at this point she was starting to think that some was better than none. Love could be fleeting, right? At least it was in her case. However, right now she just needed a male-induced orgasm.

Claire stepped off her stool and sat down at the kitchen table with her perfectly heated breakfast when Anne's cell phone rang. She didn't recognize the number, which was odd for a Sunday, but she cleared her unused morning voice and put on a cheery hello . . . just in case.

"Hi, is this Anne the party planner?" a female asked. Her words were clipped and her voice chipper, like she'd been awake for hours and already solved world problems.

"Yes, this is Anne."

"Perfect. This is Jill Monser, and I'm in a bit of a pickle, *Anne*. You're services came highly recommended, and I am in need of the most beautiful, lavish sweet sixteen party you can create. Are you available?"

Wow, way to just lay it all out there. This woman was no-nonsense. Anne had never done a sweet sixteen party. She'd only ingested half a cup of coffee this morning; she wasn't feeling particularly up to par, so she started with the basics.

"Well, Mrs. Monser, when is your party scheduled?"

"That's the problem, *Anne*, when I say a pickle, I'm putting it mildly. We had everything set for the Millard Country Club in early July, but they had a disaster and now we have to start from scratch. I need everything. A new venue, DJ, catering, lighting, decor . . . and I need it to happen before the end of June."

Anne almost dropped her mug. *Lighting?* Wow. "Oh! Okay. Well . . ."

She'd seen the story about the sewer disaster on the local news. Extensive damage, so the club was using the opportunity to renovate the old building. Millard Country Club was only for the very wealthy, so this Mrs. Monser would probably have high expectations. But she'd

also have lots of money. Anne couldn't even imagine—
no, she actually could. Pictures of what she would want
to do were already flowing through her mind. The only
rub was the time frame.

"I realize this is not ideal, *Anne*," Jill went on, obviously sensing her slight reluctance to take the job. It was
also a little unsettling the way she kept using Anne's
name, as if she were a child receiving a scolding. "But
my daughter is counting on this. I've been promising her
a sweet sixteen party for her entire life, and I need to
make sure it's parallel to none."

"Well . . . Jill, let me think for a minute. I'd certainly
love to—"

"Oh thank you, Anne! I just wasn't sure about you
when the referral came from a man, but then I Googled
you and realized you're the *My Perfect Little Life* Anne
and I was thrilled. Your work is just precious, and exactly what I'm looking for. The perfect mix of class and
handcrafted. I should have thought of you myself. Can
you put together a plan and meet me for coffee tomorrow? We can discuss specifics."

What was left to say? Could she do this? Yes, she
could, and she wanted to. But who was the man who'd
referred her? It must have been a dad from one of her
parties. "Okay, sure, Jill. Where would you like to meet,
and might I ask the name of the person who referred you?
I always like to show my appreciation for referrals."

Which was the truth. Word of mouth had made her
what she was, and she liked to send personalized thank-
you notes to those gracious enough to think of her when
they spoke with friends and family.

"Wonderful, let's meet at Callie's Confections. I know

she does the blog with you and she has a low-fat coffee cake that I can't get enough of. Oh, and her services were already enlisted for the cake by way of the club, so I'd like to kill two birds with one stone. Perhaps you can chat with her and make sure she is fine with the new date and location you have in mind."

Anne had been smiling since the moment Jill had mentioned Callie's. It was a relief to know she wasn't in this madness alone, and ironically she did have the most perfect venue in mind, a gorgeous farm on the outskirts of town that she'd been in love with for the past two years. She wondered if she could pull it off. "Yes, I can certainly do that."

"Splendid, well then, I'll see you at nine sharp, Anne. And oddly enough, you were referred by the man who restores my husband's old cars. His name is Mike Everett. You just never know who knows who, do you? Thanks again. Bye-bye now."

The line went silent and Anne was still processing the conversation. Mike Everett, old car guy? There were a lot of Mikes in her contact list, but she didn't remember working with a mechanic or an Everett. However, she didn't ask her clients' professions, and they rarely offered up the information. A certain Uncle Mike came to mind since he'd been at the top of her thoughts, but it couldn't possibly be him. They'd just met, and he didn't seem the type to run out and brag about little girl parties he attended.

Everett, Everett, Everett. She recited the name to herself as she clicked open the Internet on her phone and typed in the key words: *Mike Everett old cars.* The first link pulled up, and she clicked it open. It was from a

site for *Muscle Car Magazine*. A photo started to un-
roll . . . slowly.

"Damn WiFi," she whispered.

"What's wrong, Mommy?" Claire asked. She was
stirring her strawberry milk and sloshing it all over the
table. Anne chose to ignore it this time. "Are you mad
at your phone again?"

"No, sweetie, everything's fine."

The photo finally loaded far enough that she could
see a fancy muscle car and two men standing beside it.
She used her fingers to zoom in and her breath caught.
"Oh my God."

There looking sinfully handsome was none other than
Uncle Mike. It wasn't recent—he looked a little younger—
but it was most certainly him. Mike Everett. He was in
jeans and a T-shirt, his hands tucked into his pockets,
his grin wide. The caption said that he'd restored the car,
a '65 Shelby Cobra, for Dan Monser. There was even an
entire spread on the vehicle. Anne didn't know much
about muscle cars, but she knew this one was gorgeous.

She put her phone down and picked up her coffee, her
mind reeling from the sudden job put in front of her and
even more from the fact that Uncle Mike had given
someone her name in the last, well, less than twenty-four
hours. What did that mean? Maybe that's why he'd driven
by the park, not to see her, but to ask her about this.
Maybe it was completely innocent. She planned parties,
and he knew someone. It meant nothing.

But . . . she should still send him something to say
thank you. She *had* to show her appreciation just like
she would with anyone else.

Five

"You better be messin' with me, man. A pink fastback?"

Mike sighed into the telephone. His frustration equaled that of his painter. Manuel was the best within a hundred-mile radius, and knew better than anyone that painting a classic American muscle car hot pink was sacrilege. Ford had produced some pink cars in its time, but this one was going to be bright. Anne's raspberry color came to mind, putting a smile on his face.

"I know man. It sucks, but we gotta get paid," Mike joked as he tapped his pen on the desk. "Monser helps to keep us both in business, so we're gonna make this the most badass hot-pink Mustang anyone has ever seen."

Manuel took a deep breath. "You're right, but it's gonna break my heart to load pink paint into my gun."

"Just be ready for me to drop it off around the second week in June, and rush it."

Mike got off with Manuel and leaned back in his chair. It was Monday and he'd been up since five o'clock working on a client's Chevelle, which was nearly done. All he had left were some minor trim pieces. The faster it was finished, the sooner he could focus on the Mustang. He usually tried to keep his shop high quality, low volume, but it was hard to say no to money, which meant it wasn't uncommon to find himself in these situations where builds overlapped and got crazy.

He glanced at the clock, noting that it was nearing one. He really needed to eat something, but he knew his mini fridge only contained some frozen burritos and a bottle of hot sauce. However, the burger joint down on Main Street knew his order by heart, so he grabbed his keys and headed for the door to the alley. He wasn't expecting to find a woman there when he pulled it open, but he did, bent over just outside the door.

The suddenness of it startled her and threw her off kilter. He could see her trying to regain her balance, but the threat of falling was imminent. He reached down to grab her arm, steadying her. A mass of golden ponytail rolled back, and he locked eyes with none other than perfect Anne Edmond.

She found her footing and stood, forcing him to let go of her arm. "You okay?" he asked.

"Yes," she said, a little breathless. "I'm sorry. I was just leaving you something."

Mike couldn't help but grin as he glanced down and took in her pale-yellow top, navy skirt, and strappy yellow heels. Between their feet sat a little pink box from Callie's bakery. A little card rested on top.

"You're feeding me again? I must look like I'm starving."

She gave him an embarrassed, sexy smile, locking eyes with him and then quickly looking away. "No. I mean, I guess yes to the feeding-you part. I just wanted to thank you for the referral. I just left a three-hour meeting with Jill Monser, and I was at Callie's anyway, and her cinnamon rolls are so good, although I really try not to eat them. But I just wanted to thank you, and your sister told me where your shop was, and—"

"Anne," he said, cutting her off. She'd been about to buzz out of control, arms flying as she spoke, but not once had she looked him in the eye for more than a quarter of a second. She did now—in fact, her pupils had dilated and her lips were just barely parted. He spoke softly. "You could have knocked, you know. I would have been really sad if I knew you were at my place and I didn't get to see you."

Her face was frozen for a beat, but then just as she had at her house, she pulled it together. Watching the realization in her expression was so damn hot. He wanted her to know it, wanted her to reciprocate. *Flirt with me, Anne, give me something.*

She smiled, and a faint blush colored her cheeks. Okay, well, that was something. "I just didn't want to bother you."

"Not possible."

"Oh, don't underestimate me. I might surprise you." She scrunched her nose. He was beginning to really enjoy that cute little habit.

He wanted her to surprise him, but probably not in the way she implied. He wanted to see her strip out of that little skirt she was wearing. Peel off her top and show him her lingerie. Was it yellow, too? Wouldn't that be a surprise? Anne looked like a gently bred southern belle, but he wanted to fantasize about her being a wildcat in bed. Okay, he *had* fantasized about that. In fact he'd woken this morning with a painful hard-on that only a shower, his hand, and a lurid mental image of Anne had taken care of.

He was imagining it right now.

"You wanna come in?" he asked. "It's kind of dirty in here. Car parts, grease, metal . . . but it's *my thing*."

She laughed, obviously remembering their conversation from Saturday. Quickly she reached down, making his breath hitch as this morning's shower scene popped into his head again. Oh God, wouldn't that be a great surprise. Instead of fulfilling his fantasies, however, she reached for the box of rolls and stood up.

"That's okay, you're busy. I really just wanted to thank you." She held the gift out to him. He glanced down at the card as he took it from her. In her meticulous little penmanship he read, *Uncle Mike*. Holy shit. Why did that seem so sexy?

"You have to come in," he said. "So you can see the car I'm doing for the Monsers' daughter. It will be the focal piece of your party." She appeared to think about it for a second. He raised both eyebrows.

"Okay, you're probably right. In fact, Jill did want a tiny replica in fondant on top of the cake. So I guess I should."

He had no idea what fondant was, but he'd agree with whatever she needed in order to get her inside. "Great."

His shop was located in an older structure owned by his friend Derek, who was a commercial building architect and contractor. Derek had bought the property a block away from Main Street near the train tracks a few years ago to house his office. The place had obviously been used as some sort of shop or warehouse before. It had a couple of garage doors off the large work space, so Derek had offered to rent the back and side to Mike. It worked out well for both of them.

He led Anne inside and set the rolls on his desk. When he turned back to her she was glancing around the small office. Worn couch, file cabinet, and oversized messy desk. He wondered what she was thinking. When their eyes met she smiled. "So Erin said you live here also?"

"Yeah, it's not ideal, only temporary." He cleared his throat, and just like that he saw himself through her eyes. He lived in a fucking auto shop. What did that say about him? He knew that he had enough money in his bank account to buy a house tomorrow, a decent house even, but he'd never felt rushed. The initial plan *was* for it to be a temporary solution, but after a while it seemed stupid to move when he worked such long hours. He had plans and dreams; they were just always for the future. In the meantime she probably thought he lived like some squatter.

He had every intention of buying a piece of land at some point. Derek had even offered to work up a simple design plan for a home, but for the past couple of years this had served its purpose. He was a single guy and saving his money made sense, but here and now he felt the need to explain the situation. Make her see that he was more than the place he went to sleep at night. But ultimately, did it even matter?

"I do have a bedroom and full bathroom, so it's not too bad for now. And you can't beat the commute, you know, until I'm ready to buy a place of my own."

She laughed. "I'm kind of jealous. No dolls in your chairs or crackers crushed on the floor. It's peaceful in here." She sounded sincere, and he really didn't pick up any judgment in her expression. Was there anything about her that wasn't sweet?

"Yeah, it is. I like turning on my music and just zoning out. No interruptions."

"That sounds nice."

"Well, come on, I'll show you the Mustang."

She followed him down the short hall and out into the garage bays. It was strange bringing a woman into his work space. Just as he'd told her, he spent a lot of time in here doing what he did best, turning rusted-out clunkers into works of art. They were always diamonds in the rough, and he took great pride into restoring them not only to their former beauty . . . but even better. And he did it alone, only subcontracting out for a few specialized things like paint, glasswork, and more extensive interior work. Between his father and some trade school auto classes he'd learned what he needed to know.

Anne ran her thin fingers along the hood of a Nova that was in primer. Then she spotted the Mustang, a small smile forming on her lips. He was impressed that she'd obviously known which one it was.

His father had loved old vehicles, from the classics to the muscle cars, and he'd shared that passion with Mike growing up. They loved nothing more than finding a neglected treasure in some field or the paper and spending hours trying to get it running. He had fond memories of working with his dad and he liked to think his father would be proud of what he'd accomplished, but sadly he would never know. Chuck Everett, his only living parent, died suddenly of a massive heart attack when Mike was a senior in high school.

What should have been Mike's saving grace was the fact that he'd been over eighteen and not sent through the system, but instead he took his life into his own hands. And as a grieving teenager, his first decision was to drop out of high school and find a new hobby, which ended up being getting-trashed-by-whatever-means-necessary. His sister had been in college, not really equipped to support him, so he'd assured Erin—who was grieving herself—everything was cool when he moved in with a few friends. The wrong friends, of course, but no one could have convinced him differently at the time.

Amazingly he finally found his way out of trouble. Part of his eventual healing had been returning to what he loved, restoring cars. The tattoos on his arm and back were the only link to that dark time in his life, a small price to pay for making it out alive. It was another reminder of how different he was from this beautiful woman standing in his space.

He met Anne beside the Mustang. Seeing it now—ugly green, spotted with Bondo where he'd tried to smooth some of the minor body work—he realized how much work was ahead of him.

"Doesn't really look like something a teenage girl would like," she said.

He chuckled. "No, not right now, but it's early yet. This is the original paint. I'll finish up the bodywork, prime it, get it painted with white rally stripes, drop in a restored 351 Windsor V-8, make sure all the trim is re-chromed, and then it will be amazing. Despite the hot-pink color request."

"I heard about that pink. Wow, hard to imagine

looking at this. Sure you can do it?" She grinned, teasing him.

He held his hand up to his chest as if in pain. "Anne, your lack of faith in me is breaking my heart. I didn't question your use of canning jars for drinking glasses."

She rolled her eyes, groaned, and then laughed quietly. "Those glasses are awesome, mister. And very trendy right now, I'll have you know."

The sound of her happiness and teasing rippled through his entire body all the way to his dick. Maybe having her in here was a mistake, because he didn't want her to leave before he put his hands on her. She walked to another car, and he watched the slide of her hand roam across the hood of the '70 Chevelle. Her nails were still manicured in her party polish, the colors striking against the shiny black paint of the car. It was a huge turn-on.

"I really like this one." She smiled over her shoulder, her beauty standing out amid the grittiness of the shop. Her little sweater and navy skirt were nowhere near improper, but that only added to the sexiness. He stepped in her direction; the breeze coming in from the open garage doors lifted the little hairs off her neck.

"It's a Chevelle Super Sport. Rare, and one of my favorites, too. It's the client's third, which seems like such a waste since he rarely drives them."

"Why would someone have something so special and not use it?"

He shrugged, good question. He understood the desire to keep something safe and precious, but then again, "You can't take it with ya," as his father used to say. "I guess some people enjoy the feeling of possession more than the thrill of the ride."

A grin teased at her lips. Perfect Little Anne didn't miss a beat.

"And which one of those are you?" she asked in a quiet voice.

He stalked a little closer, his eyes never leaving hers. When he was just a foot away his gaze traveled down, her chest rising and falling with each heavy breath she took. He could feel and almost see their attraction sparking. And now he wanted to taste it.

"Possession can be a turn-on, I guess, but there's nothing better than a good ride." His voice was low and he didn't miss the way her jaw went slack and waist dipped in, like she'd just literally lost her breath. She was so responsive, it was heady. He leaned closer and rested his right hand on her hip, his thumb stroking just below the hem of her top. Jesus, she was soft. And warm, and her perfume, floral and sweet same as the day of the party, was filling the air around them, making him dizzy.

He resisted grabbing her from both sides and crushing her against him. For one, while he wanted Anne ferociously, there was an expensive car behind her that he didn't want both of their weight leaning onto. Even in times like these he still had to think about his babies. And two, her eyes were so wide he was afraid she might panic, but he knew there was desire in there, too. He let his gaze sweep down to her amazingly full lips and then tilted his head just a little . . .

"Mike!" a singsongy voice called from the office.

"Shit." He pulled away from Anne instantly, dropping his hands.

"Oh my God," Anne said in a pained whisper. She

turned and faced the open garage door as Katie strolled into the shop.

"Oh hey, sorry, I didn't know you had a customer," Katie said, coming to a sudden halt when she laid eyes on Anne. Although her words were fine, there was no mistaking the slight bitterness in her tone.

Damn, this was shitty timing. Anne wasn't a customer; she'd brought him cinnamon rolls and a note. She called him Uncle Mike. But he didn't correct Katie, because there was nothing technically between them. Anne had turned around and was now intently staring at the Chevelle, unable to look him or Katie in the eye.

"Just let me wrap this up, okay, Katie? I'll be back there in a minute."

Katie looked between them for a moment and then slipped back into the office, closing the door behind her. He wished she'd just keep going and head home. Their Saturday evening had ended with him declining her offer of taking it back to her place. He'd even surprised himself by saying no, but extremely hot Katie had gotten sorority-girl-level wasted when they'd ended up back at the bar next door at the end of the night. The chasm between her and the sexy single mother in a pink party dress floating in his mind had shredded the last of his once well-planned Saturday night.

"Well, I really hope you enjoy the cinnamon rolls, I had one this morning and really shouldn't have."

The change in Anne's voice was like a punch to the gut. Just like at her house, things got awkward and she was trying to fix it, act like nothing happened between them. He also didn't like how she put herself down when she was embarrassed. He would've liked to see her eat the cinnamon roll, and then taste the frosting from her lips. But right now her heels were clicking as she headed for the open garage door, avoiding the office and Katie at all costs. He couldn't blame her.

"Anne, don't go."

She turned to face him, her expression carefully void of any emotion. She cocked her head to the side, as if she was trying to figure him out. "Why?"

He didn't know what to say. Could she not see that he'd been close to kissing her? That he wanted to still? She stood there in her cute little outfit, golden hair lit from the light of the open door, with a confident and un-affected mask firmly in place. A moment ago she looked like she could have melted into his arms, and now she was running. He shoved his hands into his jean pockets, still quiet. Katie was waiting, and he certainly didn't want her to come back out and upset Anne more.

"Never mind, thanks for the rolls."

Her eyes searched the pavement in front of her for a second before she glanced up at him. "You're very welcome. Thanks again, Mike."

And she walked away, around the side of the building toward the alley where her car was parked. For a split second he wanted to go after her. Apologize for the interruption and beg her to let them rewind back to five minutes ago. He'd wanted to kiss her more than anything, and he was pretty damn sure she'd wanted it, too. Twice now he'd let her walk away uncomfortable after getting close to him.

"Damn it," he muttered under his breath.

When he heard her engine start up and gravel popping beneath tires he went back into the office to find

Katie sitting on his desk. Her legs rested in the chair and her sheer black bra was completely exposed, her T-shirt tossed over the computer monitor. *Shit*.

Why wasn't he turned on? He was still a man, and she had a beautiful body. But this wasn't the time, and she wasn't the woman he wanted to be with. She opened her mouth before he could tell her that.

"I'm a little embarrassed about Saturday. I've never gotten that drunk before."

He highly doubted that. She'd thrown back rum and Diet Cokes like a champ, but giving her the benefit of the doubt was the gentlemanly thing to do. "No big deal, we've all been there."

She crooked a finger at him and leaned back a little. "But we didn't get to have any fun."

No, they didn't, and at this point he wasn't interested. A shame really, he didn't find half-naked women in his office every day. Okay, he never found half-naked women in his office, so he wasn't sure how to gently tell one that she wasn't wanted. He feared there was no good way to go about it.

"Katie, listen—"

Her mouth dropped open and she set up. "Are you fucking kidding me, Mike Everett?" I'm sitting here on your desk like this, and you start with 'Katie, listen'?"

She stood up and grabbed her shirt, making him feel like the biggest asshole. He also felt responsible for letting down the male race everywhere for denying such an easy offering. But he honestly couldn't explain it. No, that wasn't really true; it definitely had something to do with the box of cinnamon rolls that had been a foot away from Katie's ass on his desk.

"I'm not stupid, Mike. You should have just said you weren't interested before Saturday, although I don't get what happened. You asked me out. We've been flirting for weeks."

She was right, they had been. But something had recently changed. He wished like hell it hadn't, things would have been a lot easier. "Katie . . ."

"Oh no, don't you dare." She pulled her shirt over her head and picked up her purse. "I thought you were a nice guy. I liked you a lot. I really thought this was . . . *something.*"

He raised an eyebrow, his expression showing his obvious bewilderment, he really thought they'd been on the same page about things being just for fun. *Shit.* The rage in her eyes neared hysteric proportions.

"You're a total asshole," she growled before slamming the door behind her.

He closed his eyes and dropped into his chair. How the hell had this day gone so wrong? Two women had shown up and both had left in anger. That had to be a real talent. Thinking of Anne's gift reminded him of the card.

He leaned forward and snatched it up before lifting it to his nose. A little bit of her floral scent clung to the paper. He flipped it over to look at her handwriting again. *Uncle Mike.* He smiled. Who would have thought it could be so sexy? He definitely didn't think of Bailey when Anne used the endearment.

Inside the envelope was a small note card covered with yellow polka dots. In the bottom corner was a swirly *A* monogram. *Women.* He opened it up and read.

Mike,

You may have regretted staying at a little girl party, but I'm very glad you did. Thanks so much for the referral. It means a lot that you thought of me.

Anne

Anne couldn't possibly know all the ways he'd thought of her, many of which he probably shouldn't have. The thing he was thinking now was equally dangerous, and that was how much he'd hated letting her go.

Six

Fridays were by far the busiest day at Callie's Confections, so Anne had started coming in to help in the mornings. She did it without pay because Callie Daniels was one of her best friends, and it was nice to get out of the house. Plus, the bakery was good business for the blog and vice versa.

She'd met Callie two years ago—right after she'd moved to Preston—at the local Saturday-morning market. Anne had sampled some of Callie's blueberry scones and nearly died on the spot, they were so good. The next two Saturdays she had bought something different, and everything was amazing. On the fourth week Anne convinced Callie to do a guest blog post. It had been on how to make those to-die-for blueberry scones. Of course the post was a huge hit, as she'd known it would be, and the followers had fallen in love with Callie's witty personality and her yummy food. The next step had been making Callie a permanent part of *MPLL* and Anne's life. Now she and Callie were close friends, spending a lot of time together working on the blog along with

Lindsey, and also occasionally collaborating on parties. Callie was one of the hardest workers Anne had ever known. Plus, the woman was gorgeous, yet Anne had never seen her date since they'd been friends.

Despite the hard work and all of their various sacrifices, it was nice to have two other people whom you clicked with. While Anne and Callie covered the party and food side, Lindsey was their expert Junker and had been gone for the past two weeks on a trip to the East Coast to antique. Anne envied the ability to just up and leave, but she knew her friend loved it and would accumulate some great project pieces for her thriving business and for the blog. The accomplishments of Anne's friends never ceased to amaze her, and their blog readers benefited from their many talents. She was especially proud of the bakery and was happy to know that the blog had helped make Callie's dream come true.

This morning Anne had already made three types of coffee, frosted some cupcakes, and was icing cinnamon rolls when Eric rolled in, designer sunglasses on his tan, chiseled face. Behind her Anne heard Callie sigh loudly.

"Do you realize that if you were on time the sun wouldn't even be up yet? The very act of putting those glasses on your face means you have taken the risk of walking into a very annoyed boss, Eric." Callie washed her hands in the prep sink and headed for the walk-in fridge.

Anne was surprised when Eric remained silent and didn't take the bait and engage in the banter he and Callie were so fond of. Callie obviously noticed it, too, because she peeked out of the walk-in and caught Anne's eyes. She nodded at Eric, and Anne shrugged. Eric was folding pastry boxes, a mindless, uncreative task, one that did not meet his very specific idea of his job description since he considered himself a creative genius.

Callie walked over to her friend and squeezed his arm. "What's goin' on, E?"

He replied with a sniffle. Callie looked at the ceiling and bit back a groan. Anne knew that Callie adored Eric, they both did, and he was a huge part of what made Callie's bakery a success. But he was twenty-six and liked to imagine that every guy he dated, or spent the night with, was *the one*. Anne and Callie both thought that at one time his naive romantic notions were adorable; now they were just part of their routine.

Anne and Callie had both told him repeatedly that finding the right guy was nearly impossible, no matter gay or straight. Men mostly had one thing on their mind, and it wasn't how they could make one person happy for the rest of their lives. Ironically Eric was also one of those men, but his relationship motto seemed to be *Do as I wish, not as I do*.

"I'm sorry, sweetie," Callie said. She rubbed circles onto Eric's back. "Did you and David break up?"

Anne looked over her shoulder. He shook his head but continued folding pink-striped pastry boxes. The logo on them matched the logo on Eric's pink work T-shirt, the same shirt that squeezed at the muscles across his back and shoulders. He was a beautiful man, toned and broad. It was such a shame for the women in Preston that he didn't have a little more swagger and a lot less Lady Gaga in his life. Not that it stopped women from flirting with him daily. Lucky for Callie he realized that turning on the charm with the female customers was good for business.

Callie dropped her hand, rolled her eyes at Anne, and then turned him around to face her. "Well then, what happened?"

"I broke up with *him*," he said quietly.

Callie sighed dramatically. "Why in the world did you do that? He was gorgeous, and very into you if your constant desire to overshare is any indication."

"That he was." Eric looked up with a wistful expression on his face before turning back to folding boxes. "But he wanted too much too fast, and it was making me feel suffocated."

"*Eric!*" Anne and Callie said at the same time.

Callie held up her hands. "What the hell do you really want out of life? You know what, hold that thought because I'm afraid the answer could be multifaceted. Are you gonna be okay? Because it's Friday and we're about to be swamped."

He gave a small nod and finally put down the box in his hand. "Yes, being busy is good."

"I promise I'll make it up to you. We bust ass today and tonight we go to Smokey's, okay? Sound good, Anne?"

"Oh . . . I don't—"

Callie shot her a glare.

"Of course," Anne said changing her tune. "Smokey's sounds like fun."

A grin spread across Eric's face. Callie definitely knew how to speak the guy's language. Smokey's was a bar in town that drew a decent crowd on the weekend, students from a nearby college making up a huge part of the clientele. It wasn't always ideal for Anne, but Callie and Eric—who were only twenty-seven—loved it. Anne usually had a good time once she got there, but dancing never called to her the way it did the others. She was just getting way too old. Plus she often didn't want to spend her weekends away from Claire. Unfortunately Claire was with her father this weekend so she had no easy out.

Yet after all of her recent embarrassments with a certain mechanic, maybe it was just what she needed. Mindless fun and flirting could be just what the doctor ordered to forget the sexy Mike Everett.

Callie grabbed the tray of fresh iced cinnamon rolls from Anne and headed for the front of the store while Anne and Eric prepped more trays. She was always reminded how impressive it was that Callie had managed to build such a lucrative business in just a little over a year here in Preston. When they'd first met she was baking out of her apartment, taking custom orders, and selling at the farmers' market. Now she was selling out daily, and still doing custom orders every week—at least her kitchen was now commercial. On top of that she managed to post new recipes to the blog twice a week, and the readers loved Callie's recipes. Some were twists on classics and some were her own personal creations. All were delicious.

By nine o'clock Anne had done all she could to help so she filled her travel coffee mug and said good-bye to Eric, hoping that maybe he and Callie would be too tired by the end of the day to go out dancing that evening, but even she knew there was not a strong chance of that.

* * *

Two times now Mike had experienced the pleasure of treats from Callie's Confections, but he'd yet to step foot in her shop. He'd seen it, of course, but he kept a pretty low profile in town save for the bar next door, the burger place, and the gas station. If he went out for a big night it was usually in the city. He wasn't really a "local bakery" type of guy, so he was a little surprised at his desire to stop into the shop.

No, he wasn't that surprised. All he'd done was think of Anne since she'd left his place earlier that week. He didn't want to call her since she hadn't technically given him her phone number. He was kind of hoping he might run into her at Callie's. A bell jingled when he opened the door, and Callie stood behind the counter writing on a pad.

"Good morning," she said in a cheery voice without lifting her eyes.

Before he had a chance to speak the door from the back swung open and a young, built guy came through it, bringing with him the scent of fresh-baked sugar cookies and a whiff of what almost smelled like Anne's flowery aroma. Mike hesitated for a moment; the scent was strong enough that he wondered if she was here. Was she back there with that guy? The thought bothered him for some reason—a lot, but before he head time to ponder his reaction the guy sporting the pink CALLIE'S CONFECTIONS tee spotted him and his eyes grew wide.

"Well *hello*, how can I be of service?"

Yeah, Mike didn't need to worry about *this* guy coming on to Anne. Now . . . coming on to him, that was a different situation. He glanced at Callie, who had finally looked up from her paper. Her smile was large and smug.

"I knew it. No one eats my goods twice and doesn't become addicted."

Mike watched as the guy behind the counter raised an eyebrow at her.

"And by goods, I mean the ones I'm selling," she said with a smile. She ran her hands along the top of the glass display case. "The ones in here."

Mike smiled at her joke but had the grace not to comment. Callie was really cute, she just wasn't the woman he'd thought about continually.

"There are only two cinnamon rolls left, Uncle Mike. Shall I put them in a box for you?"

He chuckled and scratched the back of his head, surprised at her use of the pet name. Did that mean Anne had mentioned him? He liked the thought that she must have.

"Okay sure, that'll be great," he finally said after gazing at all the offerings. "They *were* really good. Obviously, that's why I came."

"Of course it is." She grabbed a small box behind her and filled it with the two cinnamon rolls. He noticed she was smiling at something behind him. "Anything else? Coffee? Eric just brewed a fresh pot."

Mike glanced over his shoulder at Eric, who quickly feigned tidying up the stir sticks. Mike was pretty damn sure the guy had been looking at his ass. "Sure, that sounds good."

"Great." She tapped his purchase into the register. "That will be eight dollars and sixty-four cents."

He was a little shocked by the price of two cinnamon rolls and coffee, but he pulled a ten out of his wallet. He quickly considered ways to casually fish for some information about Anne but felt ridiculous; he was a grown-ass man, for God's sake.

"I know, my goods aren't cheap, but they're worth it. As you well know." She gave him a wink before she continued. "However, Mike . . . I will give you some very important intel for *free*."

Could he be so lucky . . . or so obvious? She shoved the register drawer closed and handed his change over the counter. She loaded up a little handled bag, throwing in some napkins and a plastic fork as she spoke.

"Poor Eric broke up with his boyfriend this morning," she said with an over-the-top pouty frown.

Mike straightened up a little as he glanced once more at Eric and cleared his throat. "Sorry to hear that, man."

Eric nodded. "Thank you. I'll be okay eventually."

"As you may have learned," Callie continued, "the only way to get over one guy is to get drunk and get under another one, you know?"

Is she serious? "Uh, do I know that? I'm not so sure," Mike said, befuddled.

"Don't worry, Alpha Mike, I have a point. So me, Eric . . ." She nodded toward her friend and then leaned over the counter and spoke slowly as she handed Mike his bag. ". . . *and my very best party-planning girlfriend* . . . are going to Smokey's tonight. Okay?"

Ha. He liked Callie. Best wing woman ever. He smiled slowly and nodded. "Okay. Thank you."

"You're very welcome. Eric has your coffee." She nodded behind him.

Mike turned and Eric was standing there waiting, coffee prepared and in hand. "I assumed you took it lightly sweetened and creamed, was I right?" Eric said with a wink.

"Yeah. Great, thanks." Mike swallowed, ready to get the hell out· of there.

"Oh and if you want your mind blown . . . stick those buns in the microwave for twenty seconds." Eric nodded at the bag.

"Uh . . . all right. I'll try that." He carefully took the to-go cup from Eric's hands and left the building shaking his head at having just had one of the most useful, yet uncomfortable conversations of his life.

Seven

Standing in her teeny walk-in closet, Anne let her eyes
wander over all of the unflattering options with a heavy
sigh. She had no idea what to wear to a bar on a Friday
night, but it really didn't matter because no matter what
she chose she would feel out of place.

Weekends without Claire were always a combination
of joy and misery for Anne. On one hand, there were
few mothers who didn't dream of some time to themselves, a reprieve from the never-ending questions, snack
preparation, and bedtime routine. On the other hand, she
hated not knowing what was going on when Claire was
with Scott.

It wasn't that she worried for Claire's safety or that
her daughter wouldn't feel loved. Scott may have grown
out of love with his wife, but he still adored their child
and for that Anne was grateful. No, it was the little things
that she worried over, like how did Scott respond when
Claire mentioned her mother. He may not *say* anything
negative, but many thoughts weren't expressed through
words. Or did Scott realize how vulgar prime-time

television could be these days? Or that a mere five minutes of Claire exploring his iPhone could potentially
rob her of her innocence forever?

But she had to let it go. Scott had rights, and they were
currently outlined by a biweekly visit starting from Friday after school and lasting to Monday morning. The
thing that really chafed was that Claire always spent the
Sunday night with Scott's parents, which conveniently
meant that he never had to get Claire and himself ready
on a school or work morning. In Anne's eyes, you weren't
a card-carrying parent until you juggled breakfast, school
papers, and the drop-off line while simultaneously trying to put on mascara. But she liked Scott's mother, so
she tried to get over that, too.

Most Claire-less weekends involved work, reading,
and too much time on the Internet, but Callie had
other plans for them this Friday evening. Anne stepped
out of a black skirt and tossed it onto the floor along-
side the other three outfits she'd just tried on and re-
jected.

"This one would be amazing." Callie pulled out a
black scoop-neck sleeveless dress. It was tight from waist
to boobs. The belted skirt was overlaid with black lace
and pleated out to just above Anne's knee. She loved that
dress, but . . .

"Nope, can't wear it. See this yellow shirtdress?"
Anne asked as she pointed to the dress in question in
her closet. "From behind it on back are all outfits that
are too small. Yellow dress forward are fat clothes." She
held her hands out game-show-host-style.

"Fat clothes, my ass." Callie dropped her arms in frustration, black lace dress still in hand. "Anne, you have

a totally hot body. What is wrong with you? Guys check you out all the time."

Anne wrinkled her nose. "No, I'm chubby." She pointed to her stomach in order to prove her point.

"Good heavens, woman, you're crazy. I have that, too."

Callie's comment was laughable. Their stomachs had nothing in common except a belly button, and Callie's was much more visible and sexy. She had the sleek and strong body of a dancer. Callie had spent all four of her college years on her university's elite dance team squad, and her figure was still reaping the benefits. It was unfair that she now made a living taste-testing pastries and still managed to look the way she did.

"Anne, try the damn dress on. I invited you out, so I get to pick your clothes." Callie yanked the dress from its hanger and tossed it to Anne.

"I've never heard that rule before." Anne pulled the dress over her head, shimmied it down past her boobs, and stood in front of the full-length mirror.

"Holy shit . . . this dress is so happening tonight." Callie bent down into the closet and shuffled her way through the mess that was Anne's shoe stash. A muffled screech came from the darkness before Callie pulled back holding one old cowboy boot. "And these are going with it."

"What? I'm not twenty anymore, Cal, I'll look like a hooker at a rodeo in that outfit."

"I know, right? It'll be perfect."

"What does it even matter? I thought this night was about Eric. We should be trying dresses on him." Anne sat on her bed and slipped a worn cowboy boot over her sock. "Where is he anyway?"

"He just texted that he's on the way," Callie said.

"I wish Lindsey was back so I had someone to hang out with while you two get your party on." Lindsey was always fun, but lower-key than Callie.

"Well, then I'm glad she's not back yet, because you need to have a good time tonight. As much as I love Lindsey, you two enable each other to be fuddy-duddies at the club."

"Not sure if Smokey's qualifies as a club."

"It's as good as we're gonna get in Preston, and sometimes I have to dance."

Anne stood up and took a final glance in the mirror. She had to admit, she did feel kind of hot in this outfit, even if it was squeezing her top half a little too much, so much so that she didn't even need a bra. She needed a confidence boost after the week she'd had. It was lucky that Mike had gifted her with the referral of the Monsers' party because she'd been grateful for the distraction.

One source of pride for the week was that she'd managed to book the venue she'd been pining over. It was a beautiful farm just outside of Preston owned by a lovely older couple. The property was one Anne had admired for years. The farmhouse was large and idyllic with a long porch and large pillars. The massive old barn out back was the most perfect setting for the party, rustic yet spacious, and it hadn't held livestock or hay bales for quite some time so prepping it wouldn't be too much work.

When she'd stopped by on Wednesday she saw that the elderly woman still maintained a beautiful and extensive flower garden behind the house. Anne's mind had gone wild with all her ideas of guests mingling in the garden, and then the main party in the barn. Luckily she'd come equipped with cupcakes and ready to beg. It had worked, and she'd talked them into letting her rent the property for the Monsers' party.

After that she'd hired an amazing band for the "mock-tail" hour, and a popular DJ for the dancing, and had lined up interviews with several caterers. Things were moving along nicely for her first major project, and it kept her from thinking about how ridiculous she felt for being pulled into Uncle Mike's sexy trap not once but twice in a matter of seventy-two hours. Okay, almost kept her from thinking about it.

The moment she'd caught a glimpse of the young, big-busted woman in Mike's shop, she'd felt like a complete idiot. Anne had been silly to even consider a fling with Mike Everett. It was probably a blessing in disguise that the woman had entered and saved her from making a complete fool of herself. She could never compete with the perky blonde.

With a sigh, Anne turned back to the mirror and pushed her own breasts up and together, considering her reflection. These things had nursed a child, for heaven's sake, but they weren't too bad. She was still a pretty firm C cup, and nothing was facing south, thank goodness. With another sigh she turned and walked into the bathroom where Callie was touching up her own makeup.

"Maybe there will be a hot guy there. One look at you in the slutty-cowgirl getup, and you could get lucky tonight." Callie teased.

"I'm not looking for a hot guy. I'm a lost cause when it comes to men."

"You never know. I have a good feeling about Smokey's tonight," Callie said.

"Psssh. The last time you had a good feeling every hottie that approached our table ended up hitting on Eric."

"I know, and he was such a cocky little brat about it," Callie said as she picked at her curls once more. She then turned to Anne and gave her a head-to-toe perusal. "You look so hot, Anne. Let's do this."

Sunday through Thursday, Smokey's would fall into the "local dive bar" category. But every other Friday and Saturday they hired a DJ from the city, which drew in enough bodies that it could be considered a club—according to Callie. Not normally Anne's scene—okay, never Anne's scene, as she'd never really developed a taste for sweating bodies and loud thumping music. But it was fun to dance, and she was having a really good time. Now that she knew who Mike was, and that he lived and worked next door, she just hoped that he didn't walk over and have a beer. Tonight was about forgetting the man existed.

About six dances and three drinks in, Anne was hot and thirsty for something not alcoholic so she headed for the main bar and squeezed her way in to ask for a glass of water. Several middle-aged women sat flirting with the beefy bartender who looked like he'd just left his motorcycle gang. He was slightly scary with tattoos and a goatee, but when he saw her and gave a wide smile, his features softened almost to the point of handsomeness. He handed her a glass of water, which she gulped, when one of the middle-aged women spoke to her.

"Aren't you Anne from the crafty website?"

She swallowed her water and wiped some sweat from her forehead. "Yes, I am." It was a little embarrassing to be asked that in a place like this. This wasn't her kind of hangout, and it definitely didn't match the tone of her blog, which was pretty wholesome and family-centered. As her small newspaper column gained popularity locally, this happened more often.

"Are you here with a date?"

"Oh no, just some friends out having a good time," she answered with a smile.

"That's what Friday night is for, right?" The woman closest to her motioned to the bartender. "Have a shot with us before you go. We're fans."

"Oh . . . no, I shouldn't."

"Aiden, give her a shot," one woman said. Her vibrant red hair was in a sassy updo and her face had been pretty once upon a time, but she'd obviously lived a hard life. Anne put her hand up in protest.

"Just following orders." The bartender slid a shot glass in front of Anne with a wink. She didn't want to be rude, so she lifted it and they all clanked glasses before she threw it back. The liquid burned down her throat and she held back a cough. "Oh wow. That was . . . that was really good."

The redheaded woman laughed; not one of them seemed to struggle with the fiery drink. Anne thanked them and insisted she find her friends, but first she entered the dimly lit women's restroom and yanked a crunchy paper towel from the dispenser. Resting it between her dress and the counter, she leaned toward the mirror. She took another paper towel and patted at the light sheen of sweat on her brow as she reflected back on the past hour. Besides the recent shot, two men already had bought her a drink, which meant she had a healthy buzz and was feeling confident. That was about her limit; she never liked to get out of control.

Though not a complete stranger to male attention, even Anne was shocked by *two* free drinks from men. That was cause for a celebration . . . and maybe another pair of cowgirl boots. The guys had even been cute. Anne washed her hands and tousled her hair, which she'd left loose and wavy. She had to admit she looked good tonight. Maybe if she'd worn her hair down around Mike she wouldn't have looked so much like a "customer." With a promise to herself not to think of Uncle Mike again, Anne left the restroom.

It was still a little early by club standards so it was not yet a total crush, but the place was what Callie liked to call "promisingly packed." Meaning the chances of finding a hot guy to dance with were pretty good, but it wasn't so crowded you lost your friends in the crowd.

Anne headed back to the table where her friends were seated to find one of her drink suppliers waiting for her. He grinned when he spotted her across the room and pushed off from the side of the booth. *Oh gosh.* What was she getting herself into?

The deep bass of the dance music seemed to match each of his steps as he prowled toward her, weaving through the high-top tables. Anne couldn't help looking past his manly swagger at the two goofballs she called her friends giving her the thumbs-up behind him. Eric even pretended to claw like a tiger, his face imitating a growl. Anne really loved those two.

She met her sexy free-drink man at the edge of the dance floor and he slid an arm around her waist, pulling her in close before he spoke. "We need to dance."

She looked up into his eyes as he finished off his beer. She wondered how old he was. It was possible that he was nearing thirty. Maybe. He was probably closer to twenty-five. But who the hell cared right now? Her limbs felt light and tingly. He reached out and set his empty bottle on a nearby table then pushed his body into hers from chest to thigh, backing her into the crowd of moving bodies.

The friction of his firm torso against her warm languid one was making her head spin. She wrapped her arms around his neck and moved to the music. It was nice to look into a man's face and see something more than friendliness in his eyes. Although she'd been pretty damn sure she'd seen that earlier this week in Mike Everett's face . . . nope, she wasn't going to think about him.

She refocused on the cutie in front of her and smiled as one of his hands brushed against her rear and finally palmed it full-on. The worst part was that she allowed him to keep it there. What was wrong with her? It was one thing to look like a rodeo hooker; she hadn't planned on acting like one, too. But she couldn't seem to stop herself, or care.

She turned her head to the right as the handsome stranger ground his body against her. Callie and Eric were dancing beside them now, and they looked good dancing together. For a moment Anne thought about what a bummer it was that they couldn't be a couple. Of course Callie was a dancer, so she always made whatever move she was doing look incredibly hot.

Anne did a 180 in her partner's arms so she could face her friends, and maybe cool the dude off since his hands were getting a little too aggressive. Callie danced up to Anne's front, a huge grin on her face. Anne could feel all of her sexy stranger moving against her backside, the strong smell of his cologne lingering in the air.

Callie wiggled her cute small body up against Anne's. Watching Callie move—or do anything for that matter— usually resulted in Anne questioning her own sexiness, but tonight she didn't do that; the feel of the cute guy behind her was all she wanted to think about. They all danced together for a moment before Callie leaned close. "He's really hot, don't you think."

Anne nodded and the hand resting on her rib cage squeezed as if he'd heard the conversation. Those damn club whispers were not as intimate as one hoped.

Callie got even closer to Anne's ear. "Don't look now, but someone to your right is not enjoying our super-sexy show." Anne's body tensed as Callie and the stranger behind her kept her in a tight gyrating sandwich. Someone was watching her dance like a floozy to this song about riding some guy's pony? *Great.*

The music was loud and thumped through the floor all the way to her nerve endings. She turned her head toward where Callie had indicated as a warm hand slid up her thigh, pulling her dress higher.

Her eyes adjusted to the dark area beyond the lights of the dance floor, and she met gazes with none other than Mike Everett. *Shit.* His eyes were slightly hooded and his lips in a tight line. He was leaning against a high table watching her dance. Another guy sat beside him talking to some woman with her cleavage on display.

For a fleeting second she felt embarrassed. This was not how a mother or a woman over thirty should act. She would regret it tomorrow, but tonight her alcohol-influenced brain was telling her to let loose . . . a little. Who cared what Uncle Mike thought about her, and no one else she knew well was here besides her friends.

However, that didn't keep Anne's gaze from travel-ing down his shoulder to his biceps, flexed and pushing at his shirt where he leaned onto the table. His large hand was wrapped around a beer bottle. He was so gorgeous she could feel the heat of embarrassment flush her cheeks again, or maybe it was the shot she'd tossed back a few minutes ago. She was such a fool for having crushed on him.

Eric returned from a trip to the bar and handed her and Callie a bottle. Anne grabbed hers, threw back her head, and took a long drink before she looked back at Mike, whose eyes hadn't left her. The colored lights were hot, and a bead of sweat escaped her hairline. She lifted her arm and brushed the drop of sweat from her face.

Her dance partner, still behind her, took that as some sort of invitation and pulled all of her locks up in his hand. She felt a small tug as he pulled her head to the side a little and then lowered his lips to her neck. Anne gasped at the feel of his hot breath and wet lips. It was a little domineering, and she pulled away, throwing an innocent smile over her shoulder before she looked back at Mike. He had turned away and was now also talking to Cleavage and her friend Even-More-Cleavage. Screw him. Why was she even giving him a second thought?

The song changed, switching up their rhythm and her

partner spoke into her ear. "I'm gonna go get another beer. Don't leave this spot."

Anne nodded, a little relieved. Callie grabbed Anne's hand, pulling them together. The song that came on was obviously popular because more bodies had closed in around them, shielding her from Mike's gaze.

"Holy shit, that was so fucking awesome," Callie yelled over the music, obviously intoxicated.

"What do you mean, that was so awkward. He pulled my hair. What the hell?" Anne used her palm to massage where the strange lips had touched her. She was done with this guy. It would probably be wise to get lost in the crowd before he returned.

"Did you see his face? There is nothing hotter than a guy brooding and jealous." Callie's eyes were wild with adrenaline, and Anne realized she hadn't been talking about Caveman Hair Puller. Callie stood on her tiptoes trying to see Mike over Anne's shoulder.

Anne shook her head as Callie grinned, dancing again to the music. She was still young enough to enjoy this kind of drama. Anne had to admit it was kinda fun. She hadn't done this sort of thing ever, not even in high school. She'd always been too busy trying to be a good girl, get good grades, and make the honor roll. In other words, she hadn't had a lot of fun—all her own doing, of course. Her parents had never put pressure on her. She did that all by herself.

But then a sobering thought struck. What if Callie was wrong and Mike was glaring at her because she was acting like a promiscuous cougar at a bar full of college kids, not because he was jealous? He probably never imagined she would be at this place, and now he was no doubt disgusted with her behavior.

Damn it, she should feel good . . . and happy. And she did; the buzz she had going made her feel warm all over. But she would feel a lot better if she didn't have to witness Mike picking up other women. She turned her attention back to Callie, Eric, and the music that was blaring across the dance floor. Mike could think what he wanted. She was done caring. Tonight was about forgetting him.

Eight

Thankfully Mike was sitting directly under a speaker so he could barely hear the woman in front of him talking. He nodded when it seemed appropriate. Her smile indicated that she was appeased, and so did her hand resting on his thigh. He tended to avoid Smokey's on the weekends because this was not his idea of a good time—too loud, too crowded, and too many drunken idiots. Since he'd spent his early twenties one step away from death or incarceration, he was unfamiliar with the frat-boy party way of life. When had he gotten old? He came to a bar to chill out, have a beer, catch up with Aiden who let him drink cheap in exchange for tune-ups and oil changes, and, yes, occasionally flirt with someone. But this was madness. He couldn't believe Anne was here, but sure enough she was.

He risked a look back to the dance floor. He could no longer see her, and he didn't know if that was good or bad. Watching her body move in that dress, especially before she'd known he was watching, was hot as hell. But seeing that jackass put his mouth on her had been almost more than he could stand. The anger that pounded through Mike's body when the fucker had pulled Anne's hair had surprised him. He wasn't the jealous type, never had a reason to be, but something about the sight had made his jaw twitch and his fingers flex.

Bodies parted just long enough to see that Anne and her friends were dancing alone. He stood up, forcing the woman's hand from his leg. "Excuse me for a minute," he yelled over the pounding music.

He gave a slight nod to Derek. He'd told his friend exactly why they were here tonight in order to get him out. Derek wasn't into the club scene, either, although he was picking up women like he was made for it. No surprise—his friend had the rich-guy look going for him. He just didn't get out much between making tons of money and caring for his seven-year-old son. Not that his friend was a money-hungry asshole. He was as kind and humble as they come, but he did do well for himself because he was a hard worker. Maybe Derek should hook up with Anne—they both had kids and knew what it was like to be a single parent. He was high-class, had a college degree, and could give Anne everything she deserved.

Nope, just the thought of it made Mike's blood boil hotter. Sweet little Anne deserved many things that weren't taught in school—things he knew very well, and he was going to be the one to give them to her.

He made his way to the far side of the dance floor, ignoring wandering hands and the suggestive smiles of the women dancing. He knew exactly where he was going, and when he found himself standing directly behind Anne Edmond, he relaxed and breathed in deep. Her scent filled his nose and her hair fell down her back, the colored lights making it sparkle. He'd wondered what it would look like down, and just as he imagined, it was incredibly sexy. In fact, everything about her was making him hard at the moment.

She stopped dancing and leaned into her friend to talk. Over Anne's shoulder Mike met Callie's eyes and winked. He owed her for making this happen. Callie grinned and turned around to dance with Eric, who gave Mike a huge smile.

Very slowly Mike slipped his hands past Anne's elbows and wrapped his arms around her waist. She jumped and then relaxed a little, obviously thinking her overeager dance partner had returned. With one hand she lifted her beer to her lips and began to move to the beat, but didn't melt against him. Mike was sure he could still sense a little tension in her torso, still thinking she was with her previous dance partner. Maybe she hadn't been into the prick after all . . . Mike held back a grin.

She was obviously a little buzzed, so it took her a second to realize something was off, but he knew the minute she did by the instant freezing of her body. She jerked her head to the side.

Mike chuckled behind her and leaned in to her ear, letting his lips brush against her hair. "Are you done punishing me, Perfect?"

He couldn't deny that the way her limbs immediately relaxed into him when he spoke was a complete turn-on and made him relieved. He wanted her to touch him and feel comfortable doing it, wanted her to feel safe. When he pulled her firmly back against his body, she lifted her chin, the crown of her head rubbing against his collarbone as she turned to speak.

"I don't know what you're talking about," she said loud enough to be heard over the music.

He tightened his grip on her waist as he growled into her ear, "I think you do, Anne."

She wiggled within his arms and twisted her body around to face him, looking straight into his eyes. She was beautiful tonight. Her dress showed off her soft shoulders, and the leather of her boots looked amazing next to her tan legs. He glanced down, taking in the sight of her breasts pressed against his chest.

His hands tightened on her hips before sliding down her backside and gently easing up her skirt so he could get a hand beneath it just below her butt. Anne gasped when his palms hit her bare skin. The fullness of her short dress cascaded around his hands, concealing anything indecent. He exhaled hard, loving the feel of her, the softness of her warm skin. Finally having his body flush against hers was better than he expected, and he tried not to think about how moments ago she'd been this close to another man.

He leaned in and ran his tongue along the soft lobe of her ear before he spoke. "Watching you out here was driving me fucking crazy."

He felt a small tremor race through her and then her chest move against his own with each of her deep breaths. They were cheek-to-cheek, and he adjusted just a little, slanting his eyes down to see her. The roughness of his stubble scraped at her tender skin, and when she tilted her face up to meet his eyes he immediately took advantage of the position. This should have already happened, and it would have if they hadn't been interrupted in the garage. He would be damned if it didn't happen tonight.

He dipped his face down and lightly brushed his lips to her soft, full ones, tempting her with light kisses. She was still at first, but it didn't take her long to respond, and when she did it wasn't just her mouth that reacted. Her whole body once again molded against his, and the slow movement of her hips pressed his growing erection into her lower stomach. She drew in a quick breath through their kiss, subsequently torturing him more. He coaxed her lower lip into his mouth and sucked lightly, and he swore he heard her moan even over the noise.

After a moment she pulled free of his hands and kiss; she briefly looked into his eyes before leaning in and taking control, crushing her hot mouth into his. Mike groaned against her as he ran one hand up the length of her, from her hip to the side of her breast, the other hand cradled the back of her head, angling her face just the way he wanted it.

The intensity of the moment was explosive, messy, and wet. Anne's hands found their way to his neck, and she hung on tight as her right leg shifted forward, perfectly pressing her center against his upper thigh. He rocked into her, knowing the friction would be just what she wanted, and his intuition was rewarded when she threw back her head, eyes wide. Her lids fluttered as he continued to press their bodies together to the rhythm of the music.

He could feel the people around them, hear the bass pounding in his ears, but right now his attention was focused on soft, warm Anne. He dipped his head once more and ran his lips along her jaw as he trailed his fingers up her rib cage. She was still flat against his chest, so nobody saw when he slipped his hand between them and laid his hand against her breast, and gently squeezed.

Anne's head snapped up as if she needed a breath, her hands grabbed at both sides of his face, pulling him back to her. He was ready to kiss her again but she leaned into his ear and made him as hard as a rock with her sexy voice. "I want you. Bad."

It was his turn to shiver, because he was not expecting to hear those words. He'd known Anne was attracted to him, but he didn't know what to expect tonight and had come prepared to work for what he wanted. And it looked like work he would, just in a different manner than he'd originally expected. He had no problem there—he was ready to give her whatever she wanted. He lowered his head to her ear again as her hands clutched his biceps. "You're gonna have me, Anne. Tonight."

Nine

Anne allowed Mike to lead her through the pressing bodies at the bar but pulled back when she realized they were heading for the door. He turned to look with questioning eyes, and she jerked her head toward the table where Callie and Eric had reconvened. He nodded and turned to follow her, obviously understanding that she needed to tell them she was leaving.

She'd said she wanted him. She even said *bad*, and he'd taken it as an invitation for immediate action. Of course he had, because if she was honest with herself that was exactly what it had been. Hell, it had nearly been a plea. Was that what she had intended? Going home with sexy Mike Everett? She wanted to, yes badly, but now that his tongue wasn't part of the equation her senses were coming back, reminding her that just a few hours ago she was cursing his existence. But God, his touch was amazing, those strong hands, his hard chest, and that very talented mouth. What woman could say no to that?

She made her way across the bar toward her friends with Mike at her heels. When they reached the booth his hand landed on her neck. The gesture was a little possessive; his rough thumb stroked a path toward her hairline, sending a chill down her spine. Everything about him made her nerves tingle with impending ecstasy. His muscular arms had enveloped her on the dance floor, and having his hard thigh between her legs had given her a hint at what his naked body would look and feel like all over. There wasn't even a question that this man knew how to make her feel good; just thinking of him could induce orgasms. Not that she'd done that. Today.

The music had grown louder in the last hour, or maybe she was a little too intoxicated. Either way she leaned down to speak directly into her friend's ear, but before Anne opened her mouth Callie beat her to it with a smug grin. "Leaving so soon?"

Anne cocked her head to the side, annoyed at being so predictable. But God, yes, she was leaving, and she was excited and scared and overwhelmed. A shot glass full of something pink and orange sat in front of Callie untouched. Anne picked it up and downed it in one motion, ignoring Callie's weak protests. If she was going to leave this bar with Uncle Mike, she couldn't lose her buzz. Some extra liquid confidence couldn't hurt. "I'll call you tomorrow."

"You better." Callie smiled and said good-bye to Mike, who had waited patiently behind Anne, his fingers running lightly across her back and neck.

Anne gave a small wave to Eric, who winked at her as he danced in the booth. She turned back to Mike, and he held his hand out to her once again. She grabbed it, pushing down the unsure thoughts that were bubbling to the surface of her mind.

There was no mistaking that he wanted this—*right*? He'd come to her on the dance floor, and accused her of punishing him. Had she been punishing him? That hadn't been her initial intent, but it had felt amazing to see the irritated look on his face. To know that seeing her with another man had made him feel a hint of jealousy. She wasn't used to anyone showing possession of any sort, but it was arousing.

Now here she was, following Mike as he waved to the burly bartender as they headed for the exit. Random thoughts pinged through her foggy brain, trying to make sense of the incredibly hot man leading her out the door. Did he come here often? What did he expect from her? Were they going to go all the way? Had she worn sexy underwear? Had he ever had sex with someone over thirty? The last one was doubtful.

The main parking lot was behind Smokey's, accessible by stairs. Anne breathed in the balmy night and without thinking gripped Mike's hand as she considered how many drunk idiots had fallen down the wooden steps that led to the back lot. She was grateful that she'd chosen boots over heels.

"I got ya," he said, as they walked slowly and silently down the two flights.

Once they hit gravel she attempted to loosen their connection but Mike wasn't having it. He gave her hand a squeeze, keeping them close as they weaved through the cars toward the rear of the lot. His new-looking black Camaro was backed into its spot and slightly angled. It chirped as the alarm disarmed, the doors unlocked, and the engine simultaneously turned. Of course he would have a remote start.

"So you're one of those guys, huh? I hate crooked parkers," she said with a hand on her hip.

He dropped her fingers and grabbed her waist, pulling her firmly against his body. "*Hate* is a strong word, Perfect."

"Maybe," she said, embarrassed at how breathless she was. Every time he called her that name it gave her a little thrill, and also made her wonder why. She was nowhere near perfect, but hearing him say it made her want him to say it again and again. She melted into his arms and angled her head back as he nuzzled into her neck. The heat of his mouth blew against her skin and she gasped quietly as his tongue ran across her collarbone.

"I don't think you *really* hate me right now, do you?" His fingers skimmed down her side and cupped her ass through her dress. She shook her head, looking into his eyes before he leaned in again to press his lips just below her ear. Just when she thought she might die from the sensation of his tongue lightly touching her, he pulled away and patted his palm against her backside. "Let's go."

Well. She could hardly voice offense at his treatment when the act had every nerve in her body humming.

He pulled open the passenger door and she sat down, the taut leather seat gripping her hips on both sides and leaning her back as if she were in a race car. He shut the door and she took a deep breath. The cool air was already lowering the temperature. She watched as Mike entered the other side and settled in, messing with an illuminated screen on the dash and then finally grasping the stick shift between them. It was totally hot seeing him behind the wheel of such a sexy car.

His eyes met hers and the corner of his mouth lifted in a naughty smirk as he put the gear shift into reverse and then pulled into the night. Even from the passenger seat Anne could feel the power of the car, engine low and rumbling as it vibrated through her body. She could have watched him driving all night, his long masculine fingers gripping the stick, his solid arms stretched out to palm the steering wheel. There wasn't anything about his physique that didn't melt her from the inside out.

They approached the longest straightaway on the route to her house and he dropped into second gear, showing off and taking it faster than was legal in a residential area. When he swung into Anne's driveway she giggled, the last shot of alcohol settling into her bloodstream.

"Were you trying to share with me the *thrill of the ride*?" she said with a grin.

He opened his door and put one foot onto the concrete before looking at her. "I'm about to share something with you . . . but that wasn't even close to the thrill of *this* ride." He shifted in the seat and leaned toward her. Apparently her body was now trained to respond because she instinctively met him halfway. His lips swiped at hers once, twice, and then he pulled back a little. They were still close as he whispered, "Get out of the car, Anne."

She slammed her lips shut and exited the vehicle. Stepping up to the garage door keypad, she spoke over her shoulder. "You're kind of bossy tonight."

Anne began to type in her code—Claire's birthday—when Mike's body molded against the back of hers. Both of his hands settled on her hips as the door rumbled to life beside them.

"I'm sorry, but I've been thinking about you all week, and I don't want to wait any longer to get my hands on you." He swept her tousled hair to the side and placed his lips on her nape. The sensation was maddening, and her fingers latched onto the wood frame of the garage door. This man and his roaming mouth were dangerous.

"Do you have a thing for my neck?" Anne asked as her body instinctively pushed back into his. He placed another wet openmouthed kiss on her ear, sending a jolt of pleasure straight through her torso and settling heavily between her thighs.

He pushed his erection against her backside once more as he spoke. "I have a thing for all of you."

A chill ran through her and she moved aside, making him follow her into the house. The garage entrance was off the kitchen and she flipped on a light switch, filling the room with warmth and brightness. It was the best lighting they'd seen each other in all night.

The harsh change of scenery brought her back to reality and with it the realization that it had taken less than a hot second for her to bring Mike back to her house to have sex. Because that was what this was about, right? All of their conversation had been about bodies and touching and *rides*. Suddenly she wasn't sure she could look him in the eye.

Club-Going-One-Night-Stander wasn't the role Anne was accustomed to playing. She rarely allowed herself to become intoxicated, and she hadn't had sex since her divorce. Now in her own home, surrounded by her real life, she was beginning to digest what was really happening and it was a little overwhelming. Maybe seeing her at Smokey's made him think she was a different kind

of girl. She'd sort of felt like a different girl, that was
for sure. There was no way he would be calling her perfect after this.

Unable to control her conflicting thoughts or her fidgeting, she grabbed the bag of coffee out of the cabinet
and headed for the coffeemaker. Her feel-good drunk-
enness was waning in the bright light of her kitchen and
forcing her to view this situation for what it was. A huge
mistake.

"Anne," a warm, low voice said behind her. She
stopped leveling a scoop of beans and straightened her
back, but she didn't turn and face him. He spoke again
in a slightly amused yet soothing deep tone. "What are
you doing?"

"I'm making coffee, sound good? I think I drank a
little too much and this should probably help—" She was
cut off when an arm reached around her and took the
tablespoon from her fingers, dropping it in the sink and
sending beans clinking against the porcelain.

"I love coffee in the morning, but at night I like other
things. And this night those things include you naked."
His sexy words and the way he brushed his fingertips
along her shoulder sent bumps racing down her arm.

She turned slowly, taking in the full effect of a well-
lit Mike Everett. He was a beautiful sight with his square
jaw and rugged features. His hair was a little too long
on top and styled by running his fingers through it, and
his deep-set blue eyes made her weak in the knees. It
was shocking to know that this handsome man was
standing here, in her kitchen, wanting to touch *her*. She
gave him an awkward half smile. All of this was just
too good to possibly be true.

"I feel like I'm losing you here, Anne," he whispered as he brushed a strand of hair from her forehead. It was so gentle and yet incredibly intimate.

She relaxed a little. "I'm sorry. It's only now that we're here I just . . ." She didn't know what to say. She didn't want to change her mind, especially when her body wanted to attach itself to his and never let go. Seeing Mike naked would be the best thing in the whole world, but him seeing *her* naked sounded like the absolute worst form of torture. Why did her brain have to become active in moments like this? He didn't wait for her to finish her thoughts. He stepped closer, his thighs pressing against her skirt.

"I think you should stop thinking so hard, unless you don't want me to touch you, right here." His hand lifted to her jaw and cupped lightly. His fingers fanned out against her face, rough and callused. Good Lord, she loved the feel of them. "And here."

His opposite hand delved under her hair and behind her head, tipping her face up to him slowly. Her lips parted and she heard her own breath coming out in tiny puffs from deep in her chest. He was so close, in fact, that with every exhale she felt her breasts move against his chest.

"Now I'm gonna kiss you. And then . . . I'm going to touch you *everywhere*."

She was definitely in trouble, because all of her internal battles over this situation instantly gave up the fight with those words from his soft lips. His eyes hadn't left hers.

"Tell me it's okay, Anne." His breath smelled faintly of beer, and it mixed with his cologne to create the most perfect man scent that had ever graced Anne's kitchen. She nodded in surrender because she was a total goner. She needed to shut down those negative thoughts in her head because she wanted this more than anything.

"Okay," she whispered.

His lips closed over hers and took her mouth in a hot kiss. There was no testing and no gentleness; this was raw and unleashed passion. She gave it back, licking at him, nipping and biting just as he did to her. His hands roamed over her entire body, sending her nerves into a frenzy. When his tongue passed her lips, tangling with hers, all thoughts of stopping fled. They kissed for what seemed like an eternity, until she felt like any second she'd internally combust. Her eyes fluttered and she ran her hands over his neck, his back; then finally she returned the gesture he was so fond of and grabbed his butt as she licked into his mouth. A low growl rose from his throat. She smiled against his lips.

She could feel the return of his smile against her, their lips still touching, until he spoke. "You have a wicked mouth, Anne. Makes me wonder what else it can do."

Oh shit. The way he talked to her made her feel a little loopy; thank goodness she was resting against the cabinet. She pulled back to look into his eyes, their noses still brushing. She'd never been a dirty talker, never really been *with* one, either, but she wanted to try. "Maybe I'll show you what my mouth can do . . . if you're lucky." *Okay, that was lame.*

His eyes crinkled and his mouth went into a roguish lopsided grin. "That sounds promising, but you should know I'd never expect something I'm not willing to give."

With that he turned, led her around the island and

pulled a chair out from the kitchen table before he spun
them so that he was backing her up to the wooden surface. He pressed his face into her neck, placing small
kisses on her skin, teasing her with his lips and his
tongue. She let her head fall back as her fingers laced
through his hair. Everything he did made her crazy with
desire, more so than she'd ever been in her entire life.
The way he spoke, kissed, touched.

"Lie down," he whispered against her neck.

Anne's eyes opened and she yanked her head up to
stare into his face when she realized what he wanted.
"What? On the table?"

He patted the wooden surface behind her. "Lie down
and rest your sexy cowgirl boots right here." He patted
a hand on his thigh.

Anne was frozen. There was no way she could lie
down and display herself like a buffet—not that the idea
didn't have her insides turning to hot liquid. "People eat
there."

He chuckled and grabbed her around the waist.
"You're catching on."

She gasped, and her heart pounded at the vision in
her mind. She wanted to do it—she wanted to feel his
mouth on her—but paranoia and her extreme self-
conscious nature were sabotaging her. Shit, she wished
she had a bottle of wine to chug real quick.

He leaned into her, forcing her legs to part so he could
stand between them. A quick kiss landed on her lips as
one hand found its way under her skirt. His warm fingers skimmed her upper thigh, across the front, and finally found their way to her center as he cupped her with

his large hand. He really knew how to get his way. Every sensation was driving her mad.

He kissed her again, their tongues fondling each other, and she felt her body being angled down until finally her shoulders hit cool wood. As soon as she was flat on the table Mike's mouth began to work down her front while his free hand teased her nipple through the tight dress.

Anne arched her back, pushing against his palms, and he rewarded her eagerness by drawing the bodice of her dress down until one breast came free. She had never, ever experienced anything like this.

"You're so fucking beautiful, Anne." His mouth closed over a nipple, warm and wet, and he drew it slowly into his mouth, the suction matching the throbbing of her core, which she desperately wanted him to touch skin-to-skin and not just through the cotton of her underwear.

As if she'd spoken the thought out loud, one finger angled perfectly above the right spot and applied a light pressure, making her moan. Mike lifted his body from hers, leaving her aching. She raised her head off the table and glanced toward her knees to see him sit down in the chair, his eyes half lidded meeting hers. His expression was predatory as he pushed her skirt up her thighs. Anne let her head fall back and clamped her eyes shut so as not to be blinded by the bright light over the table.

Logic and that insecure side of herself still reeling from a broken marriage were telling her to stop him, cover herself, close her legs. In fact she must have been trying to do just that, because both of his hands grasped her inner thighs and held them firm as he spoke. "Let me see you, Anne."

Mike applied a little more pressure and thankfully Anne let her legs fall open, revealing her black panties and pale inner thighs. The sight of which nearly undid him. He could tell this hadn't been easy for her, offering herself up this intimately, and the fact that she'd done it for him was incredibly gratifying.

His hands rested on her inner knees and he traced a finger up her smooth skin, along the cleft of her thigh, and enjoyed the tremor that radiated through her body. One fingertip teased her panty line up and down, and he felt her tense.

"Oh God, Mike." Her words came between short breaths.

"You don't need to be shy with me, Anne." He stood up again and leaned over her, taking in her flushed cheeks and shut eyes. Her lips parted on a soft whimper as he ran his finger one more time up and down her damp panties. "Your body is telling me how much you like this."

"I do like it . . . I just . . ." she said in a small voice.

Mike stopped instantly and jerked his hand away to settle on her thigh. She opened her eyes and looked at him. He wasn't used to getting turned down at this point in the game, but despite what Katie said earlier in the week, he wasn't an asshole. If Anne wasn't into this, he'd stop.

He hovered above her warm body, one arm propped on the table next to her waist. "Too far?"

When she didn't respond immediately, he began to ease off her, but she grabbed his arm. "No, I lied. I mean . . . I didn't lie, but I do want this. Really bad, it's just . . ."

"Just what?" He gently smoothed her hair away from her face because he couldn't seem to keep from touching her in any way she'd allow him to. Maybe things were happening too fast. Even if it didn't happen tonight he knew he'd be willing to wait. Maybe he needed to slow down for her sake.

"Are you sure *you* want it?" She asked. Her eyes looked wary at the words.

He jerked his head back; a shocked laugh escaped his mouth. "You can't be serious." She raised her eyebrows and scrunched her nose. What the hell? "You *are* serious."

"I'm sorry. I'm not good at this. I'm a mom. I'm older than you. I feel a little slutty in this outfit, and you're so . . ." A frustrated groan left Anne's lips and she slapped her hands over her eyes. "Somebody shut me up."

"Done." Mike leaned down and took Anne's mouth with his, parting her lips with his tongue and fully possessing her. Not a word was leaving these lips. Anne was unsure of herself, but she'd fought that uncertainty with him time and time again now, at her daughter's party and at his shop, and it was incredibly sexy. How did she not see that? She was gorgeous, and drove him crazy with how incredibly sexy she was. Mike would just have to prove it to her.

"I'm not sure why you doubt how bad I want you, Anne." He spoke as his kisses worked their way over her chest, pulling one nipple into his mouth while he freed the other breast with his fingers. Every inch of her skin was hot and ready for him to touch if only she would stop worrying. He stood up and tugged lightly on her arm and then situated her hand against his jeans right against his erection. "Do you feel this?"

She nodded her head, lips parted, and heavy breaths lifting her naked chest up and down. She moved her fingers, grasping at his length as well as she was able to through the thick denim. The feel of her hands on him had him surging his hips forward, pushing against her palm. Lord, she had no idea what she was doing to him.

He laid his hand over hers, applying pressure and guiding them together up and down. "This doesn't see a mom, your age, or the outfit you call slutty and I call hot, and it doesn't matter because all of those things make you Perfect. You are an incredibly sexy woman, who I know for a fact wants me while sprawled across her kitchen table."

She squeezed him through his jeans, a smile breaking out on her mouth.

"So tell me what you want now," he said. "You wanna stop, we stop. You need to be sure."

She hesitated for a second, her hand still teasing him, and then slowly reached for the zipper of his fly. "I want you."

"Tell me what you want me to do." He let her continue to undo his pants slowly, her painted nails working at the zipper.

She stared at him, breathing deep. Then she whispered. "I want you to put your mouth on me."

Mike grinned and dropped back into the chair, his pants gaping open. "Thank God."

This time he didn't wait. He grabbed her boots and settled them on his thighs before pressing his mouth to her black panties. Hearing the hitch in her breathing, the way her knees fell away was so fucking hot. He slid a finger along the side of the elastic, ready to finally get a taste of her, when her right boot started vibrating against his side.

He raised his head for a moment to be sure he was hearing what he thought he was.

"Oh no, my phone." Anne set up and pulled her boot off, catching her phone in the same motion. She glanced at the screen. "Oh God, it's Scott."

What the hell? Mike slid the chair back to give her some room. Seeing her panic for *Scott* was like a bucket of cold water over his dick.

She clicked the phone on and then lifted it to her ear. "Is something wrong with Claire?"

Mike let out a breath and ran a hand over his mouth. This had to be Claire's father, a huge relief, unless something was wrong with Anne's daughter. His panic rose again.

"Have you taken her temperature?" Anne jumped off the table, pulled up her dress to cover her chest, and started pacing, which would have been slightly amusing since she now only had on one boot, but the tension and worry radiating from Anne killed his grin. Suddenly she stopped and faced the kitchen sink as she listened to whatever was going on with Claire. Mike moved to stand behind her and laid a hand on her shoulder, out of comfort, or hell he didn't know what, and without thinking she reached up to cover it with her own. The act felt . . . intimate. More intimate than what he'd been about to do while she lay on the table.

"I'll just come get her. She'll be more comfortable in

her own bed and I have a cabinet full of medicine. It will be easier." Anne dropped her hand and turned to pick up her discarded boot. "Okay, I'm on my way."

She ended the call and glanced around the kitchen before picking up her purse. "I'm so sorry, Mike. Claire's fever is a hundred and three." She met his eyes and gave him a half smile.

"Of course you have to get her. Let's go, I'll drive you." He zipped his pants, picked up his keys, and headed for the garage where they entered.

"What? No, no. I don't want to ruin the rest of your evening with a sick child."

He turned and gave her a hard stare. "Anne. I may be a horny as hell right now, but I know your daughter needs you. I'm helping."

"I appreciate your offer, but I don't need you to drive me."

"I disagree. You chased a good buzz with a shot not even forty-five minutes ago at Smokey's. I can't let you pick up Claire like that."

She groaned and laid a hand on her forehead. "Oh no, you're right. And the Preston cops patrol heavy on the weekend. But Scott lives twenty minutes away in Dansford."

Mike shrugged and reached for the door that led out to the garage. "After you."

They loaded back up into the Camaro and he started the engine. Before he backed out, he turned and lifted his hand to Anne's face, brushing her lower lip with his thumb. "One thing before we go. It won't be tonight, but I have every intention of making sure we pick back up where we left off."

Ten

Several amazing things had just gone down in Anne's kitchen, or nearly gone down, literally. But the one that was making her pulse rapid was the way Mike had caressed her shoulder while she was on the phone. Without thought she'd reached right up and grasped his hand, as if to hold it there, drawing support from him. It had been instinctual. But why?

They'd been about to have sex, nothing more. He didn't seem bothered that she'd put a stop to their shenanigans; in fact, he'd seemed genuinely concerned about Claire and getting her home safely. That wasn't so shocking, Mike was a good guy. She knew that for sure, and she assumed that since he was close to his niece he wasn't unfamiliar with childhood ailments and un- expected sickness.

The headlights lit up the long stretch of highway in front of them as the Camaro tilted into a smooth curve. This car really was amazing. Anne glanced across the center console at the large man driving. He was so incredibly beautiful, with his strong profile and straight nose. He turned and caught her staring.

"What?"

She grinned and looked back at the road. "Nothing."

There was silence for a moment and she felt a little awkward so she spoke again. "Actually, thank you, for driving me to get her. I know I should just let her father deal with this, I mean, it's his job, too, but I'm her mother."

Mike shocked her by draping his arm over the console and grabbing the hand resting in her lap. "Hey, no need to explain. Kids need their mom. All my young memories of being sick included my mom. She'd wipe my forehead with a cool cloth, bribe me into taking medicine with new toys, sometimes even sing to me. I get it. And it's no problem. You're a good mom, Anne, and I like that about you."

Anne's heart fluttered at those words. She couldn't recall Scott ever saying she was a good mom. She bit her lip and held back a tear. She brushed her thumb over his knuckle in silent gratitude, and he squeezed her fingers in reply before pulling his hand back to the gearshift to change gears. Another quick yet intimate gesture. She didn't know what to make of this night. One moment it was about sex, the next she was on emotional overload.

"Speaking of moms, sounds like you have a good one," she said, trying to lighten things up a little. She didn't miss the way Mike stiffened at her comment.

"Had. She passed away when I was seven."

"Oh, I'm so sorry. That's horrible."

He shrugged. "Thanks, but it was a long time ago." He glanced over and gave a tight smile.

Seven years old. That was only a year older than Claire. Anne couldn't even imagine her sweet, sensitive daughter going through losing a parent. The thought of a young Mike enduring that loss nearly broke Anne's heart. It didn't seem to upset him, but of course he was right, it was long ago. When he didn't seem inclined to say any more, she spoke.

"I was adopted. My early years were . . . bad," she said. He'd shared something, so it felt right to share something with him.

He jerked a little in his seat and sent a quick glance her way. "Seriously, I wouldn't have guessed. I mean . . . actually I don't know what I meant by that. Sorry."

She chuckled a little. "No biggie. I know I seem somewhat put together, but, if it weren't for my adoptive parents, I don't know where I'd be right now. They gave me a great life. My mom has a gift for making every occasion memorable. Birthdays, recitals, graduations. She never missed an opportunity to make me feel loved and special. I guess my love of planning parties comes naturally."

The car was silent for a moment, no surprise. That was kind of an awkward conversation transition. But she had made peace with her past. She was lucky that she'd been given a second chance at a happy childhood, and now she knew what it meant to be a good mother to her own daughter. She liked to think that every time she created a special memory for someone else she was carrying on her own mother's traditions.

"What you do is amazing, Anne. That party you gave Claire was insane. You truly have a talent for making things special. I'm sure your parents would say they are the lucky ones to have gotten you."

"Thanks," she said with a smile. "Sadly my dad, Wade, died of prostate cancer when I was nineteen. So looks like I have a mom, and you have a dad."

She laughed quietly and stared out the window. Mike cleared his throat.

"Actually my father died when I was eighteen."

Anne didn't speak for a moment, because she honestly had no idea what to say. Mike had no parents at all. She knew he had his sister Erin, Bailey's mother, but still. A sibling is not a parent, although Anne wouldn't really know since she didn't have any siblings—her mother was unable to have children, and they'd never adopted again.

"I'm so sorry, Mike. That's . . . I'm just sorry."

"Yeah, it sucked," he said with a heavy sigh. "Life was bad for me, too, for a while, but you get through it, ya know?"

"Yes, I do know," she said quietly. She shifted in her seat to face him. "We're quite a pair here, aren't we? One minute we're making out—and I'm freaking because I don't want you to see me naked—and now we're being completely morbid in your car while you drive my drunk ass to get my sick daughter. You have to be cursing fate for making our paths cross tonight."

He turned to her with a grin. "Not even a little bit."

There had been no hesitation. He didn't regret their ridiculous make-out scene or the fact that she wasn't capable of driving herself somewhere. Not that she was really that intoxicated now, but she wasn't confident she could pass a Breathalyzer at the moment. Mike Everett was truly a gentleman.

It felt good to let some baggage out, and in front of a hot man no less. She'd never done that before; in fact it had been months into her relationship with Scott before she'd shared the details of her past with him. Maybe that was the answer. She needed to be up front about all the ways she was less than perfect. That way there would be no room for disappointment, no chance for confusion or unrealistic expectations.

Right now he was probably figuring out that he was in over his head with her. She had some body issues and he was probably used to young hotties stripping down and showing off for him. She had a sketchy past and the biggest of all . . . a child. No guy would want to bother with all that mess. But what a thrill tonight had been, having him touch her, kiss her, and make her feel desirable. She didn't regret it one bit, whether he decided to or not.

"Thank you, Mike, for driving me. It's very sweet. I owe you."

"That you do, Perfect. We'll call it even once I've seen you naked."

Anne's mother, Marie, was the kind of woman that you wanted around when you were sick, sad, happy, or especially hungry, as her casserole repertoire was legendary. But now that Marie was seventy-one, Anne found herself worrying over her mother more often than the other way around. However, Marie would never admit it. She was insanely proud and independent. But seventy-one is seventy-one, and some things in life are inevitable, especially when battling diabetes.

Anne had grown up in a small town west of Kansas City about twenty-five minutes from Preston, but Marie no longer lived in the suburban ranch home that Anne had been raised in. Two years ago Anne had convinced her mother to move into a senior apartment complex only a short drive away from Preston.

Marie had made a fuss saying that she was "Nowhere near ready for an old folks' home."

"Mom, this is a senior living *apartment*," Anne had pleaded with her. "Your own furniture, no hospital beds, and there's even a walking trail. You come and go as you please, and you even have a carport."

A week after the move Marie had already made two new best friends, planned a trip to the Ozarks with said best friends, and started a Bunco group. Anne had been so relieved and happy for her mother. She deserved to enjoy her senior years and be surrounded by people. With a business, a blog, and a daughter of her own, Anne couldn't always be on call for her mother. The move had been ideal.

They had immediately resumed their traditional biweekly supper with Grandma Ree that had started after the divorce. It was always the Monday after Claire's weekend with Scott, and as they entered into Marie's two-bedroom apartment this Monday they were greeted with smells of lasagna and garlic bread.

"Grandma Reeeeee!" Claire ran through the living room, straight into the small dining room, and into her grandmother's waiting arms. She'd always called her the silly name, mashing Grandma and Marie. It had started as soon as Claire was speaking, and it stuck. Marie wouldn't have it any other way. She loved the name.

Anne smiled as her daughter was swept into a strong embrace by her grandmother. Claire may never know her grandfather, but Grandma Ree made up for it the best she could.

"Callie sent me with a sugar-free carrot cake." Anne set the pink cake box on the table, which was set for three. "Can I help with anything?"

"You can grab the lasagna and carry it in to the table. It's sitting on top of the stove." Marie sat in her chair and pulled Claire onto her lap. "I'm gonna cover my Claire-bug with sugar."

Anne walked into the kitchen. The sounds of smooches and giggles ringing through the air. The pan of steaming lasagna sat on the stove and the bread was in a basket. She took them to the dining table and returned to the kitchen for the salad.

Turning to the fridge to retrieve some dressing, Anne spotted a couple of doctor's appointment cards under a magnet. One was for her mother's regular doctor and one was for a nephrologist. *Huh.*

She stared for a moment, considering what that could mean. Her mother hadn't mentioned anything about the appointment. Maybe it was for a routine procedure. She was . . . elderly. Not that Anne would ever say it to her face. She grabbed the dressing and some cheese before returning to the table.

Both Claire and Grandma Ree were sticking their fingers in the cream cheese frosting on the carrot cake. "Hey, quit it, you two."

Claire broke into laughter, and the sound was music

to Anne's ears. After the fever broke Saturday morning, Anne had kept her for the day to be sure they were in the clear before Scott insisted that he pick her up before dinner that night. Fine, whatever, it was his weekend, blah, blah, blah. Claire was always happy to be with her father, so Anne could hardly make a scene. She would allow Claire to be the one thing Scott got right, as much as it killed Anne.

The three girls said a quick prayer before Anne dished up the food. As always, it was amazing. Anne was a pretty good cook, but a family of one and a half wasn't really conducive to large home-style meals, so she usually prepared simple things. Grandma Ree's Mondays were always a treat.

"So tell me about your weekend with your Daddy," Marie said to Claire.

Anne appreciated her mother's prying since Claire tended to be a little more candid about what went on at Scott's when conversing with her grandmother.

"Ummmm, we ate ice cream and went shopping for new shoes for Daddy, and his friend Dana came over."

Anne nearly choked on a bite of lettuce. She glanced at her mother, who raised an eyebrow. Anne shrugged lightly.

"Well, that sounds fun," Marie said, barely missing a beat. "What kind of ice cream?"

"Chocolate from Carey Darey."

"Yum, I love chocolate ice cream," Marie went on. Anne knew her mother was a genius at this kind of thing, so she just remained silent and ate her dinner as Marie continued in her happy, interested voice.

"Good thing Daddy got new shoes. Did you meet his friend Dana for ice cream?"

Claire picked a cucumber out of her salad and dipped it in ranch as she spoke. "Well, Daddy picked me up from my house, then we got new shoes and then we picked her up. And then we ate ice cream, and then we went home."

"Oh I see." Marie and Anne met eyes once again. This time Anne raised an eyebrow and took a drink of her water. She was feeling a little sweaty. Marie went on. "So Dana went to Daddy's house with you?"

"Uh-huh." Claire was completely oblivious to the drilling she was getting as she ate her lasagna.

It wasn't like Scott couldn't date. He was young, handsome, and available. But did he really have to do it on the weekend he had his daughter? Was this relationship serious? As much as Anne had grown to despise the man, it still grated a little deep inside.

"Well, that sounds like fun. So, does Dana have pink pajamas or purple?" Marie leaned toward Claire like she was asking a super-fun girlie secret.

Claire giggled. "I don't know, Grandma Ree. She stayed in Daddy's room during bedtime."

"Oh well, of course," Marie said as if it had been the silliest of questions.

Anne bit back a groan.

"So you liked Dana?" Marie asked.

Claire bounced in her chair, clearly losing interest in the conversation. "She was nice. She wears a lot of lipstick. I like Mommy's friend Uncle Mike better, he sings funny."

Anne froze with a bite of bread halfway to her mouth. The direction of this interrogation was about to go very wrong. She was afraid to look her mother's way, but she chanced it. Sure enough, Marie was giving her *a look*. Anne put the bread in her mouth and smiled as she chewed, trying to appear innocent.

"When did Uncle Mike sing to you? That sounds like fun."

"When I was sick. I had to leave Daddy's in the middle of the night and he sang to me in my bedroom while Mommy got me some medicine. He likes to sing 'Itsy Bitsy Spider.' It's a baby song, but he was funny."

Oh Lord, obviously Claire had gotten a second wind for conversation and was spilling all the messy details. Anne knew her mother wouldn't quit until she'd pulled everything possible from Claire's lips.

Marie laughed along with Claire and then looked at Anne as she said the next bit. "He sounds nice. So in the middle of the night you say, that's too bad. I hate to be sick, especially when I'd rather be sleeping." *Oh gracious*.

"It was okay. Mommy and Mike came to get me. Even when it was really dark, and Mike's car is fancy and really fast." Claire was on a roll. Anne wanted to put her hand over her daughter's mouth. Instead she just sat quietly while her mother's wide eyes assessed her. "And he's really big, way bigger than Daddy. He has big muscles and he carried me to my room like I was a baby."

Claire imitated rocking a baby in her arms. It just kept getting better and better.

But Claire was right, watching Mike with her daughter had been . . . strange. Strange but amazing in a way she needed to forget since she had been using him as a boy toy just hours before that. Wasn't that what they'd been doing . . . casually fooling around? She'd just decided in his car that he would probably be done with her after their night together, but the way he'd handled Claire had made everything so confusing.

Mike hadn't come with her up to Scott's door, saying it would be awkward, which was true. But once they arrived back at Anne's, he'd insisted on carrying Claire in, tucking her into bed, and when Anne had come up with a dose of Tylenol and a cool cloth, she'd overheard him singing "Itsy Bitsy Spider." She stood in the hallway like an idiot, listening to this large, unpredictable man caring for her sick daughter. Then he'd given Anne a chaste kiss good-bye and left. Claire was right about one other thing: He was much, much bigger than Daddy.

"Well, my goodness, young lady. You've had quite a weekend I sure would like to meet this big muscly Mike. Think he'd sing for me?" Marie asked with a wink.

"Grandma Ree," Claire grinned. "You're silly. Mike is Bailey's uncle. He came to my birthday party, too."

"Okay then," Anne said as she stood and started to collect dirty plates. "I'm ready for carrot cake, anybody else?"

"Meeeee," Claire shrilled.

"Oh me, too," Marie said. "I'll cut Claire and me a big piece—you'll be too busy talking."

Anne blew out a breath and carried the dinner plates into the sink. If she was smart she'd spend a lot of time rinsing and loading them into the dishwasher. Thanks to her daughter who had obviously inherited her mother's trait of the verbal vomit, she had a lot of explaining to do. But truthfully, she wanted to talk to her mother. She didn't know what to think about this thing with Mike, and she needed some maternal advice, which Marie was brilliant with.

Obviously she would leave out some of the more explicit details, but she needed to think out loud and let her mom help her figure a few things out. She liked Mike. She wanted him, but a couple of things had thrown her off balance so far. And then for the thirty millionth time in her life, Anne thanked heaven that she had Marie, the best mother she had ever been gifted with.

Eleven

Tuesday morning Mike sat down at his desk and booted up his computer. Checking the *My Perfect Little Life* blog each day had become a habit. Either Anne, Callie, or the third chick Lindsey posted daily, sometimes twice a day. He wasn't interested in most of the content as he didn't bake and wasn't interested in picking up garbage from someone's curb to paint, but he liked seeing this side of Anne.

He always skimmed through the first few comments, smiling at how much people loved Anne and how they asked about Claire, whom Anne referred to as Bug on the blog. These strangers were deeply invested in Anne's life; it was kind of crazy, but he understood. She was funny and smart, sharing just enough personal info to make her relatable without giving too much away. She had this amazing way of being a little bit self-deprecating, making her humble, all the while maintaining humor and confidence. He could see why women admired her. It was quite a gift, and if he hadn't met her, he'd want to.

Mike scrolled through photos of a pony party that

she'd done on Sunday. He guessed it was cool, if you were a five-year-old girl. It was the first post she'd personally done since Friday morning, and at the end she summarized as she usually did, often asking a question to engage the readers.

Except for this party, my weekend was uneventful and relaxing since Bug spent most of it with her daddy. I read a lot and cleaned house. Anyone else do anything exciting?

Mike sat back in his chair, completely shocked by what he'd just read. Yeah, he'd done something exciting, and so had she. She had to be crazy to say her weekend had been uneventful. Of course he didn't expect her to say *I spent part of Friday evening lying on my table with my dress around my waist so a man could lick me from head to toe,* but something. *Uneventful?*

He sat up and hit the COMMENT button. His hands hovered over the keyboard. There were a lot of comments he wanted to make. But none were appropriate for her blog. He needed to see Anne and soon.

Mike clicked the comment window closed and leaned his head back into his hands. He couldn't really blame her for leaving their episode out of her blog post—it certainly didn't fit the tone, which was wholesome, and mommish—but he hadn't stopped thinking about Anne since he'd left her that night. Or Claire. He assumed she recovered and gone back to her dad's since Anne said she spent most of the weekend away.

Claire had seemed so fragile and sweet when he'd carried her up to her room. He wasn't sure why he'd felt the need to make her feel better, but when he'd tucked her into bed, her cheeks flaming with fever, he'd just started singing. The same song his mother had sung to him when he was a child. He was a pathetic singer, but Claire hadn't seemed to care. She'd smiled, and asked him to sing it again. He even did the silly hand motions. Her sweet little grin was so much like Anne's—genuinely happy—that made it worth it.

After that he'd left, because it had gotten very weird. One minute he'd been hot and heavy with Anne, the next he was singing "Itsy Bitsy Spider." Although he liked kids okay, and loved spending time with Bailey, nothing like that had ever happened to him. Probably because he'd never been involved with a woman who had a child before.

That was why her words on the blog left him a little on edge. A huge event had happened over the weekend. He'd felt more than a little lust for Anne Edmond. But the thing that was blowing his mind was that he'd wanted to take care of Anne and her daughter. And aside from Bailey and his sister he'd never had strong feelings of that nature before. He wanted to make everything better for the two of them, even if it was just for one moment. He'd wanted to take some of the stress of having a sick child off Anne's shoulders, and make Claire happy despite a high fever.

It had been a damn long while since he'd thought about what it meant to be part of a family. To feel like you belonged somewhere, and to know that someone wanted and needed you there. He loved Erin and Bailey—and even Todd—but they were their own family unit that he would never be able to infiltrate because he was Uncle Mike. But now he was wondering what it would be like to have a family unit of his own to protect and care for. Gosh damn, he was a wreck. Years of dating and sex, and not once—ever—had a woman had him thinking these thoughts. Longing for things he'd never wanted before. But this woman, damn.

Everything about Anne turned him on, from her co-ordinated outfits to her perfectly styled hair. The same way you're attracted to a teacher or a librarian: You wanted to see them let loose a little, reveal their naughty secrets. After their night together, although interrupted, he was confident that she had an incredibly hot side to her, even if she was a hesitant to unleash it. More than that, though, he was also just drawn to Anne as a person. She was warm and sweet. A smile from her made him feel powerful and . . . happy. Not only because it was gorgeous, but because it was real and sincere.

It was too soon to know what this thing was between him and Anne, too soon even to know what exactly it was he wanted it to be. But one thing was certain: He was dying to see her again. He glanced at the calendar on his desk. Tuesday was when Bailey had gymnastics. He picked up the phone and dialed Erin's number.

"Hi, Mikey," Erin said when she picked up. It had always been her nickname for him for as long as he could remember.

"Hey, what's up?"

"Well I'm standing in the middle of Target and Bailey just threw a temper tantrum because I won't buy her a sixty-dollar jewelry maker."

"So just buy it. Problem solved." Mike could hear his niece whining in the background.

"You're joking, right?"

He chuckled. It was easy to get under Erin's skin; she

and her daughter were cut from the same cloth even if she couldn't see it. "Yes I'm joking, that wouldn't send the right message. *I'll* buy it for her."

"Mike don't you—"

"I'm kidding, I'm kidding." But he might do it anyway. He could rarely say no to Bailey.

"So what do you need, I'm getting ready to check out," she asked.

"I just called to say hey." He was a liar. "But it sounds like you could use a break. Why don't I take Boo to gymnastics for you?"

His suggestion was met with Erin's silence, only the sounds of a busy store in the background. He knew Erin would want to take him up on the offer. Her husband was gone four days out of the week traveling for his job, and she got tired of being a pseudo-single mom. He knew it. So why was she hesitating. Unless . . .

"Does this have anything to do with Anne Edmond?"

This time it was Mike's turn to be quiet. How the hell had she found out about that?

"Your silence is very suspect, Michael Everett." No more Mikey then. She meant business. He couldn't tell if she was mad or just curious, so he didn't know which angle to take.

"I just met her when I took Bailey to Claire's party." That comment gave nothing away.

"Well, I got my hair done Saturday morning at Lovely Salon and my stylist mentioned that Anne was at your shop last week. In fact it was all the talk with the ladies. I thought it was completely innocent when she told me that she needed your info to send a thank you. I never dreamed she'd make a personal delivery."

What the hell? News traveled fast in this town apparently. Mike blew out a breath. Katie was a hairdresser at Lovely. Was she really vindictive enough to spread this info? Sadly, he didn't need to think hard about that to have a pretty good answer. He'd bruised her ego, big time.

"Well, Erin, it *was* innocent. She brought me thank-you cinnamon rolls for a referral. No big deal."

"And by *thank-you cinnamon rolls* you mean—"

"Stop it. Give her a little credit. I gave her a really high-dollar referral and she brought me a gift. Just like it sounds."

"And you haven't seen her since?"

"I might have run into her Friday night at Smokey's, but it was a coincidence." Another lie. He hadn't lied to Erin in years, and he really didn't like it.

"Hmm. So she's not the reason you want to take Bailey to practice tonight?"

Okay, if he said no it would be an obvious fib and he couldn't lie anymore. Plus, his sister was smarter than that. "Maybe a little."

Erin's muffled voice invited someone to cut ahead of her in the checkout line, and considering she had a cranky little girl in tow he knew she meant business by giving up her place to continue this discussion. "I should say no, Mike. Anne is nice, and as far from your usual type as can be. She has a daughter who happens to be your niece's best friend. They don't need you coming in there and breaking hearts. That would be very awkward for me, you know?"

She was right, he knew it, but it still pissed him off a little. He wondered how Erin would describe *his type*, then again maybe he didn't want to know. He wasn't in the habit of knowingly breaking hearts. Sure, it happened sometimes, but he couldn't control other people's feelings. He never lied to women or intended to give them false hope; he just never wanted anything serious. If anybody lied, it was the women who implied they felt the same way and then quickly changed their minds.

"Erin, I'm not sure what's going on between Anne and me, but it won't be awkward, I promise."

He heard her blow out a breath. "I don't know how you can keep that promise. If I didn't crave a night to myself you would have no leverage, but you know better. Be here at five thirty."

"Will do." He ended the call and drummed his fingers on the desk. Gymnastics practice couldn't come fast enough.

Twelve

Smithfield Gymnastics had been part of Anne's life since Claire was three, and the owners took the sport very seriously. The coaches were intense, even for six-year-old girls, but Claire loved it. She seemed to thrive on the high expectations, and in the past few months Anne had started to feel little muscles shaping in her daughter's calves and forearms.

Having her best friend, Bailey, join this year had been an added bonus, and it hadn't taken long for Bailey to work herself up to Claire's level, never wanting to be out-done. Anne adored Bailey, but she was Claire's oppo-site. Strong-willed, opinionated, and a little aggressive. Not in a bad way, but she definitely was used to getting her way a lot.

Anne took a seat where she usually did, in the up-stairs viewing area that surrounded the expansive gym floor on three sides. There were always several classes going at once, ranging from toddlers all the way to ex-perienced teenagers, and they were all fascinating to watch. The girls were toned and strong, doing things with their bodies that didn't seem possible. She wasn't sure how far she wanted Claire to take the sport, because it required a high level of dedication. But for now she was letting Claire decide.

The lower-level viewing area was more popular since you could hear the more advanced coaches yelling, and some parents seemed to get off on that. But Anne didn't; she preferred the upstairs, which, while a little over-warm, was quiet and peaceful with its glass windows overlooking the gym. Today all the lights were off, prob-ably to help keep it cool, so the only light was coming from the high gym ceiling on the other side of the view-ing windows.

She often watched Claire, but she also read or played with her phone during the hour-long practice. Today—as she often was—she was the only one up there so she cracked open the Diet Coke she bought from the vend-ing machine and pulled up the trashy romance novel she'd been reading on her phone app.

She would need to remember to look up every once in a while and catch Claire on the uneven bars or mats so she could make an encouraging comment later. After about ten minutes the wooden stairs that led to the viewing floor creaked, and she quietly groaned at the thought that another parent would be impinging on her privacy. She hated having to make small talk when all she wanted to do was read.

She saw a body walking down the bench-lined hall from the corner of her eye so she turned, intent on giv-ing the formal half smile you did to people in situations like this. Instead her gaze landed on sexy Mike Ever-ett. He was in his typical outfit of faded jeans, this time with a navy polo shirt. And he had a hat on, which was new to her, but incredibly hot. His boyish smirk forced her to turn away and hide her wide grin.

"Uh-uh, Anne, don't pretend you're not happy to see me." He sat down about a foot from her and leaned to the side to nudge her shoulder with his. Her body warmed instantly with the contact. Shoot, she warmed at his mere presence, or even the thought of his presence.

She smiled at him. She couldn't help it because she *was* glad to see him—and admitted to herself she'd thought about him constantly since Friday night. Realistically she hadn't really expected to hear from him, but after their intense night together, she couldn't deny that she'd been a teeny bit disappointed when he hadn't contacted her Sunday or Monday.

In that one night alone she'd experienced so many facets of the amazing Uncle Mike, it would have been impossible not to think of him. After dinner at her mom's she'd pretty much convinced herself there wasn't really anything going on and she shouldn't worry so much, but now?

"What are you doing here?"

"I brought my niece to practice," he said with a nod down at the gym.

"Bailey has been coming here for nearly ten months and you've never brought her," she said, calling his bluff.

He grinned at this. "I had new motivation, I guess."

Anne's stomach did a flip, and she looked out at the girls on the trampoline. She really shouldn't give too much thought to him being here, but it was damn hard not to. They watched the practice in silence for a few minutes; finally he scooted a little closer, widening his legs so they brushed hers. He leaned forward and rested his elbows on his knees.

Anne took a drink of her soda and stuffed her phone into her purse. No way could she concentrate on her book now. Anyway, being around Mike was a million times better than reading about fictional people getting it on. His spicy scent was real, his muscles here in the flesh, and he came here to see her. There was no doubt.

Mike turned his head so his temple rested on his fist. "It's empty up here."

She shrugged. "It's getting hot, so people stay down where it's cooler." And it was getting warmer by the second.

"You like it hot?" He waggled his eyebrows.

"Is your mind always in the gutter?"

"Only with you."

"Pfff, I doubt that."

"You seem to doubt a lot of things about me."

Anne raised an eyebrow at him. She was not used to this kind of sexually charged banter, and clearly he was, but it made her tingly all over. She shifted her legs and adjusted her skirt, not missing the way Mike's eyes roamed over her lower half, following every movement. Thank God she'd shaved today. She'd even worn a cute little skirt and matching tank top. She felt pretty, and he made her also feel desirable.

They continued to watch for a while, he asked her a few questions about what the girls were doing as they took turns on the mat, and Anne tried to slow her racing heart. Finally he sat up straight, leaned against the wall behind them, and set a hand on her knee, which was half covered by the bottom of her skirt. She nearly shivered, but thankfully managed to keep her body in check. "What are you doing?"

He turned and looked at her, playing innocent. "What? Oh, I'm just touching you."

"I know that, but why? We're in public." *And please don't stop.*

"We're alone. And I'm doing it because you're hot and I like having my hands on you."

Oh my God. She could barely contain herself at his blatant flirtation. No man had ever been so forward with her. Part of her wanted to protest, but the deepest parts of her wanted to straddle his lap and ride out her frustrations.

He turned his gaze back to the gym floor. "Claire is really good. I'm impressed."

"Thank you, she enjoys it." They were silent for a while longer, the warmth of his skin like a brand on her own. Anne swallowed hard, trying to relax which was nearly impossible.

After a while his hand slowly slipped under her skirt. Her own palm shot out and covered his. She didn't turn, but she could feel his body shake with laughter next to her. After a while she relaxed her hand on his, which was still lingering under the hem of her skirt.

Eventually he began to move again, his hand inching higher. Anne could feel every movement, and it was the most thrilling and titillating sensation she'd ever experienced.

"Spread your legs, Anne," he said in a low voice.

"What? Are you serious? Someone could see!" Her

voice was already breathless. She let her eyes roam the entire gym; none of the coaches or athletes ever looked up here. But oh gosh, her heart was pounding.

"No one can see. The lights are out and this wall comes up to your waist. Plus they're all way down there."

"Someone might come up." She was nearly panting.

"Did you hear those stairs? Not a chance we would be caught by surprise." She heard the smile in his voice. She couldn't look at him. "Spread your legs, Anne."

She sucked in a breath and blew it out as she slowly parted her thighs. What the hell was she doing? His fingers found their way to her center and brushed her panties just like the last time he had his hands on her. She wanted to moan but held it in; of course Mike didn't have a problem. He still didn't look at her, but a low groan came from his chest the minute his finger found its way to the cotton covering her most sensitive spot. The sound of it nearly had her rocketing out of control.

"Every time I touch you here, you're ready." He turned his head her way just a little, his lips tilted up on one side. "Have you noticed that?"

Anne squeezed her eyes shut. She wanted to drop her head back against the wall and enjoy the feel of his finger circling her, or lie back on the bench and pull him on top of her. Instead she sat very still as he fondled her. He used two fingers now, increasing the speed of his movements on the wet fabric. Even with her eyes closed she could feel his eyes on her.

"I want you to come, Anne," he said, his voice low and quiet. "Right here."

She bit her bottom lip as pleasure rippled through her body, all stemming from that one spot. She was close, so close, and she wanted to whimper. She glanced down at his arm draped across her leg, his hand hidden beneath the skirt that rode up her thigh.

"Look at me, Perfect."

She didn't move. Instead she opened her eyes and stared at the far wall of the gym; everything around her was hazy and sparkling. And he'd called her Perfect again. How in the world had she managed to get this sexy man to touch her like this and think of her in that way?

"Look at me," he said again, his fingers finding a consistent rhythm, the one that was going to make her body shatter into pieces inside. She finally turned her head and met his eyes. She could feel her body begin to vibrate, and she clenched her jaw shut. A naughty grin spread across his face. He knew exactly what he was doing to her and was enjoying it, which made it all so much more arousing. Their eyes stayed locked.

"Relax and let it go, babe. We're just two adults up here, having a conversation, while I get you off under this skirt." This time he bit at his lip as he stared at her.

That was it. Her body succumbed, her thighs convulsed against his wrist, and she locked her hands onto the lip of the wooden bench as she came hard. She wanted to turn away from him, and he must have known it.

"Don't look away from me, Anne." His words were a low growl. His fingers kept moving, riding out her entire explosive orgasm. She looked deep into his eyes, which grazed over every inch of her face as if he wanted to memorize her. Normally she would have been horrified to have a man watch her face while she came, but she felt sexy, and he was appreciating the view, his expression tight and serious.

When it was over he stroked her slowly, his fingers running circles all over her underwear, which he had never even moved. Her chest heaved in and out.

"That was the hottest thing I've ever seen," he said. She gave him a disbelieving stare, but he reciprocated with a grin, his eyes in shadow from his ball cap. "And don't you doubt me for one fucking second."

And truly, she didn't. It was incredibly hot. The hottest thing she'd ever been a part of. Mike slid his hand from under her skirt and squeezed her thigh before resting it in his own lap.

Anne had no idea what to say after what had just happened. She adjusted her clothing and let her eyes search the entire gym floor until she found Claire's pink leotard on the bar. Her heart was still racing, and she took a cleansing breath and blew it upward, making her hair flutter.

Mike chuckled next to her but he was watching the gym floor also. "Was gymnastics as exciting for you as it was for me?"

"Nothing in my life has been quite that exciting." And that was no lie. Her life had been pretty damn boring until that birthday party that Mike chose to stay for. She didn't know how she felt about that. Was this just a crazy ride they were on, and she'd better enjoy it while it lasted, or something more? It was hard to tell because at first glance Mike didn't appear to be the kind of guy looking for a girlfriend with a six-year-old daughter.

The horn sounded that the hour was up and Anne felt

a twinge of disappointment as she gathered her purse and soda.

"So when are you going out with me, Perfect?"

"Why do you call me that?" she asked as she stood straight.

"Why do you think? Because that's how I see you."

"No one's perfect, especially not me."

"No, they're not, but you come pretty damn close. Your parties, your house. These sexy little outfits you wear." His eyes swept over her skirt, sending a blush through her cheeks. Did he truly find her clothes sexy?

"I would like to think I approach things with a certain level of . . . passion. But some men find that annoying."

"Some men are idiots." His eyes narrowed a little but he didn't take his gaze off her. "Passion is always sexy, no matter where it's focused."

She swallowed. It might be easy for him to say that when the stakes were low and it was all just fun times. It was up to her to keep things in check. She put a hand on her hip. "We shouldn't go out."

His expression relaxed and he crossed his arms as he gave her a quiet laugh. "You better be playing hard-to-get, Anne . . ." He lowered his voice and leaned into her. ". . . because I'm pretty sure you like spending time with me."

Full of complete sexy arrogance, he cocked his head toward the bench they'd just stood from. Anne tried not to smile, but couldn't help it. He had the nerve to laugh at her.

"You're so full of yourself," she said.

"True, but I'd like it better if *you* were full of me."

"Oh my goodness, will you *quit*." She brushed by his hard body, laughing, but he grabbed her at the last second with an arm around her waist. She turned her head to look into his eyes. He was so handsome she could barely stand it. They just smiled at each other for a moment, and she forced herself not to acknowledge the feelings that settled in her chest as he stared down at her.

The creaking of the stairs startled her. "The girls, let go."

"Say you'll you go out with me."

The stomping was reaching the top, definitely two little sets of feet. And then she heard giggles. "Mike!" she hissed.

"Say yes."

She pulled from his arms at the last second as Bailey and Claire burst into the viewing hallway.

"Uncle Mike, did you see me? I did a back handspring without a spot."

"I sure did. I thought you were gonna snap your neck, but it was spectacular." He winked at Anne. Neither of them would have noticed flames break out on the gym floor because he'd been too busy setting Anne on fire.

"I did one, too, Mommy." Claire tugged on Anne's finger.

"Well, I know you did. I saw it." Anne didn't like lying, but she sure liked the bad-boy grin on Mike's face.

The girls headed back toward the stairs to leave, and Mike and Anne followed. He nuzzled into Anne's ear, walking closely behind. "You are so going to go out with me."

"Hush," she said.

He laughed at her as the four of them made their way down the stairs and to the front door of the gym. They were halfway through the parking lot when little voices rose in anger.

"Uh-huh, she had her finger under your back." Bailey put both hands on her hips.

"Because we were supposed to," Claire insisted. Anne had never heard her daughter so irritated—well, with anyone but her.

"Hey, hey, hey," Mike said as he and Anne caught up to the two bickering girls. "What's the problem?"

"Claire had a spot with her back handspring and I didn't. So mine is better," Bailey said.

"I coulda if I wanted, but Coach Jen said not to. Bailey didn't listen."

"Nh-uh."

"Yeah-huh."

"Okay, okay." Mike squatted down between the two frazzled six-year-olds.

Anne wondered what he was going to say, because she knew Claire was right. The rule was you had to have a spot till level 5, but she wasn't going to put his niece in her place.

He pulled Bailey close to his body and looked into her eyes. "I'm super proud of you for your back handspring. But is there a rule about having a spot?"

Bailey was quiet, obviously not wanting to admit she'd disobeyed. Anne glanced at Claire, who had her chin lowered watching Bailey and Mike. These two girls were like oil and water, but they managed to be inseparable. How did it always work like that?

"Answer me, Boo." Bailey shook her head back and

forth, ponytail flying. Mike let out a breath and looked at Claire. "I bet Claire can tell me the rule, can't you, Claire."

Claire nodded eagerly and stepped closer to Mike. "No spot. No stunt."

Mike nodded and looked back at Bailey. "Is that right, Boo?"

Bailey's shoulders slumped, and she nodded. Mike continued. "I think they have those rules to keep you safe, Bailey. It sounds like you need to say sorry to Claire."

Still squatting, Mike held out the hand that wasn't resting on Bailey to Claire. Without hesitation Claire slid right into his open arm. Anne swallowed hard, watching the episode unfold. All of this was because of Mike. The way he was sticking up for her daughter made her want to cry and kiss him all at the same time.

"Bailey?" Mike prompted.

"Sorry, Claire."

"It's okay."

Mike quickly kissed Bailey on the head and patted Claire's back. He palmed each little girl's hair with a large hand and pretended to knock their heads together, banging his fingers instead. Riotous giggles ensued. "You two are a couple of knuckleheads."

Mike stood up and stalked toward Anne. "Don't think I haven't forgotten that you owe me an answer, Perfect."

Nope, she hadn't forgotten, either, and after what she'd just witnessed she knew her answer. As if she hadn't decided already. There was only one thing left to say. "Yes."

Thirteen

It was Wednesday, one more day of uninterrupted work time until school was out, so Anne decided to spend the morning working on the blog at Callie's shop. The bell tinkled as she entered and she ducked into the front corner table by the window to wait out the five-person line.

Anne set up her work space, which consisted of her laptop, phone, pen, and notepad. Then she sneaked behind the counter where Eric slipped her a mug so she could hit the coffee station. She never paid for coffee at Callie's. She used to try but gave up after Callie refused her money over and over. She did, however, insist on paying for baked goods because she wanted to support her friend's business. She might occasionally turn a blind eye when Callie slipped something extra in the bag for Claire.

When the line cleared and things settled down, Callie came and plopped down in the chair across from Anne.

"I'm ready. What happened and don't you dare leave a detail out."

Anne grinned. She couldn't help herself. This morning she had texted Callie that she was coming in because "things are happening." Any other time of day her friend would not have bothered to reply; she would have called back and demanded to be told right away. But Anne knew that mornings at Callie's Confections were too busy for that. Instead Callie had texted back a short and sweet message. *You're evil*.

Over coffee and a caramel pecan sticky bun—her personal favorite—she proceeded to fill her friend in on the events from the last few days, leaving only *tiny* details out. No need to be graphic. Callie's mouth hung open the whole time. When she was done, Anne leaned back, a huge smile on her face. At some point Eric had joined the table.

"God you're so lucky," Eric said. "I'd give anything to get a piece of that action."

"Me, too. Anne, this is crazy. Who would have thought, meeting a hottie like that at a kiddie birthday party?"

"I know! I just don't know what to think. I mean, what do I do?"

Eric leaned in. "You do what any smart person would do. You let him give it to you all night long."

Anne laughed and covered her eyes with her fingers. "I want to, I do. Is that horrible? Would you guys think less of me?"

"Uhhh, have we met?" Eric asked.

"No kidding, Anne. We've had to listen to stories from Eric that make us question our entire moral compass, yet we still love him. And I'm just dying to live vicariously. So *please*, go out with him, take him home, and seal the deal."

"It's just, I'm not that kind of woman. I don't have casual sex or mess around. What if people found out? I plan children's birthday parties in this town."

"Sweetie, how would anyone find out?" Callie picked off a bite of Anne's roll as she spoke. "And so what if they did? You're a grown woman. You're not married. What you do with Uncle Magic Fingers is nobody's business." She popped a gooey pecan in her mouth.

Anne sighed. That was all true, but she'd always been overly concerned with doing the right thing. Although she had a very public platform that grew larger every day, she still went out of her way to avoid drawing unnecessary attention to herself. All her life, she'd worked hard—in school, sports, clubs—to make her parents proud, and they'd always told her they were. Their love and support had been unwavering. Maybe she was just a natural-born worrier. Her choice of things to fret about may have evolved to things like her daughter, her business, and how she looked naked, but the stress was still the same. The thought that anyone would find her lacking scared her, but this—this kept feeling right despite the fear of it all.

She wasn't clear what Mike's intentions were, and she'd been pretty sure they were just fooling around, but now that he'd asked her out on an official date she wasn't sure what to think. Was going to dinner first just a nicety? A means to an end? Or was something more at play?

She had a hard time believing Mike might be interested in something more than a physical relationship; he just didn't seem like that kind of guy. But he also hadn't seemed like the kind of guy to work out an argument between two little girls. Anne still warmed thinking of it. She didn't even tell Callie and Eric about that episode or about the singing to Claire, because somehow that had seemed like something more. How did a person process that information?

"So you told him yes, right?" Callie asked. Eric had gone to the counter to help a customer.

"Yes, we're going out Saturday night."

Callie did a little dance in her chair. "Yay! I can't wait to hear about this. Do you need me to watch Claire?"

The question reminded Anne of how much she loved Callie, always ready to help her out without a second thought. But this time she didn't need help. "Actually, Mike arranged for Claire to stay the night with his sister and Bailey."

"Oh wow, well that's nice. That boy isn't giving you an out, is he? Claire will be excited about the sleepover."

"She's already got her bag packed." Anne chuckled.

"Okay, now it's my turn for good news," Callie said. She had a mischievous grin on her face.

Anne's eyes widened. "What? What kind of good news? Are you seeing someone?"

"Oh Lord no, I don't have time for that shit." Callie shuffled in her seat, her eyes sparkling. "Even better, I'm officially the brand-new Preston High Pantherettes Dance Team coach."

Anne's jaw dropped and then she squealed like a little girl before speaking. "Oh my gosh, that's amazing." She reached out and grasped Callie's hand. "When did this happen?"

"I just found out yesterday that it was for sure. I applied a couple of weeks ago when a customer informed me they fired the last coach. I just knew I couldn't pass it up. I'm sorry I didn't tell you, I just . . . I wasn't sure if I'd get it."

"Callie, don't apologize to me. I'm so happy for you. You're going to be amazing. I can't wait to stand in the bleachers and cheer your girls on."

Anne thought back to when she was in high school. She and Callie would not have been friends because they would have been in completely different social circles. Callie of course would have been cute, popular, and captain of the dance team. Anne would have been the girl in the library studying to get a 105 on her math test. The two types didn't usually blend. But that didn't matter now; in fact, the thought made her laugh.

She couldn't help but imagine who Mike would have been. No doubt the bad boy with the loud car who skipped class and melted hearts with his stare. Also the one who made out with a different girl every weekend and had fathers everywhere reaching for their guns. Yep, she wouldn't have gotten a second glance from a teenage Mike. Not that she could have anyway, considering he was years younger than she was. She decided not to think about that because she was getting a lot of looks—and touches—from him now. Anne snapped out of her daydream and realized that Callie was chatting about drill team camp in July and costumes. She pulled it together and nodded. She was so happy for her friend.

"So how will this work with the shop?" Anne asked.

"Well, I told the principal that ideally the girls would practice right after school four days a week. That's our slow time, so Eric will just close up the shop for me on Monday through Thursday, and maybe a few other random times. He's been really great about this. Of course there will be games and such, but they will be in the evenings. It will all work out, even if I have to hire someone else. Dancing was my life for so long, and I miss it terribly."

"Wow, that's so great, I'm glad you're doing something with your talent, Cal. And you know I'll be willing to help with the shop whenever I can."

"Thank you, Anne. That means a lot. Let's hope I don't make a fool out of myself. Now, next on the agenda, let's discuss this gigantic cake for the Monsers' sweet sixteen party."

Friday night Mike stepped out of the scalding-hot shower and grabbed the towel from the wall rack. It had been a long day, the majority of which included his body doing unnatural things. Not the good kind that included a partner, but the ones that involved him leaning so far over the engine that his calves cramped or lying on his back under the car for an hour. He couldn't complain, though; he made a living doing what he loved, even if he had to frequently pop ibuprofen to get through it.

He scrubbed at his wet hair and then used the towel to wipe the steam from the mirror. Hot showers at the end of the day were a necessity to wash away the grease and the smell of old car, and to ease the muscles. Today's scrub had included another bonus: thoughts of Anne, which, if he was truthful, were becoming a habit. Jesus, he smiled just thinking of her.

The way she'd looked at him the other day, his hands stroking her, her release hitting her while their eyes locked. He'd replayed the scene over and over in his head a million times since Tuesday. Tomorrow's date couldn't come soon enough.

After brushing his teeth and throwing on a pair of basketball shorts, Mike sprawled out on his tiny double bed. He flipped on the TV and tried to relax as he switched from channel to channel. Nothing was capturing his attention. Either that or he was incredibly distracted.

He picked up his cell phone and glanced at the time. It was just after ten o'clock. He suddenly had a painful urge to talk to Anne and he wasn't sure how to feel about that. He'd dated a lot of women, some he'd liked a lot, and some were . . . okay. But never before had he craved conversation with a woman like he had Anne. He wondered if it was too late to text her.

He flipped to the news and watched a story about the rise of skin cancer in teenagers who used tanning beds. Yep, the news pretty much sucked. He turned the TV off and picked his phone back up. Fuck it, he was gonna do it.

MIKE: You awake, Perfect?

He stared at the screen, willing her to respond. After five minutes he considered just calling. Or maybe not. She was probably asleep, or not by her phone, or maybe she just chose not to respond. *Or maybe you need to get over it.*

He laid his phone on the tiny bedside table and was reaching for the lamp when the phone dinged. He snatched it up and opened the message.

ANNE: Yes. Can I help you, Uncle Mike?

He grinned. Damn, he loved it when she called him that. It reminded him of the day he'd first laid eyes on her in her pink dress with flowers from head to toe. She'd been so beautiful. She was always beautiful. He typed out a reply.

MIKE: I certainly wish you were here to help
     me.

He was relieved to see the bubble pop right up that let him know she was typing.

ANNE: And how exactly would I be of service?

And even more relieved to see that she was willing to play along.

MIKE: That's a dangerous question, Perfect.
     What are you good at?
ANNE: I don't know.
MIKE: I don't believe that. I can think of many
     things.
ANNE: You're trying to butter me up.
MIKE: Good idea, can we do that tomorrow? I'll
     bring the butter.
ANNE: Butter is bad for you.

MIKE: I like things that are bad.
ANNE: YOU'RE bad.
MIKE: But you like me.
ANNE: Yes I do.

He hadn't been sure how she would respond, but her easy admission made him grin.

MIKE: I like you too.

What was she going to say to that? What did he want her to say? And why the hell was he lying here in bed worrying about shit like this? He wasn't thirteen anymore. This was fucking ridiculous.

ANNE: I'm excited for tomorrow. I better get to sleep.

Ah, she was going to put a stop to it. Okay, so maybe it had gotten a little awkward. What the hell was he doing?

MIKE: Good night, Perfect.
ANNE: Good night, Uncle Mike.

Lying back in the darkness, Mike tried to make sense of everything he was feeling. In a very short period of time things had started crossing into uncharted territory. He liked women, he enjoyed them, and he respected them. But he *liked* Anne. He hadn't been lying or trying to butter her up. Well, maybe a little. He was still dying to see her naked. But it was more than that. If he knew tomorrow had no chance of nakedness, he would still want to be with her. Talk to her, listen to her laugh, date her.

Getting to know Anne in person was amazing, but the combination of the real Anne and the one he read on her blog made her dynamic and interesting. He sometimes felt like he was peeking in on something sacred and private when he read the comments she exchanged with her readers. She was a special person, to everyone. Even if someone left a not-so-kind message—which really chapped his ass when it happened—she replied with friendliness, validating their opinion and trying to find a common ground. She had a sort of kindness and class that many woman he met didn't. He admired her, and he'd never felt this kind of awe for a woman he was attracted to.

It occurred to him that they had never discussed her blog. Strange. Would she never mention it to him? He realized he really wanted her to share every part of herself with him.

Fourteen

Saturday afternoon Anne scrolled back through the previous evening's text conversation with Mike. She'd probably read through it ten—or a hundred—times.

I like you too.

Four words that made her heart pound in excitement and panic simultaneously. She liked lots of people in varying degrees. The degree was a critical part of the equation, so what was it between the two of them? Sparks definitely flew when they were together, but that kind of heat was physical. Surely he couldn't have serious feelings for her this soon. They really didn't know that much about each other, though they were starting to.

He'd shared some of his past, and she'd shared a little about herself with him, about being adopted. But in truth her blog followers still knew more about her than Mike, and yet he'd already given her a mind-blowing orgasm—practically in public. She'd thought of that incident more than a hundred times for sure, and it never failed to bring a smile to her face.

"Why are you so happy, Mommy?" Claire asked as she stepped into Anne's bathroom.

"Oh nothing, baby. Actually, I'm excited for you to go to Bailey's tonight. You have to promise me you'll be on your best behavior."

Claire sat on the toilet seat lid while Anne applied her mascara. She'd decided to put some waves into her hair and leave it long. She'd gone a little more dramatic on her eyes and even lined her lips. Mike had said to dress casual and she honestly wasn't sure what that meant to a guy so she'd chosen some navy shorts, a white embroidered tank top, and strappy leather sandals.

She'd even gone to the nail salon downtown and had her toenails painted a bright red to match the chunky beaded necklace she'd picked up at Sweet Opal Designs. It was one of her favorite little boutiques down on Main Street and was owned by Brooke Abbott, who was quickly becoming a good friend to Anne and the other *MPLL* ladies.

"I promise to be good. Can I take my flower pillow?"

Anne used her fingers to put the finishing touches on her hair. "Of course. Are you about ready?"

"Yep." Claire scrambled off the toilet and into her bedroom to retrieve her things.

Anne was to have Claire to Erin's house at two o'clock, and Mike was picking her up at three. She wondered why so early but didn't ask any questions. She was looking forward to the surprise.

After loading Claire and her overnight items into the car they headed a little way into the country to Erin's.

Anne had been there only once, when Claire had been invited to Bailey's party in February. Although the girls were best friends, she didn't know Erin and Todd Wilson very well. She did know that he was gone most of the time traveling for work, which was why she had assumed that Mike was Bailey's father because she'd never met him. Remembering that day when he'd introduced himself made her smile. She'd been quite happy to hear that he was Uncle Mike.

Anne pulled into the long driveway and parked in front of the white colonial home. She didn't know what Todd or Erin did, but they obviously did well for themselves. She gathered up the pink suitcase and flower pillow and followed Claire up to the front door.

Anne was beyond nervous about the conversation she was about to have with Erin, even though they'd already spoken briefly. Erin had called Wednesday morning and invited Claire to spend the night, not-so-subtly joking that her brother had strongly suggested it was necessary. They'd both chuckled awkwardly and made the arrangements. Anne hoped Erin was truly okay with this; she didn't want to do anything that might affect Claire's friendship with Bailey.

The front door opened and Bailey rushed out to throw her arms around Claire's neck before both girls disappeared into the house. Erin emerged onto the front step in a pair of yoga pants and a T-shirt.

"Hellooo," she chimed. It sounded cheerful enough, but Anne didn't know her well enough to be sure what the other woman was thinking. "Come in so we can talk, it's getting hot out here."

Great.

The interior of the house was well decorated in a perfect combination of modern and country. Anne liked it a lot and told Erin so.

"Thanks, I think I finally got it how I want it." She plopped down on a leather couch and nodded for Anne to do the same. "Now. Tell me of this magic you worked on my brother."

Anne went still in a plaid wingback chair and raised her eyes to Erin's. A huge grin had broken out across her face. Anne swallowed and tucked a hair behind her ear. "I'm not sure what you mean."

Erin leaned in. "He has never seemed so excited about going out with a woman. I love him dearly, but he doesn't necessarily have the best track record. He would die if he knew I was telling you this."

Anne shook her head, trying not to put too much stock in the information. "I won't tell him."

A rumbling engine pulled Anne from the couch where she sat nervous and waiting. She didn't want to get caught peeking out the window, so she decided to just open the front door and step outside. The shiny black Chevelle that she'd mentioned liking in Mike's shop pulled into her driveway. She couldn't help but smile.

The driver's-side window was down, and when Mike's eyes found her he returned her grin with a huge one of his own. He shut off the car, got out—and Anne lost her breath. He looked insanely hot in khaki shorts and a dark-gray T-shirt. The way it clung to his chest and biceps made her mouth go dry. He had on sunglasses and once again a hat. The whole ensemble should have looked boyish, but nothing about him could be anything but manly. An incredibly laid-back and sexy man, she thought as he made his way to her.

It took her a moment to realize that his approach was predatory, far from hesitant, and before she knew it his hands were cradling her jaw and his mouth was on hers. It was a firm kiss, skin pressing into skin, and then he pulled back for a second before nipping at her top lip. Her jaw had gone slack at the complete hotness of it. How had he gained this power over her in such a short time? Her body responded to his in an embarrassingly primal way every damn time.

His hands slid down her neck and settled on her shoulders as the heady scent of his soap and aftershave washed over her. This close she could just barely make out his eyes meeting hers through the dark lenses of his sunglasses. "How are you, Perfect?"

She'd heard it so many times now, and yet she couldn't help a blush at the name. She feigned annoyance but couldn't deny the warmth that spread through her body every time he said it. Not only because she loved the sound of a pet name for her on his wicked lips, but also because of the implication. He saw her as something special, and something desirable. It was still hard to believe, but his actions—and his words—were very convincing. Her only fear was that he would realize that she was, in fact, so imperfect.

"I'm good, *Uncle Mike.*" She tried to sound flirty and seductive as her arms settled on his hips, but it came out sounding slightly dorky to her ears. His reaction indicated he was good with the way it came out because he pulled her body flush against his.

"Have I told you how much that nickname turns me on?"

"No, you haven't."

"I'm not sure what that says about me, but I can guarantee you that it's only hot from these lips." He swiped at her bottom lip with his thumb. "I can also guarantee you that the females who call me Uncle Mike can almost always expect me to give them whatever they want."

She scoffed. "Whatever they want, huh?"

"Yep."

"Good to know. I'll save that little nugget of information for later."

"Mmmm." He nuzzled into her neck one more time and laid a quick kiss under her ear before pulling away. "You better."

"Let me get my purse." Anne stepped back into the house and leaned against the wall. She was struggling to wrap her mind around what was happening. She'd been married for nearly five years and never, not once, had Scott ever been this happy to see her. Never had he greeted her with such passion and enthusiasm. She had known Mike not quite two weeks. It was their first official date, and his hello had left her wanting to drag him to her bedroom.

To be fair, she'd never minded Scott's lack of enthusiasm now that she thought about it, but it seemed it was only because she didn't know any different. Now that she'd experienced what it was like to be the recipient of such affection, she wasn't sure she could ever settle for less. And that was a shame, because when this little fling fizzled she would be left constantly looking for its equal.

She grabbed her purse, locked the front door, and

headed back outside. Mike was facing the street, and she took a good look at the back of him. He was amazing from every angle. This was the first time she'd seen his legs. They were toned, as she would have expected, muscular, and tanned with a dusting of dark hair. She wondered what it felt like to walk around the world looking like an Adonis. Must be nice.

He turned when her shoes hit the steps and reached out to take her hand. The small gesture affected her nearly as much as the hello kisses. He was passionate *and* thoughtful, and super bossy when it was appropriate, which was so hot. He really needed to reveal some flaws soon or she would be in a lot of trouble.

"So, while this was my favorite car in your shop, I think I recall that it belongs to someone else. That *possession* guy, right?"

"That's the one, and we're driving it somewhere for him. Hope you don't mind." He came around to the passenger side and opened the long, heavy door. Anne slid in, and the backs of her thighs caught on the leather tuck-and-roll upholstery. She braced herself on her hands and lifted her butt to scoot over.

"Sorry, Perfect, these old cars aren't like the cozy rides we're used to these days, but they have their own charm, you'll see."

"It's just fine. I like it," she said. He grinned and shut the door with a heavy thud. It sounded as if it was a hundred pounds of solid steel. Maybe it was. The front seat was a long bench style with an armrest that was folded down between the two of them. The dash was deep and black vinyl, the dials vintage looking; even the knobs and controls were big metal pieces. The one modern feature was an aftermarket stereo with iPod connection and digital display.

Mike sat down in the driver's seat and turned toward her. "The seat belt is a little different in here." Pivoting onto his side, he pushed over the armrest, found the seat belt beside Anne's hip, and laid it across her lap. "Now you stick it into the part by the door."

She found the latch and waited while he settled into his own seat belt and then started the engine. It was deep and growling, reverberating through her torso. His newer Camaro felt powerful also, but this had another quality; it felt . . . raw. It even had its own scent, although she couldn't place it . . . it smelled like engine and leather and . . . *old*.

They headed out of town, but instead of getting on the main interstate, Mike veered onto a southbound two-lane state highway that would lead them into Kansas. She had no idea what his plan was, and she really didn't care. She could drive through the country all day beside him, some classic rock playing faintly in the background.

Once again, the sight of Mike driving was amazing. His left hand gripping the large vinyl-wrapped steering wheel made his forearms look firm and large. He fit into the interior of the car as if it had been crafted around him. She looked at his face and noticed his eyes sliding to the side behind his glasses, trying to look at her while he drove.

This particular vehicle was an automatic, which left his right hand free. Suddenly he rested his arm faceup on the center console between them. Hand open, he tapped his palm with his two middle fingers, a clear invitation for her to rest her hand in his, and the simple intimacy of it made Anne's heart flutter. Refusing would have been rude, and of course she didn't want to be rude, not to mention she wanted to touch any part of him she could. She lifted her hand and laid it against his, their inner arms warm against each other. He instantly threaded his fingers with hers and squeezed. Simultaneously it felt like a vise clamped down on her chest.

If she had been alone, she would've cried. Not including the birth of her daughter, nothing in Anne's life had felt as right as this moment, skin touching, driving fast, beautiful country, and bright-blue sky. Every time she was in his presence another layer of Mike exposed itself, each one sweeter and softer than the last.

What was the saying—*Better to have lusted and lost than never lusted at all*? Or had she just made that up. Either way it didn't matter, because that's all this was, right?

Fifteen

Nearly forty-five minutes in the car and Mike hadn't let go of Anne's hand the entire time. He couldn't break the connection because he felt like some kind of energy had been passing through their fingertips, like their heartbeats had begun to pulse in perfect rhythm. He also hadn't been able to stop glancing at her thighs in those little shorts. Against the black seats they looked so smooth and inviting, and he knew part of the reason he'd gripped her hand was to keep from touching her anywhere else. There would be plenty of time for other things, and he intended to show her that this was more than sexual chemistry. Although it was so definitely a lot of that.

The last few times they'd been together had involved heavy petting and even heavier breathing, which had been amazing, but he wanted her to know that he could also be a gentleman. There was more to him than a hot time, and while he was damn good at hot times, he wanted more with her. He'd been on plenty of dates of the normal variety. Normal for him usually included food, movies, and an awkward morning after. However, he wanted his morning with Anne to include another round of lovemaking and then breakfast in bed. He wanted this date to be perfect.

On the drive they'd discussed Claire and Bailey, sharing silly stories of things the girls had said and done. He loved how animated her voice had gotten as she'd discussed her daughter; he would have brought anything up to hear her keep talking like that.

"I don't think I've ever been this far south of the metro," Anne said as he pulled into the small town of Green Mound.

"Well, then you're in for a treat, Perfect. Small towns may lack in some things, but Green Mound puts on a fantastic Pie Days Festival."

"Pie Days? Did we drive all this way to eat pie? Not that I'm complaining, I love pie."

He grinned at her as he steered the car toward the town square. "Me, too. There will inevitably be some serious pie eating, but that's not all. You'll see."

They drove slowly as families walked the streets, probably coming to and from the center of town where all the action was. Mike had been to Pie Days for the first time last year, drawn for the same reason, the car show. Two of his clients had mentioned how big it was in the region and he'd dragged Derek with him. Eating pie with Anne would be much more entertaining than doing so with his friend.

"Wow, there are tons of people. The town isn't even that big, it must draw quite a crowd." Anne slowly pulled her hand from his and turned to look out the window.

His palm was damp from holding on for so long. He missed the feel of her against him.

The cars on display were lined in several lots off to the side of the square. He pulled into the final one and rolled down his window to talk to the man in charge of registration. Mike had agreed to drive his client Dave's Chevelle down to meet him even though he was still waiting on one minor part before he could call it *done*. The man in charge of the car show motioned to where Mike should park, and he backed into a spot next to Dave's red '69 Chevelle, which Mike had worked on last year. He didn't see him standing around, so Mike assumed he must be off wandering the rows of cars.

"All right, Perfect, you ready?" Mike said as he parked and exited the vehicle.

Anne stepped from the car with her purse, her head turning and taking in the rows and rows of cars. "Wow, this is quite a sight. I can see why you like this. All these cars . . . it's totally your thing. Do you come to shows like this often?" They began to walk down the aisle, checking out the cars on display.

"No, not really. I enjoy working on the cars and driving them, but I don't get to do these things often. It's basically a lot of old guys for the most part." He teased, but the truth was, car shows were a little painful. He used to go to a lot of them with his father, and these men and their conversations about horsepower and renovation projects reminded him of what he was missing with his dad. He would give anything to spend an afternoon at a car show with his father, but that would never happen again. "I used to, though, with my dad, when I was young and even into high school. We'd try to find an event every weekend in the summer. We'd walk around checking out everyone's work, talk about how we would have done it better." He laughed, a subtle ache shooting through his chest. He hadn't thought of those moments in a long time. Damn, he missed his father. He missed his mother, too, but he was so much younger when he'd lost her that the pain of her loss wasn't as acute. His dad had become his everything.

"That sounds nice. I can't wait to share some of my hobbies with Claire."

"And what would those be?" He reached out and laid his hand on her lower back. He loved touching her. He'd once again just shared something personal with her, without really thinking about it, and he was hoping she'd open up a little more about her life. Preferably her blog.

"Oh, you know, making things pretty, parties, decorating. I like taking pictures, too. I even brought my camera today. I'm pretty much always taking pictures."

Mike knew that she took a lot of photos for her site, but unfortunately she didn't say that and he wasn't going to push. For some reason she was choosing not to tell him about it, and he wondered why.

They continued down the row they'd parked in, cars lining each side, some with their hoods open, some fancy, some in early stages of renovation. There were hot rods from the 1930s and '40s all the way to the beefy muscle cars of the 1960s and '70s. Each one held a different appeal and had its own fan base. Mike could appreciate them all, but had always loved the look of muscle cars of the '60s and '70s, the roar of the engines and the sturdiness of the long steel front ends.

"If you like old cars," Anne said, interrupting his thoughts, "how come you drive a new one?"

"Well, the main reason is that I want to know for sure my car will start when I get in it," he joked. But it was the truth. "Old cars come with their own quirks, and they require a lot of maintenance—which I love, don't get me wrong. I've owned quite a few, but my enjoyment comes from finding something that needs a little love and attention, fixing it up, and then selling it. Making a profit is fun, too."

"I bet," Anne said with a smirk.

"Someday I'll find a '69 Nova to trick out just the way I want it and keep it. Maybe someday I'll have a kid to work on it with. Who knows?"

He felt Anne's eyes on him, and he wondered what she was thinking.

"Mike Everett?" a man's voice called out. Mike turned to find a middle-aged man walking toward them. He wore a Hawaiian-style button-up shirt, but instead of flowers it was covered in multicolored Mustangs. He was the typical guy you found at these things. Mike stuck out his hand.

"I'm Mike. Have we met?" The man grinned and took Mike's hand in a firm grip. His body smelled of alcohol and aftershave, and his bulbous nose was sprinkled with broken blood vessels, letting Mike know exactly what kind of guy he was dealing with.

"Not yet, but I've heard a lot about you. I'm Keith Meyers, friend of Dave's. He said you're amazing. I've got a GTO that needs an overhaulin' and Dave said you're the only guy I should consider."

"Well, that's nice of Dave. He's been bringing me his

rides for a few years now. I'd love to take a look at your GTO, but unfortunately I couldn't get to it for another few months or so."

"That busy, huh? Well, good for you. I'm in no hurry. Used to do the work myself, but these days my arthritis gets in the way." He leaned back and patted his giant beer belly, a chuckle rumbling from his open mouth.

Anne laughed quietly beside Mike, and the sound drew both men's attention. Keith's gaze roamed over Anne a little too long, and Mike felt his blood pressure rise. This jackass might find that *a few months* could turn into forever if he wasn't careful.

"This your lady, Mike? You scored yourself quite a looker. I'm jealous." Keith laughed at his wit and gave Mike a slap on the back. Mike managed not to budge and not to smile.

Keith sensed that his humor wasn't going over well and reached for the pocket on his shirt. "Well, shoot, I don't have a card on me. Why don't you give me yours?"

"No problem," Mike said as he grabbed Anne's hand and backed up a step; thankfully she followed. "I don't have a card on me, either, so I'll just get your info from Dave tonight."

"Oh, oh yeah, good idea."

Mike gave a half wave then turned and pulled Anne close to him as they joined the throng of people wandering the square. She didn't mention the interaction and he didn't, either. For a moment he'd felt proud to have his work talked up in front of Anne like that; then the guy had to be a dumb-ass and fuck it up by ogling her and making ridiculous comments.

Dealing with men and cars inevitably involved men

behaving like men, some worse than others, but he didn't want any of that macho bullshit directed at Anne, especially from the men who did business with him. There was already a stigma connected to blue collar work, he knew that. Just like he knew he would never be in her league, but damn, he wanted to show her that he could be worthy of her.

The late-afternoon air was heavy and filled with the scent of funnel cakes and kettle corn. Children ran through the green, which was dotted with tented booths and food trucks, teenagers loitered, and Mike enjoyed that the crowd pushed Anne's body closer to his. After a while he bought them a beer at a booth from the small local pub and then walked across the street into a parking lot full of carnival rides.

"Claire would love this." Anne looked around as she held her beer out to Mike. "Will you hold this a minute."

"Sure." He had to drop her hand to take the bottle, and he stood there watching as she fished through her purse and pulled out her camera.

"This way I can show her what I did while we were apart," she said with a smile. She turned back and forth, snapping photos of the Ferris wheel and the colorfully lit ticket booth.

Mike didn't doubt that she would share many of these photos with Claire, but she'd also taken a photo of the little beer stand, even an up-close shot of the rows of vintage-looking beer bottles. He knew she wouldn't be bragging to Claire about all the alcohol she drank. She was taking photos to share on her blog, he was certain. For some reason she didn't want to discuss it with him.

Why? It didn't make sense. Her blog was a large part of her life, he could tell. Would she tell her blog readers who she'd been with at this small-town carnival? He wanted to think she would, or at the very least say she'd been on a date, but he had a feeling she wouldn't.

He wished the thought didn't bother him. He didn't want to be Anne's secret, although he wasn't sure what he *did* want. To date her for sure, but more? He hadn't processed that yet. Was she ashamed of him? Mike knew he was no wealthy catch; he didn't wear a suit or have a corner office. But he had a job, he did well, and he knew Anne was attracted to him. Maybe she just didn't want to share more of herself with him. That thought just plain sucked.

She stuffed her camera in her purse and grabbed her beer. "Thanks."

"So you plan parties, right? Is that all you do?" He was officially probing. Great, his man card was now in jeopardy of being revoked.

"Ummm, pretty much."

Mike's jaw tensed. Although they were walking again they hadn't rejoined hands. "So how do you generate business? Word of mouth, or do you have a website?"

She was silent for a moment but he didn't turn and face her; he only looked ahead as they headed back toward the rows of pie booths. *Don't lie to me, Anne.*

"Um, yeah, I do have a website where I share party ideas and such on a blog. It's not a big deal, and most of my parties are referrals."

"Well that's good. Word of mouth is the way to go," he countered. She hadn't lied, but she sure as hell wasn't offering anything more, and he didn't quite know what to think about it. She clearly wanted to keep that part of her life private, which was ironic because that part of her life was also so public. Obviously he was right, and she wanted to keep it private from *him*. "So a blog, huh. That's cool, you must put a lot of work into keeping that up."

He didn't miss the way her body tensed at his words.

"No, not too much work. Like I said, it's no big deal. Just another tool for business, I guess." Quickly she regrouped and reached out to grab his hand. Damn, he loved her doing that on her own, and her smile . . . it was enough to let her avoidance of the blog thing go for a little while. He wanted her to touch him, wanted her to want him, and he wanted her to reveal herself to him. For once in his adult life the tables were turned on him. He was offering himself up, and the person he wanted was keeping him at a distance.

The hours went by too quickly as they rode the Ferris wheel, played ridiculous games, and checked out lots of cars. She didn't even mind that part. She loved hearing him talk about it, and he never hesitated, knowing the answer to every one of her questions, even managing to make it interesting. She had no idea that varying headlight styles, vinyl tops versus metal, and engine parts could be so interesting. It was very possible, though, that she just loved the sound of his voice, the sparkle of his eyes, and how much he genuinely seemed to enjoy telling her about it all.

Dusk was now falling, the pinks and purples of the sky blending with the carnival lights. The sound of the carousel was nearly overpowered by the song of crickets and the laughter of happy people. The atmosphere was perfect as she stared down at the pie smorgasbord resting beside her on a bale of hay. Mike had bought the sample plate, which included small pieces of cherry, apple, French silk, and Dixie—a pie she'd never heard of. It looked delicious.

The only thing that was killing her mood was the thought that she hadn't been completely honest with Mike when he'd asked about her site earlier. It had been right on the tip of her tongue to tell him all about *MPLL*, but she'd held back, fearful. His comment about how much work she must put into it was what shut her down completely. She loved her work on that site, was proud of it even, but in some ways it had led to the demise of her first marriage.

Scott had accused her of caring more about her image as the perfect homemaker than about her real home, more specifically, about him. He'd blamed her for the lack of intimacy in their relationship, which he said was why he'd resorted to cheating. She wasn't stupid, her brain knew that was crap; plenty of marriages lacked intimacy—even happiness—and that didn't mean spouses always cheated. But in retrospect she knew she carried part of the blame. She had pulled away from him in many ways. All of it had been . . . painful.

What she couldn't reconcile was why she felt the need to hide it now, from *this* man. She knew he was not like Scott. But it wouldn't be long before he realized that a ready-made family was a lot to handle. What if her busy life—her party planning, her newspaper column, her blog—was the final straw, and he'd decide that none of her baggage was worth the hassle? Pretty soon he'd see that she was not as perfect as he imagined her to be.

Another part of her hesitation was that she was sort of embarrassed for him to read it. She wrote about parts of herself she wasn't always capable of sharing face-to-face, said silly things, told funny stories about her life. The pitiful thing was that the deeper part of her, the one she tried to push down, wanted to share it with him. Wanted to know what he thought. Besides Claire and her mother, and of course Callie and Lindsey, the blog was what Anne loved more than anything in the world. It had saved her, given her purpose, an identity, and a way to provide for her daughter. It was a part of her that felt special, and she wanted him to be impressed by it.

He returned with a stack of napkins and large soda and sat down straddling the hay bale, his knee pushing against her thigh, the plate between his legs.

"I wasn't really thinking if it would be okay to share, do you mind?" He lifted the Styrofoam cup in question.

"No, I don't mind," she said. He handed her a fork and lifted the plate, holding it between them.

"Which one you trying first?" He lifted an eyebrow.

"Let's see." She lifted her fork and scanned the plate. They all looked heavenly, and if she was alone she could probably put a good dent in each one. Not really something she wanted to brag about it. "I think I'll try the Dixie, because I'm curious."

"Good choice, me too, but ladies first." He waited for her to fill her fork with a bite and then watched as she lifted it to her mouth, his eyes darted back and forth between her lips and her eyes. She chewed slowly, unexpected flavors exploding on her taste buds.

"Mmmm, there's chocolate in there. Almost like pecan pie with chocolate."

Mike responded by filling his own fork and taking a bite. His eyes widened and he spoke around the pie. "Oh yeah, that is good."

She smiled and took a bite of the apple. It was delicious, the crust flaky and the filling gooey and cinnamony. "Oh gosh, that's good, too."

Next was the cherry, a little tangy for her taste, but the crust was yummy, almost like a sugar cookie. She moved on to the French silk, saving it for last because she knew she would love it. What was not to love about rich chocolate mousse and a creamy topping?

Once the smooth filling hit her mouth she moaned, her eyes flitting shut. She leaned on her thighs, letting her fork dangle in front of her. "God, that one is complete heaven."

"You're a sexy eater, Perfect." She looked up to find Mike still staring at her, his fork lax in his hands. It was darker now, so he'd removed his sunglasses and turned his hat around backward.

"Oh my gosh, how embarrassing. You were supposed to be eating, too."

"I was until I realized watching you was a lot more enjoyable. Sit up."

She did as he asked and he grabbed her thigh, shifting her to face him a little. He picked up his own fork and loaded it with another bite of the French silk before he held it up to her lips.

"What are you doing?" She couldn't help smiling.

"I'm feeding you. Now open up."

Anne parted her lips and watched his eyes take in the

movement as he slid the fork into her mouth. She willed herself not to be self-conscious about eating for a man, because it was incredibly erotic knowing that he liked it. And all she had to do was glance down to be completely sure.

His lips slid slowly into a wicked grin and he adjusted his shirt to cover the noticeable tent between his legs. They both started laughing and before Anne knew it he was setting the fork down and putting his hand behind her neck, pulling her in, pressing his lips to hers. The taste of cherries and chocolate mixed as their tongues met over and over. She lifted her hand to his shoulder, the firmness of his muscles reminding her of how incredibly perfect *he* was. She realized she hadn't seen him without a shirt yet, and suddenly she was dying to.

A low groan came from Mike's throat as he licked at her bottom lip. "I want to feast on you, Anne," he mumbled against her mouth and kissed her cheek, then her jaw. She loved him calling her Perfect, but she loved her name on his lips even more. It told her he knew exactly who she was, it wasn't a dream, and he hadn't made a mistake. He wanted her, Anne Edmond, thirty-two-year-old single mother. He thought she was perfect and sexy, and she would cherish this time with him, let him give her memories that would last her forever. Maybe it would be enough.

Her eyes shut as his hand lifted up to cup her jaw. He gave her a small smile and they finished the pie, discussing what they liked about each one. After he lifted the final bite of French silk to her lips, he tossed the plate and napkins in a trash bin near their seat. "You ready to go? The car judging should be over by now."

"Yes, I'm just going to go to the restroom real quick since we have a good drive ahead of us."

"Okay, there's a convenience store across the street. I'll walk over with you."

"No, no. You wait here. I'll be right back. It's close."

She stood up and grabbed her purse off the ground before she ran into the Casey's gas station across the street from the square. There was a small line, but she got in and out of the small store and made her way back toward the crowd. The night had brought out a louder, younger group, and she jumped when a hand closed over her arm. She expected it to be Mike, but she turned to find two women.

"Sorry to startle you, Are you My Perfect Little Life Anne?"

"Oh gosh, yes, I am. Hi!" This had happened several times in the past, and it never ceased to amaze Anne and make her blush. She was no celebrity, but she did have a following. Thanks to her newspaper column and some local magazine coverage, some readers now knew she lived in the area and recognized her. She was always surprised to find how much people felt like they really *knew* her. Like they were friends. It was sweet . . . albeit a tiny bit awkward.

"See, I told you it was her. I'm Cecille, known as beezlebub379 in the comments, and this is my daughter-in-law Patty, or Pattypie." They both beamed, and Anne collected herself quickly.

"Of course, it's so nice to meet you both. I recognize both of your screen names, you've been readers for a long time. That means a lot."

"Since nearly the beginning," Patty said with a grin.

"We adore the blog. Is Bug with you?" The woman glanced past Anne.

"No, I'm sorry, she's not. What a small world. Do you live here in Green Mound?"

Sure enough they did, and Anne chatted briefly with them. She glanced around, hoping Mike was nowhere near enough to overhear the conversation. How embarrassing to have to explain.

"You should come by and try Patty's cherry pie. It wins blue ribbons, and she just started using an adaptation of Callie's Perfect Crust."

"Oh, I think I did . . . the cherry you said? The crust was my very favorite." Patty grinned and gave her thanks as Anne kept up the nervous glances from side to side. "I'm so sorry, I do need to run, but I'm so glad you stopped me because it was so, so nice to meet you both. I'll tell Callie you love the piecrust. She'll be thrilled."

She tried to graciously run off and turned around to instead run right into Mike. "Oh, hi."

"Hi. Who was that?"

"Oh." Anne swiped some hair out of her face. How did you admit to someone on a first date . . . *Well, I'm kind of special and my blog gets over twenty thousand hits a day.* "Just some women who had looked at my site before. We were just chatting for a minute."

"They recognized you?"

"I know, isn't that weird?" She laughed awkwardly and then scrunched up her nose. She hated that nervous habit.

"Yeah, that is weird." He stared at her for a minute, a small smile working at the corner of his mouth. "Must be some site for people to recognize you from it. You sure you're not famous?"

Oh God. Her throat nearly closed up, and she stifled a small nervous chuckle. "No, why in the world would you say that? It's really nothing." It was silly to try to explain it away; the only good explanation was the truth. But she wasn't ready to go into that.

Mike was still grinning when he took her hand again. "Okay then, shall we go?"

She nodded and took his hand. He led them back through the carnival all the way to the car lots, which were less full than they had been when they arrived, empty parking spots dotted the aisles. It was now fully dark, and the folks lingering were dark shadows. Right now she just wanted to get him home and touch him, kiss him. Do all the things she'd been fantasizing about. She needed to get him out of her system.

When they found the Chevelle, two blue ribbons were stuck under the windshield wiper.

"Look at that," Anne said. "What did you win?"

He opened the huge metal passenger door, and she stood cradled between it and the interior as he read the ribbon. "Best in Class Chevelle and Best in Class Year. Technically Dave won, not me."

"Except you did all the work. That's amazing." Anne grabbed the front of Mike's shirt and pulled him against her. He looked surprised for a second and then wrapped his arms around her waist. "I'm impressed, Uncle Mike."

He was quiet for a moment. The dim interior light inside the car just barely lit his handsome face as he lifted a finger and ran it down her cheek. "*Are* you impressed, Anne?"

She didn't know how to respond to that. He suddenly seemed very serious, like he had something on his mind. She swallowed and answered him, her voice coming out in a whisper. "Yes, I am."

"Because I'm impressed with *you*. All of you. Everything. I like . . . *everything* about you."

He kissed her, thank goodness, because she'd had no idea what to say to his admission. It was as if he didn't want her to reply. He only wanted to assault her mouth with his lips and his tongue. His fingers dug into her ass and squeezed, pulling her against him, his erection pushing into her lower stomach. His mouth was hot and his lips forceful as his tongue tangled with hers, both of them trying to conquer the other—but she really wanted him to win, she wanted him to lay her down on the bench seat of the Chevelle and strip her naked. She wanted him fully tonight.

"Come home with me," she said with her head tilted back as his lips pressed small kisses to her neck. "Please."

She felt his chest rumble against her breasts, and he let out a groan before stepping away from her. "Get in, Anne."

She stood there for a moment completely confused. When he made his way to the driver's side and got in, she followed suit. She wanted to hurry back to her place, finally make this happen, because she wanted him so badly.

She felt him looking at her as she buckled her seat belt, and his silence mixed with his previous comments were making her a little paranoid. "Is something wrong?"

"No." A heavy sigh left him, and he started the engine before turning back to her. "It's just, I want you like crazy, Anne, but you need to know, I'm not sleeping with you tonight."

"Okay," she whispered. Embarrassment swept through her body in a wild rush, then quickly turned to anger. "But why? I thought that's what we were doing tonight. What was the point of arranging a sleepover for Claire? Also, we didn't get to finish last time. I want you, and you want me. And who says it's all up to you anyway?"

"Let me explain, Anne," he pleaded, grabbing her hand.

She sat back against the leather seat and stared out into the night. She wanted to scream or throw a tantrum. Seriously, what the hell was his problem? Their kissing had nearly undone her, and he said he wanted her, but he refused to have sex with her?

"Things between us . . . it's hot, right?" He didn't wait for a response and she didn't offer one, but she turned to look into his eyes. He didn't look angry, he looked like he was as affected as she was. His thumb swept back and forth over her fingers, making it really hard to focus. "It's been intense, and I want it to linger. I guess. I don't know. But I don't want this to be all about the physical. I like you. A lot, and I want to *know* you, Anne. Is that possible?"

Her stomach threatened to drop through the floor of the car. What was he saying? He wanted a relationship? This was supposed to be simple, fun, and *easy*. So why did his words make her happy, confused, and want to cry all at the same time? Because it was entirely possible that the minute he really knew all of her he wouldn't be quite so impressed. She had a mommy blog, she'd failed at her first marriage, and her stretch marks were noticeable. She was so not perfect.

"I'm not sure, Mike. I think . . . I need to think about it." He swallowed, and she swore his jaw twitched.

"Okay, you think about it, I'll be waiting, Perfect." With that he pulled out and headed out of town and back to Preston.

Sixteen

The rest of the weekend had come and gone, it was now Monday and Anne hadn't heard from Mike. It was killing her. For something that she'd wanted to keep easy, it was taking over all her thoughts. This was far from no-strings-attached because all of her strings were pulled tight and begging for Mike.

She'd spent the morning sitting on the couch with her laptop loading some photos from Pie Days, typing up a blog post about the small town and the crafts she'd seen there and the cute little pub that carried bottled beer from local towns. Her followers loved stuff like this; within five minutes she had thirty-two comments. She smiled and closed her laptop, only to stare out the front window. Thinking. More thinking. Wasn't that exactly what she'd told him she needed to do? Maybe he was waiting for her to contact him.

Clearly she was far from ready for a relationship; she was a mess. *I want to know you.* His words kept repeating in her head. Why did she feel the need to keep things surface with him? She should share her passion for the blog and her work, let him know how successful they were. It wasn't something to be ashamed of. It was on a public medium, yet . . . it felt like revealing something personal and private. It felt like he would know everything about her, have any reason at his disposal to find her lacking, judge her, and end things altogether. And now telling him could be weird because she hadn't been entirely up front about it from the beginning. She almost just wished he already knew, but it was no surprise that a hot young guy didn't peruse the Home and Hobby section of the Sunday newspaper or read lifestyle blogs online.

She knew what people typed into a search engine that landed them on her blog. Things like "DIY princess party," "how to make paper flowers," or "easy desserts." Men didn't read her blog, well, at least not men like Mike Everett.

"Grandma Ree's here." Claire came bounding down the stairs. "I saw her from my window."

"What?" Anne stood up and glanced out to the driveway. Sure enough, her mother's sedan was sitting there. Anne went to the front door and met her mother on the porch.

"Hey, Mom, I didn't know you were planning on stopping by. You should have called. I could have had lunch prepared."

"Oh no, honey, I hadn't planned it, just thought I'd swing by after my doctor appointment."

"Well we're glad you did."

Claire ran to her grandmother and wrapped her arms around her thighs. "Hi, Grandma Ree."

Anne went to the kitchen to get her mother a glass of tea while she and Claire hugged on the couch. Anne loved how close the two were, and she was grateful that she could give her own daughter the kind of early childhood she'd never had. Those early years were important, they stuck with you even if you couldn't remember the details you remembered the feeling of being loved. Or the lack of it.

When Anne returned to the living room her mother was wiping a tear from her eye, and Anne's heart plunged. All at once she put together the pieces: doctor's appointment, unexpected visit, the nephrology appointment card she'd completely forgotten to bring up.

"Claire, why don't you run up to your room and play?" Anne asked, trying to sound casual.

"What's wrong, Grandma Ree?" Claire didn't let go of her grandmother's arms.

"Oh, it's nothing, Clairebug, I'll come up and play with you in a minute, okay? Why don't you get all the Barbies in pretty dresses for us, they'll have a party when I come up."

"But—"

"Claire, now please," Anne said, a sharp edge in her voice. She didn't want to frighten Claire, but Anne needed to know what was going on with her mother immediately. Claire walked slowly up the stairs, looking once over her shoulder. Anne couldn't blame her daughter; it was disconcerting to see Grandma Ree cry, and she knew that for her to let it slip in front of Claire meant she was struggling.

"What's going on, Mom?" Anne set down beside her

mother on the couch and handed her a box of tissues. Marie plucked one and swiped under her eyes.

"It's my diabetes acting up. No big deal."

"Obviously it is a big deal. What do you mean, acting up? Your blood sugar's too high? What do we need to do, change medicine?" Anne hoped she didn't sound as panicked as she felt. They'd dealt with the diabetes for years now; as far as she knew her mother was keeping it in check with diet, medication, and insulin when needed.

"Well, it's a little more than that, actually." Marie slumped her shoulders and rested her hands in her lap. She met Anne's eyes. "The nephrologist says that I'll probably need to start dialysis within the year."

Anne felt sick to her stomach. Her reply came out strangled. "What? How did this happen?"

"Apparently, it just happens sometimes, no matter how good you are. Anne, I've been living with this disease for twenty years. It's taken its toll on my kidneys."

For a moment they were both silent. Anne didn't want to cry. She knew if she did it would upset her mother, but despite Anne's wishes, the tears pressed on her eyelids. She took a deep breath and forced them to hold tight. She could cry alone tonight for all the ways she was hurting today.

"What do we need to do, Mom? Is it reversible?"

"We could slow it, but eventually it will probably need to happen. At that point dialysis is usually just a way to buy some time; eventually I'll possibly need a new kidney. Or not, I *am* nearly seventy-two."

"No, no, no. Don't talk like that. You're still young.

You drive, do your own laundry, and cook your own meals. And I *need* you." Anne's eyes were burning again, and this time she couldn't stop it. One traitorous tear ran down her cheek. "Can't I give you a kidney? People do that all the time."

Marie smiled through her own silent tears. "I don't think I'm okay with that, Anne. You have an entire life ahead of you and a daughter to raise. I can't have you risk surgery for me. Plus you're healthy now—but what if you were diabetic someday? I'm not comfortable with that."

"Well, it's not entirely up to you."

Marie's eyes widened, and she laughed. "Oh, it's not, is it? Are you going to force me down on an operating table?"

Anne smiled, but the pain was acute in her chest. "No, but if we can't get your diet under control, and this dialysis doesn't help right away, if things get bad, I'm doing it. You hear?" And she meant it. Marie Harris had saved her once; Anne couldn't live with herself if she didn't use the opportunity to return the favor.

"We'll see, sweetie. Now let's stop this crying. It's not happening tomorrow or the next day. The news was just, well, I'm just a little scared, that's all." Marie fanned herself with her fingers and then slapped her hands against her thighs. "Now I'm gonna go play with my Clairebug. No more tears."

Anne watched her mother walk up the stairs and couldn't help notice how slow she took it. Marie Harris was getting old, and now she was sick. Her body was *failing*. It was part of life, but it wasn't fair. Fate could

throw you a curveball in the blink of an eye. The only
thing that mattered was the people you cared for and the
moments you spent with them now . . . today.

Anne grabbed her phone and without thinking it
through opened Mike's contact. She was hurting and
scared, and nothing else had seemed more natural than
reaching out for him. *Shit*. She typed out a text and then
hesitated for just a moment, her finger hovering over the
SEND button. Their conversation from Friday night raced
through her mind. *I like everything about you, Anne. I
want to know you.*

ANNE: Are you busy?
MIKE: Busy, yes. But not too busy for you.

She smiled at that. Why did he always say just the
right thing? His ability to know just what she needed was
really making it hard to keep this casual. Her tears threatened one more time, which was completely insane. How
could this be happening, now, with this man? She hadn't
been looking for him, or anyone. But everything about
him was so . . . perfect.

ANNE: I've been thinking of you.
MIKE: I'm glad, Perfect. I've been thinking of
    you too.

A wave of relief spread through her entire body as
she read the words. When he dropped her off Friday
night, there hadn't been a lot of conversation between
them, just a quick kiss and a whispered good night. Before she could formulate a reply her phone dinged again.

MIKE: Been thinking about anything else?
ANNE: Maybe. Claire and I are going to the
    park for a picnic soon. Want to come?
MIKE: Yes.

She couldn't believe how quickly he'd replied. Her
heart pounded as she saw he was typing again.

MIKE: When?

She glanced at the clock. The picnic idea had been a
spur-of-the-moment decision. She didn't want to ask her
mother to leave so she did some figuring in her head.

ANNE: 1:00.
MIKE: What are the rules?
ANNE: What do you mean?
MIKE: Around Claire. Can I touch you? Or are
    we friends?

Warmth radiated through Anne's cheeks. This man
made her feel things she didn't know were possible. Silly
things from songs and movies seemed not so silly anymore. A heart could quicken, a breath could catch, and
a few words could make you feel alive. She wanted to
feel this, but it was dangerous. He said he wanted to
know her, but for how long would that last? How long
did she want it to last? Was it even possible that this could
turn into something real? Was she crazy to even give that
consideration? She didn't want Claire to be hurt or confused. *She* didn't want to be hurt or confused, although
she was already one and fearful of the other.

ANNE: You can touch me a little when she's not
   looking. If you want.
MIKE: I want. I'll try to keep it to a little.

She giggled lightly but shut herself up as Claire and
Grandma Ree came down the stairs. Anne caught her
mother's eyes on her and felt embarrassed. She'd filled
her in a little about Mike, but not with these latest de-
velopments. She knew what her mother would say. *Have
fun, Anne, worry when there is something worth worrying over.*

She would try that, have fun today, but she would still
be worried about her mother because that something was
worth everything.

Mike stared down at his phone with a huge grin on his
face. He couldn't help it. He'd been waiting for her to
contact him and she'd finally done it. He had planned
on toughing it out, but he'd known he wouldn't have
made it another day before he'd given in and called her.
However this victory was sweet.

"Good God you look like fifteen-year-old girl grinning at your phone like that," Derek said as he walked
into Mike's shop through the large bay door.

"Fuck off." Derek and Mike had been friends since
grade school, and they'd always communicated through
shit talking and foul language. It worked for them. They'd
lost touch a little after high school when Derek went to
college and Mike chose the wrong path for a few years,
but they'd picked back up five years ago like nothing had
ever happened. He still hadn't told Derek everything
about those few years after his father died, and like a

true friend, the guy didn't pry. But Mike knew if he ever needed anything, Derek would be there for him. It didn't need to be said.

As an architect and contractor, Derek was all business. His firm was doing deals left and right for projects large and small. The guy seemed to work eight days a week unless he was with his son, Tanner. For that reason they didn't hang out often enough, despite the fact that they worked out of the same building.

"What's going on?" Derek walked over to the little fridge in the corner and helped himself to a beer. "You sexting?"

"With your mom." Mike laughed at his own joke while Derek tossed obscenities his way. Mike pushed off the worktable he'd been leaning on. "I've got a picnic date in an hour, so if you came to shoot the shit you better make it fast."

Derek sputtered against the rim of his beer bottle. "A picnic date? Who the hell with? That chick you left Smokey's with last Friday?"

"Yep, but she's not *that chick*, her name is Anne. We're taking her daughter to the park." Mike met his friend's eye, daring him to say something.

Derek blew out a breath. "Okaaay." He contemplated for a moment and then tilted his head to the side.

"Damn, who'd have thought? Mikey Everett settling down and playing house."

"Shut up," Mike growled as he headed for his office. He heard Derek follow him.

"You know what you're getting yourself into, right? It's kind of parent code, no kids involved unless it's . . . *something*." Here it was. Mike knew that Derek took the whole "kid in the relationship" thing very seriously. So seriously he was pretty sure no woman Derek dated ever met Tanner. Shit, Mike took it seriously, too, although he'd never experienced it before.

Mike sat down in his chair and Derek reclined on the old couch waiting for a reply. Derek had been burned badly by his ex. In fact, she managed to keep burning Mike's friend, something that really pissed him off. Derek was a great father, but he didn't get to spend near enough time with his son.

"Well, maybe it is *something*. A big maybe. I haven't figured it out yet, but her daughter is a friend of Bailey's so it's not too weird."

Derek took another swig of beer then pursed his lips before he finally spoke. "Fair enough. What's she do?"

"She plans parties. And something else." Mike grinned and angled his computer monitor so Derek could see it from the couch. He only had to go to his drop-down screen to pull up the site since he'd visited it a million times. "Look at this."

"My Perfect Little Life? What the hell is this for?"

"It's Anne's blog. It's like . . . crazy popular."

He angled his head to see the main page, only to find a new post and the photos she'd taken of their Pie Days date. He hadn't seen that yet, but he instantly recognized the beer, the Ferris wheel, and the rows of muscle cars. He scrolled through quickly, scanning her commentary. Nothing, oh no wait, she'd gone with a friend. A *friend?* He didn't say anything because he'd be damned if he let Derek know—

"Didn't we go to that last year?"

"Uhhh, not sure." Mike scrolled down to the comments, ignoring his question.

"Wait, no we did, go back up. That was the Pie Days thing in Green Mound, you dragged me down there for that car show. Damn, that was the best pie I'd ever had in my life."

Mike didn't respond, just kept reading through comments. She could have at least called it a date. But a *friend?* She couldn't be serious.

"You took her there didn't you? So why'd you just get all bitchy? You not want her to talk about it?"

"First of all, I did not just get all bitchy," he spit out. Okay, maybe he sounded a little on edge. This woman did this to him. "But no, that's the annoying part." Mike sat back and Derek leaned forward to pull the mouse toward him. He continued to look through the site as Mike went on. "She hasn't even told me about this blog. I mean she's said she has a blog, but she hasn't told me about how huge it is. Two strangers recognized her at this Pie Days thing and yet she completely downplays it with me, says it's no big deal. It's a big fucking deal, I know because I've been reading every day. Each post gets like . . . over a thousand comments. It's nuts."

Derek grinned.

"What?" Mike asked.

"You read it every single day?"

"Dude, focus. I'm just wondering why she'd hold back from me. She shares so many things about her life, and yet this is the second time she's noticeably left out that she's been seeing me."

"Maybe she's trying to protect her privacy, and yours.

And sorry, but you are getting all bent outta shape, like a woman. "

"And you cried during *Forrest Gump*, dickhead. Anyway that would make sense, but why won't she tell me about it?"

Derek shrugged but kept reading, probably only half listening, which was fine. Mike wasn't really looking for advice, only venting.

"Well listen to this, you're gonna love this comment from twenty minutes ago." Derek laughed and wagged his eyebrows.

"What? Read it."

"What the hell kind of name is Pattypie?" Derek asked.

"Just read the damn comment." Mike remembered Pattypie, and it had been all he could do not to walk right up behind Anne and make her really uncomfortable . . . but he hadn't.

"All right, damn." Derek cleared his throat than read. "So glad we finally got to meet you, Anne, you are the sweetest thing. Your boyfriend was also the hottest piece of man meat we've ever seen. Yay for you, Anne! You deserve to be happy."

Mike grinned. *Well, well, Perfect. You've been outted.* "No shit? Read farther down."

Derek scrolled the wheel of the mouse, a smile creeping up on his face as he mouthed *bitch*. "I can't believe we're doing this, stalkin' on this chick's website. Looks like just a bunch of 'woohoos' and 'yays,' and several demands for pictures of the 'man meat.' You're famous, jackass."

"Unbelievable." Mike felt a little smug, but he'd feel

a whole lot better if Anne would just tell him about her damn blog. "Well, she's gonna have a hard time denying things now."

"You've got to be shittin' me." Derek's humor had turned to irritation with the outburst. "That's Lindsey Morales."

Mike sat up and leaned forward to see what Derek was looking at. He'd gone to the bio page. Mike looked at the third woman, the only blog girl he hadn't met yet. She was pretty, beautiful even. Her dark hair sparkled in the sunlit photo of them in the grass. Her dark eyes were exotic and her skin a deep tan. "Look who's stalkin' now. You know her?"

Derek took a deep breath and blew it out. He fell back on to the couch, visibly shaken. "Yeah I know her. Or did know her. We dated, in college. She was . . . damn. I haven't seen her in years."

Mike looked at the monitor again. He was pretty sure based on random conversations that Derek had dated quite a few girls in college, but there was obviously something about this one that had his friend pretty undone at the discovery. He wondered what it was, but didn't ask.

"She's pretty hot," Mike said. Derek glared at him. *Interesting.*

"Have you met her?" Derek asked.

"No, and I don't know anything about her because Anne doesn't talk to me about this blog, remember? But hold up, Lindsey does posts about painting furniture and other old shit."

Derek smiled at that. "I'm not surprised, she was an amazing artist."

Mike scrolled down to the individual bios and he

heard Derek's breath suck in as he leaned forward to look at the head shot of Lindsey. Mike had to agree, she was definitely gorgeous—there was no denying that. Derek read silently and Mike waited, unsure of what to make of Derek's reaction to this woman. Either way he didn't have time to sit here and figure it out.

"Here." Mike jotted down the website on a sticky note and handed it to Derek. "I won't make you embarrass yourself by asking. Take this and stalk on your own time. I gotta get to the park, it's ten till one."

Derek reluctantly looked away from the screen and got up before snatching the post-it note from Mike's hand. "Fine, I'll go. But I came by to let you know I started making a sketch and design for a house. You need to get out of this shithole and I had a little extra time."

"Extra time, you?"

"Well . . . relatively speaking. But I told you I'd do it and I was sorta in the mood. I'll let you know when I'm ready to get your input."

"Ha, nice try. You never want my input."

"Good point. I'll just do it my way." Derek headed down the little hallway calling out over his shoulder. "And just so you know, *Forrest Gump* is sad as hell, asshole."

Mike laughed, sat back in his chair, and looked around his office. He'd never planned to stay here this long, but he'd never been in a hurry to purchase or build a house on his own or for himself. It seemed like something you did when you wanted more. A family. Was it coincidence that Derek brought it up now that he found himself attracted to a woman who was the epitome of home? He shouldn't put much thought into it. Things with Anne were still at the beginning stages, although he couldn't deny that he'd never had feelings this strong for a woman before.

Right now he just couldn't wait to see Anne. He wondered if she'd read the blog comments yet. Would she mention it? 'Fess up about how popular her blog really was? The ball was in Anne's court now. It always had been, really.

Seventeen

Anne heard Mike's car before she saw it, which made her stomach quiver with anticipation. His sleek Camaro pulled into the spot next to her SUV, and she watched as he stepped from the driver's seat, all masculine grace and sexiness. Even in jeans he was breathtaking, and she was ridiculous for ogling. She turned back to the playground as Claire came down the slide and then spotted him.

"Uncle Mike, you're here," Claire squealed. She hit the ground and took off running. For a moment Anne envied her daughter's disregard of propriety as she threw her arms around Mike. Anne wished she could do the same, but instead she walked slowly toward them. Mike patted Claire on the head and then whispered something into her ear that sent her into a fit of giggles as she skipped back to the play equipment.

The wide smile on Mike's face made Anne dizzy. He came close and grabbed her hand before lifting it to his lips and brushing a soft kiss to her fingers. "You look beautiful today, Anne."

"Thank you." She glanced down at her black twill shorts and gray tank as they made their way toward the wood-chip-covered play area. She'd attempted a casual look by putting her hair in a low ponytail, but of course she'd spent extra time on her makeup.

She dropped his hand and turned to lead them to a shaded bench off to the side where they could speak in private while still watching her daughter, but when she turned around Mike was making his way up the steps of the equipment and running after a laughing Claire. When they made it to a big wood-slatted bridge, Mike put an arm around Claire's waist and lifted her tiny body over his head, causing panic to well in Anne's body. What if he lost his balance, or dropped her? When he dangled Claire over the edge, pretending he might do just that, Anne froze. She stood up and tried to speak over Claire's hysterical giggles. "Okay . . . that's enough."

Mike met Anne's gaze, and his grin went wicked. He let Claire drop a little more, her laughs mixed with happy screams. Anne glared at him and spoke in a warning tone. "Mike."

He pulled Claire upright and squeezed her to his chest. "I think we about gave your mommy a heart attack." He gave Claire a quick kiss on the head and gently set her feet safely on the bridge.

Anne's heart stopped, not from the near-death experience of her daughter, but the way Mike handled her. Watching him with Claire was almost painful, that swift innocent kiss, the way Claire smiled at him and laughed. It was like the two of them were long-lost friends. Anne swallowed hard and sat down as a breeze blew her ponytail into her face. Why did he have to make everything so confusing?

Mike jumped down from a plastic ledge on the play equipment and jogged toward Anne. At the last minute he glanced over his shoulder. Claire was just sitting atop a slide facing the other direction. With his body shielding the action he leaned in and kissed Anne on the mouth, his tongue quickly sliding against her lips. Before she could respond he pulled away and sat next to her on the bench. She caught her breath and looked at him.

"I'm glad you could come," she said, loving the way her insides fluttered every time he kissed her.

"I'm glad you asked." He leaned back against the park bench in an overwhelmingly male way, legs wide and an arm draped behind her. They were silent for a moment while she collected herself after that sexy kiss. He seemed to know how it affected her, his grin smug as he watched Claire play. She needed to bring them back to more appropriate territory.

"So how is work on the Monser car coming along? I can't believe the party is so soon."

"I know, don't remind me. It's going into paint in a couple days, then it will be frantic installation and details until it's done. I hope she appreciates it."

"I'm sure she will, Jessica's a nice girl. A little spoiled . . ."

He leveled a gaze at her. "A *little*?"

"Okay, very spoiled." Anne laughed. "I can't imagine you'd want to drive a pink Mustang to Pie Days."

He chuckled, and the sound was masculine and sexy.

"Hell no, that would be a huge blow to my ego. It's bad enough working on it, knowing it will soon be the color of bubble gum."

They were quiet once again as they watched Claire play. A few more children had shown up.

"So, I wondered if you might like to come over for dinner Friday evening." Anne twiddled her fingers in her lap. Mike turned to face her, his thumb absentmindedly brushing against her neck.

"You know I would."

There he went again, saying the perfect thing. She lifted a brow and couldn't help smiling. "Well, good. Claire will be with her father again."

"Sooo, we'll be alone?" His playful grin made her insides melt.

"Yes, is that okay?"

"That's a silly question, Anne. But tell me this, are we trying this out? Something more than just . . . sex?"

"But we haven't had sex yet," she said playfully.

His grin made her giddy. "Trust me, I know all too well all the things we haven't done. I'm dying to fix that."

"Me, too, and yes, we are getting to know each other. For real."

He smiled, turned back to the playground, and they sat in silence for a while as Claire went down the slide over and over. After a moment he scooted closer. "So what's for lunch? I'm starving."

"Just turkey sandwiches, chips, and grapes. I'm afraid it's a rather child-friendly meal. Hope you weren't expecting anything fancy."

"Sounds good. And that is fancier than my average lunch, just so you know." He turned back to the playground, his fingers still tracing lazy circles against her nape. The slight roughness of his skin sliding up and down against her own sent shivers through her body.

"I figured we could sit at that picnic table over—"

"What the hell is that chump doing? Claire was going for that swing." Mike stood up and stalked toward the far end of the playground. To be honest, Anne had stopped focusing on her daughter when Mike's skin met hers.

Now she watched as Mike approached the swings where two older boys, at least twelve, had commandeered both swings. Claire stood warily off to the side as one boy motioned to the other while Mike closed in on them. They exchanged a few words, and Anne was sure she heard an apology from an adolescent voice. Then Claire put her hand in Mike's outstretched one before he lifted her onto the swing.

Anne had to bite her lip to hold back the emotions that boiled over as she watched Mike push her daughter on the swing ever so gently. He'd protected her, stood up for her, and put a smile on her sweet little face. How had this happened? Anne considered all the events that had transpired in just a few short weeks as she listened to Claire's happy voice tell Mike heaven knew what. Probably something horrible like "My mom can eat a whole pizza by herself" or "My mom's tummy has stripes on it." But she really didn't care. She just wanted to be sure she did whatever she could to preserve this feeling, because at this point she knew the loss of Mike would devastate her and Claire both.

Friday finally came and Anne cradled her cell phone between her ear and shoulder as she tossed her asparagus with garlic and olive oil. Callie had called on and off all day to check in, and Anne owed her friend big for that. She'd been a wreck for days thinking about this date. What she'd cook and which outfit to wear. She hadn't invited a man to her house . . . well, ever, really.

"So what main dish did you decide on?" Callie asked.

Anne let the screen door slam behind her as she went to the backyard to light the grill. "Steak. That's good, don't you think? All guys like a slab of meat, right?"

"I don't know about all guys, but I certainly like a slab of meat," Callie snorted on the other end of the line.

"You have the filthiest mind."

"Guilty. So, dressed and ready? He should—"

"Oh gosh, I just heard the doorbell," Anne said, her voice hushed into a whisper.

"Oh my God. Well, go get it and do me proud."

Anne said good-bye and ran inside to the small bath off the kitchen to give her looks a final once-over. She'd chosen to wear a simple peach summer dress that she thought did nice things for her upper half since it was snug up top and swingy and feminine on the bottom. A nice mix of classic and sexy, at least she hoped. Her hair was down and wavy and her makeup just the lightest touch dramatic.

When she opened her front door Mike's cocky grin nearly had her melting onto the porch. He held up a six-pack of bottled beers from the local brewery in one hand and a bottle of wine in the other. "Wasn't sure which was appropriate."

"Hmmm, maybe both." She stood back and held the door open.

"I like that idea." He stepped in and looked her up and down. "And you look . . . absolutely stunning."

She didn't want to blush but there was no hiding it. Having such an attractive man give her a compliment would never get old. His compliments truly made her *feel* beautiful.

He headed for the kitchen and she followed, watching as he shoved the beer into the fridge, but not before grabbing himself one. He looked over his shoulder. "You want one now?"

"Sure. I was going to grill some steaks, so I thought we could hang out on the patio." No need to mention that she'd already had a glass of wine to calm her nerves.

"That sounds good." He twisted the top off the beer and handed it to her. They went out to the backyard. The sun was still level with the treetops, warming the patio where her favorite new outdoor furniture was situated. Lindsey had found the table and four chairs sitting outside an apartment complex's Dumpster last fall and completely transformed them with a coat of paint and some custom paisley cushions. Anne loved them.

"Everything inside smells amazing. What else are you making?"

"Asparagus, and twice-baked potatoes . . . with cheese and bacon." She gave him a flirty wink and turned to the grill.

"Cheese *and* bacon? Are you trying to seduce me, Perfect?" He stood behind her and ran his fingers down her bare arm as she laid the meat on the hot grates. The sizzle matched the sensations running through her nerves.

"It's possible."

"Oh it's very possible . . . and easy. So easy it's not even necessary." He laid a small kiss on her shoulder and then sat down in one of her puffy patio chairs.

"Not necessary?" she balked. "I might remind you that on our last date you flat-out told me you weren't having sex with me."

He pursed his lips tight to hold in the beer that threatened to escape with his laughter. She watched his neck move as he swallowed. Everything on his body was appealing and made her think of all the things she wanted him to do to her. Things she wanted to happen tonight.

He managed not to choke before finally speaking. "Don't think I didn't want to be with you. Doing the gentlemanly thing isn't easy with a woman as hot as you are."

She shook her head, sat down across from him, and took a drink of her own beer. Her cheeks were already flushed from the alcohol, the heat, and the way he made her feel. She wanted to flirt with him. "So how did you deal with that frustration? Did you, uhhh . . . think of me? When you got home."

He raised an eyebrow and then turned toward the yard, a huge grin on his face. When he looked back at her he made his expression serious and cleared his throat. "Let's see, did I *think* of you? Are you asking me what I think you're asking me, Perfect?"

"Mmm-hmm," she murmured around the rim of her bottle as she drank. He knew exactly what she meant, and she was shocked at herself for asking such a personal question. It may have something to do with the wine already flooding her system, but she didn't regret it.

"I've *thought* about you every day since I met you." His eyes bored into hers and the words washed over her like a magic spell, setting every nerve ending aflame. She tried not to show any reaction, but she knew it was not possible as she shifted in her chair.

She wanted to let her eyes roll back and sink into the chair to experience the full pleasure of knowing the sexy Mike Everett had touched himself while thinking of her. Where was he when it took place, in the shower, in bed, at his desk? Oh God, it was one of the most erotic things she had ever imagined. She'd definitely have to revisit that image when she was *thinking* of him.

"Now you're supposed to tell me you've thought of me, Anne." He was still watching her intently, his arm resting lazily across the table, beer in hand.

"Speaking of being a gentleman, that's not very gentlemanly to ask a question like that."

"Good thing I wasn't trying to be a gentleman then. Plus, you asked me first."

Anne bit her lip, trying not to laugh. He was right, of course, and she didn't want him to be any way other than the way he was right now, unapologetically naughty. She stood up and headed for the back door. "Would you mind checking on the steaks? I'll get everything else ready."

"Of course." He took one more swig of his beer before standing up. "And you're forgiven for evading my question. For now."

In the kitchen she pulled the vegetables from the oven and put them on serving dishes before she collected a few condiments, put it all on a tray, and retreated outside. Their dinner proceeded with conversation about the Monser party, Bailey and Claire, their night at the Pie

Days festival, and a few other random subjects. All fairly safe topics, but in the back of her mind, she just kept wondering if he was going to stay the night. The way they'd joked when he arrived suggested maybe he would, but she wasn't sure. She'd assumed they'd do more on their last date, but they hadn't. Now she wasn't sure what to think.

At some point they opened the bottle of wine and laughed over stories of their childhoods, and she told him about a few of her more interesting party jobs. When she brought in the dirty dishes he followed her inside and helped himself to the plate of brownies on the kitchen table.

"These are amazing. I hate to ask but did—"

"I made them. Callie isn't the only one who can bake something yummy," she replied.

Despite telling him repeatedly that he could sit down and relax, he helped her load the dishwasher while they chatted. As she leaned forward to turn off the sink, she felt his large hands on her shoulders and she let him turn her around. He leaned into her, his length nestling against hers. She was beginning to think there was something about her kitchen that turned him on.

"This was nice," he said. "Just . . . being together like this."

She nodded, unable to speak as the brush of his skin against hers lit fires through her body. His eyes roamed over every inch of her face, her lips, and her eyes until he finally leaned in, his lips sliding against hers. He tasted like chocolate and smelled like sexy man.

Each time they kissed felt like a revelation, or a discovery. This time she was going to make sure it was also a declaration; this wasn't going to end without her getting everything from him. The first time she was fearful, the second time he'd pulled back, but this time, this time it was going to happen. No fear, no interruptions, and no hesitation.

She deepened the kiss, sucking at his tongue and letting her hands roam over his body, up his chest and through his hair. He did the same, his palms cupping her behind and grinding her against his body.

"Don't leave," she whispered. His mouth worked its way down her chin and then her neck as his hands slid up her torso to caress her breasts.

"I'm not going anywhere."

She let out a breath as he pulled away to look at her again, a smile working at his lips. "You were sexy as hell on that table. And I should know because I see that vision every time I *think* about you . . . but tonight . . ," He pulled on her arm, backing up, and leading her toward the hallway. "Take me to your room."

She couldn't help the grin forming. Without hesitation she took the lead and he followed her up the stairs. She could hear the swish of his clothing behind her and as soon as they crossed the threshold of her bedroom he wrapped his arms around her waist from behind, pulling her back against his bare chest. *Oh yes.* She needed to see him, but it was dusk and she'd purposely closed all her blinds earlier for just this occasion.

His hands cupped her breasts as his lips found the crook of her neck. She moaned and lifted her arms overhead, grasping the back of his head to pull his mouth harder against her. When his fingers found the zipper at her side she sucked in a breath. He lowered it slowly, and she shivered when his warm hand landed on her skin.

"I love how soft you are," he said against her neck.

She turned into his embrace, letting her own hands explore all the ways he was definitely not soft. Her eyes had adjusted to the dimness and she could see that his chest was incredibly firm and covered lightly with dark hair. The edge of a tattoo ran down the side of one bicep, which was unexpected but very sexy. His muscles moved beneath her fingers as she let them drift down to his stomach. The sound of his ragged breathing made her smile, and she looked up and found him watching her.

They stared at each other, chests rising and falling as he pushed the dress from her shoulders. Slowly it slid down her body, exposing her bra, then her waist; when it finally pooled around her ankles she let her eyes drift closed. Standing in front of him so exposed had her heart racing and mind thinking of all the possibilities. What was he thinking? What would he say? It was dark, but she could see him, so he had to see her at least a little.

"Look at me, Anne." His voice reminded her of a caged lion, low and growly, but holding back power, completely in control.

She opened her eyes. Gazing at him made her realize that her distress wasn't warranted. All she could see was desire in his expression.

"Now tell me the truth. Did you *think* of me?" he said. She paused and he tilted his head to the side, his eyes narrowing playfully until she couldn't help but be honest.

"Yes," she whispered. She couldn't believe she'd just admitted it.

His lips pursed and he inhaled deeply, nose flaring as a look of intense satisfaction ran over his face. That reaction was worth a little embarrassment. His grip on her tightened and he began backing her toward the bed. His forehead met hers and he spoke against her lips. "Did you think of me in this room?"

"Yes."

"In this bed?"

She nodded, her fingers clutching his arms.

He ran his tongue against her mouth, parting and taking over her lips as he lowered her to the bed. He stood watching her as she scooted back toward the pillows. From this angle the blinds allowed a small amount of light to spill in, highlighting his torso. His stomach was rippled with muscle, and the sight of him made her feel hot and needy.

She continued to stare as he pulled a strip of condoms from his pocket. He ripped one off and tossed it onto the bed at her feet, dropping the others onto the bedside table.

She couldn't help laughing. "You have big plans for later?"

He grinned while he undid his jeans and pushed them off, his underwear with them, exposing everything. No shame, no hesitation, and he had absolutely no reason for it. His erection was thick and perfect; his entire body was made for fantasy. "I have enough plans to keep you busy for days."

His hands hit the bed, making it dip under his weight as he prowled toward her. Grabbing an ankle, he pulled it to the side, his eyes never leaving hers. She bit her lip, promising herself she was just going to surrender completely to this. She'd left all her anxiety downstairs. She was going to give herself the pleasure of experiencing this fully without regret or insecurities.

He lowered his body between her thighs, his length resting against her center, and he groaned, rubbing against her. "I want you so bad, Anne. Everything about you is so fucking sexy I can hardly stand it."

"I want you, too." She rose up and pushed her pelvis against him, loving the hissing sound that left his mouth. His back bowed and biceps bulged. Not only was the power of his body a turn-on, but it made her feel sexy and feminine.

Immediately he lowered his mouth to her breast, licking the round top of one while pulling at the cup of the other until a nipple was free for his mouth. He devoured her, sucking and fondling until she was grinding against him, her fingers digging into his back.

He shifted his weight, ran his tongue down her stomach, and then moved to her thighs. He looked down between them at her body and used one hand to tug at her panties. She lifted her lower half off the bed and helped pull them down, tossing them onto the floor. He spread her legs wide so he could place light kisses where her leg met her body. It tickled and she fought back a giggle, the feel of his shoulders shaking let her know that he was laughing at her reaction.

"I'm trying to drive you crazy, not make you laugh," he teased. His breath was hot on her sensitive skin, and she shivered when he hovered right where she wanted him most, his lips just barely touching.

"Mmm, don't stop," she panted. "It's working."

He blew lightly on her most sensitive spot and then

lowered his head, his nose brushing each nerve ending. She could barely stand it, but the pleasure was so intense, the anticipation so thrilling, when he finally flattened his tongue and ran it all the way back up she nearly exploded. "Oh my God, Mike."

He didn't stop. He licked her over and over, sliding in and out. His hands pushed her legs wider, holding her still while every instinct wanted her to squeeze them shut against the sensations that were so raw and intense. He finally settled on the one point of tenderness that would bring her to release, flicking his tongue, bringing her to a state of frenzy.

"Come for me, Anne," he said as he brought one hand up her breast, squeezing her nipple and making her moan.

"I will . . . please." She could barely speak, every word a challenge as her mind began to shut down, her thoughts colliding, the room going out of focus. His mouth resumed its position on her, sucking her into his mouth and she felt her body turn into a meteor, a fiery source of energy rushing toward something only to explode on impact. Her stomach dipped and her entire body shook as he ruthlessly drew out her pleasure until she sank into the bed, her limbs heavy and sated.

Still weak from the hottest orgasm of her life, Anne slowly opened her eyes and realized she hadn't even noticed him move to his knees. He was rolling the condom on, and watching his fingers close over his shaft was the hottest thing she'd ever seen. He stroked himself, knowing she was looking, and then grabbed her hand, guiding her fingers around him, forcing her to take over the task.

This was nothing like feeling him through denim; this was heaven. His hips moved back and forth, pumping himself in and out of her fist and she knew it was a vision she would never forget. She looked into his eyes to find him watching her.

"You really are perfect, you know that?" he said in a low rumble.

Emotion poured through her; feelings this intense could not be described, only experienced. This virile and sexy man was more than she could have ever imagined, and the combination of his words, her nakedness completely exposed to him, and her hands on his body—it was like a fairy tale, a hot naughty fairy tale.

He pulled her hand up, grabbed under her knees, and pulled her body toward him in two quick jerks, and she nearly blushed at how much she liked the feel of him manhandling her. He didn't ask permission, he just took, which made her shiver with excitement. Nestled between her thighs he widened his stance until he was level with her opening and held her steady, slowly sliding inside, one hard inch at a time. His eyes were on hers and his lips tight as he breathed in and out.

"Shit, Anne." His head bent down so he could watch them join. "You feel so good." He pulled out again and she let her eyes drift shut so she could focus on all the electric sensations that stemmed from their connection as he entered her all the way.

He picked up speed, in and out, over and over, and the pleasure built inside once again. Never had she had two orgasms in one night, never in her whole life, and one night with Mike Everett was going to top all she'd ever known. It wasn't a surprise; he was amazing.

Beautiful, intoxicating, and so wonderful and loving she could melt.

His hands left her thighs and she opened her eyes to find him leaning down to kiss her, his tongue going deep into her mouth as his body pushed into her hard and steady. His kiss tasted like sex, and he growled deep in his throat as she grabbed his ass and pulled him closer.

He leaned on his elbows and stared down at her, each thrust making a puff of breath escape her. "I'm gonna come, baby," he whispered. "I want to feel you . . . right now."

Her body responded to his endearment, and his bossiness, sending her into a second orgasm so intense she could die of the pleasure.

He slowed down as he climaxed. Each time he entered fully he ground against her, a long growl emanating from deep within his chest. When he finally fell against her body he was damp with perspiration and she wrapped her arms tight around him, wanting to keep him there, afraid for him to meet her eyes. She feared that all the emotion would show in her face. Mike was more than she expected, so much more.

Eighteen

Anne's bedroom was painted a soft blue, so light and peaceful that when the morning sun fell against the wall it was nearly white. Mike didn't dare leave the bed, or even move a muscle. Anne's warm naked back was nestled against him, her round bottom pushing against his hip. He didn't want to wake her, but even more he didn't want her to leave his side. In sleep she was completely uninhibited, her body falling naturally into what was most comfortable.

If he looked down carefully he could see the curve of her right breast and just the very tip of a nipple. He would be still all day just to drink in this sight of his Perfect Anne. A few strands of her hair tickled his chest; they smelled like flowers.

He'd been awake for a while and once more he let his gaze roam across the room and touch all the things that made it so suited to the sleeping beauty beside him. On the wall across from the bed was a large landscape painting of a garden of wildflowers. It was pretty, although not normally his thing. He wondered if Anne ever lay in this exact spot staring at it.

Below the painting sat a large white dresser. On top was an old wire stand that held at least fifty necklaces. Who could wear that many pieces of jewelry in a lifetime? Next to it was a framed picture of Anne and Claire. They were in a field and from what he could tell it was taken at the same time the ones on the blog bio page were. He loved those photos of Anne and he wanted to get up and look closer, but he wouldn't dream of moving.

Everything about her home made him feel happy and warm. It was the kind of place a child was raised to feel loved, and it made him glad to know that Anne was giving that to her daughter. He was envious, and not for the first time since he'd met Anne, it made him want more from life, sooner rather than later, which was a scary realization. He thought back on Derek's announcement that he was working on a house plan for Mike. How was this all coming together at the same time? The idea of taking care of Anne and Claire—it made his chest ache. He wondered if she could ever see him as that guy, or if she only saw him as in it for the moment. A guy who worked on cars, who lived at his shop and had dirty fingernails more often than not.

Anne—now awake apparently—shifted beside him and rolled over. He looked down at her face, which had a pillow crease on one cheek. She looked adorable and he smiled at her. "Good morning, Perfect."

She laughed and gave him a muffled "good morning" as she tucked her face into his chest to hide it. He wrapped his arms around her body and pulled it against his, loving the feel of her leg naturally winding between his.

"I like that painting on the wall. It's pretty."

She lifted her head to look at him, laying her cheek on his chest. "My mother painted that in college. It used to hang in my parents' bedroom and I loved to look at it. When she moved into her apartment, I asked her if I could hang it in my bedroom."

They were quiet for a while and then he heard her sniffle, the sound sending a panic through his body. He shifted to try to see her face but she was now facing the foot of the bed. "Anne, what's wrong?"

She took a deep breath and blew it out, but he could see her hand rise up to swipe at her eyes. "Nothing, I'm sorry."

"Hey, come here." He tugged at her arm, and she finally gave in and looked up at him. Her eyes, already puffy from sleep, were now pink from tears. "What's going on?"

She gave a halfhearted smile. "I was just thinking . . . it's nothing."

"Anne, we just spent the night together and you're crying. Saying *it's nothing* is not an option." An ironic notion; usually he would have avoided emotional conversation at all costs. Not because he was an uncaring asshole, but because he never knew what to say to a woman when she cried. And . . . well . . . maybe because he could be a bit of an asshole. His past MO was a little uncaring only because he never wanted to send the wrong message—but not with Anne. He couldn't let this go without an explanation.

"It has nothing to do with last night. It's just . . . I recently found out my mom's health is worse than we thought. She's diabetic and may need to start dialysis soon."

"Jesus, Anne, seriously?" Without thinking he pulled her in closer to his body. She snaked her arm across his waist and held him tight. He loved the feeling of her seeking comfort from him. He wanted to hold her, make it better.

"Yeah, she just told me about it a few days ago."

He wasn't sure what to say. "I'm so sorry to hear that. Has she been sick for a while?"

"She's been diabetic for twenty years. But needing the dialysis is a new development. I guess I didn't realize how bad things had gotten. I have a feeling she kept me in the dark on a few of her doctor's appointments. She's always tried to protect me."

"Well, of course she has. Isn't that what a mother does?" He brushed her hair out of her face and let his fingers tickle over her back, enjoying the warmth of her soft skin.

"You're right, but I'm a grown-up now. I could've handled it. And of course I offered to give her one of my kidneys."

His heart stopped at the announcement. The thought of Anne going through an operation, and a major one at that, felt like a heavy weight on his chest. But the sadness in her eyes was killing him, too, and if one of his parents were alive, he'd have offered the exact same thing. "What did she say?"

"She said no. So typical of her, she was adamant that

she wasn't going to take that route. It makes me feel help-less."

"You know she's just trying to do what's best for you." He understood her frustration, but he couldn't deny he felt a wave of relief.

"I know she is. She's such a good person. But she doesn't deserve to spend her final years fighting to be normal."

"Of course she doesn't, and you don't deserve to watch your mother go through it. Maybe when it's time, she won't want to leave you and Claire and . . . she'll be ready to reconsider."

"I hope so. I can't imagine losing her." She laid her cheek against his skin and ran her hand through the hair on his chest. "I'm sorry to be a downer."

"Anne, look at me." She lifted her head again and met his eyes. "Don't ever apologize for telling me what's on your mind, no matter what it is. I want you to tell me things. Okay?"

She stared for a moment, blinking her sleepy eyes, and finally nodded, her chin resting against his chest. "Okay," she whispered.

Her head fell to the side again, her now damp cheek on his skin. He looked up at the ceiling, all his thoughts jumbling in his brain. He had lost his parents young, and his grief nearly led him down a path that easily could have ended his life. When he thought about that, he didn't feel worthy of the woman nuzzled against him, but God how he wanted her. He'd been proud of himself for finding his way, making something of himself. But Anne made him want more, not only for himself, but for her.

She was beautiful, yes. Sexy as hell, definitely. But his attraction to her was about more than that. Her love of people made her irresistible. Her natural ability to make others feel important, special, and loved. She had this quality, it was like an aura around her. He wanted her constantly.

He felt her hand tentatively slide down his stomach under the sheet, and he knew what was coming, although he had to admit it surprised him. She was full of surprises, his perfect Anne. He braced himself, knowing that after such an emotional episode he should just hold her, but when her warm palm grasped his erection he could only let his eyes drift close as her hand ran up and down the length of him.

They'd had sex twice last night and he had woken up thinking about it. How many times had he found himself in a woman's bed in the morning and dashed out like fire was biting at his heels. But not this morning. He'd wanted to feel her lying close to him, hear the deepness of her sleepy breathing, and wait for this moment when he could have her again in the morning light.

She continued to stroke him as she shifted, positioning herself under the sheets so she had one leg on either side of him, her ass hovering above his calves. He immediately knew her intent, and thank goodness he was right when she leaned down to take him fully into her mouth. The silence was broken by the wet noise her lips made as she ran the length of him over and over. That was definitely the most glorious sound known to any man.

He looked down at the sight of her mouth on him, all of her hair swept to one side, her cheeks sinking in on the uptake. The view made his breath catch, and he bit back a groan. It was the sexiest thing he'd ever seen. "That's so good, babe . . ."

A soft whimper came from her throat, and the sudden increase in pressure and intensity nearly brought him off the bed. He reached up and caressed her jaw, loving the way it shifted; knowing that it was moving with the intent to bring him pleasure made him crazy. He was going to come soon and as much as he wanted to finish inside the heat of her mouth, he wanted something else even more. "Come here, Anne."

He pulled lightly on her arm and she rose up, her lips shiny and swollen. The sight of it nearly had him undone. Her face fell a little. "You didn't like it?"

He let out a strangled laugh. "Are you kidding me? I loved it. But I want to be inside you even more."

She hesitated for a moment and then grabbed the sheets, pulling them around her body like a cloak as she sat up and positioned herself above his hips. He let it go while he grabbed a condom from the bedside table and rolled it on. The sheet she kept wrapped around her clued him in to the fact that she felt less confident with light filling the room, but he wouldn't let that come between them. He tugged at it gently. "Let go of the sheet, Perfect."

Her wary eyes met his, and then flicked to the window where the brightness of morning penetrated through the blinds. If she only knew how beautiful she looked like this, her features softened from sleep and her hair wild. She wasn't Stepford perfection right now, but she was still perfectly unkempt and sexy, which was exactly how he wanted her. She was beautiful, and he'd have to convince her of that fact.

He pulled lightly at the sheet again, which she seemed to have in a death grip. "Anne, it's just me, and I love looking at every inch of this body. I want to watch you take me inside you."

He looked at her and swore he saw a shiver run through her. Slowly she released her hold on the fabric. He pushed it off to the side and sucked in a breath at the sight of her completely exposed. He could see her nakedness but his eyes stayed right on hers, her expression intense, and he imagined she was willing him not to look down. *Too bad, Anne.*

His gaze swept downward leisurely. Her breasts hung heavy and perfect against her body, nipples tipped up and firm. Ready. He ran a hand from her chest to the peak and rolled it. He didn't look at her face again but he could hear her ragged breathing, see her chest rising and falling.

His other hand went to her waist, which dipped in perfectly above the beautiful swell of her hips. It wasn't firm, it was soft and beautiful, and just the way a woman's body should be. Why couldn't she see herself the way he did? She was made for him. The thought jarred him, because in that second he knew that he never wanted any other man to see Anne like this. Just the thought made anger coil in his gut. He pushed it away and refocused on her, his hands running along the shapeliness of her hourglass form. "You're too beautiful for words, Anne."

He heard her swallow hard as he lifted her up lightly. She pressed her knees into the bed and raised her body to just the right spot. He watched as she sank down, bringing him inside, parting and filling her. He swore under his breath at the sight of it, so perfect.

The intensity of the moment was strong, the sensations so acute that he could barely breathe. The amount of blood rushing through his body caused his ears to roar like a river rushing through his head. His only thought was to take her, make her his. It was a primal urge, the desire to claim her body in this way, and he'd never ever experienced a need like it. He guided her up and down, his hands still on her hips as they rocked back and forth.

"*Mike.*" Anne's breathy voice was more than he could handle, and he slammed up into her body, each stroke bringing him closer. He could feel her tightening around him, and she leaned back to rest her hands on his thighs. The view of her from this angle was breathtaking, making it harder to hold off. He ran his finger over her exposed folds, finding the spot that would bring her to completion. She moaned as he stroked her, and he couldn't take it anymore. She was gorgeous, her body rocking back and forth on top of him.

"Anne . . . I can't."

"I'm coming." Her hips quickened their pace, grinding against him, her ass brushing him, all of him, with every move. His thumb continued its motion on her clit while his other hand tightened its hold on her waist, pushing her back and forth until he came hard, their sounds of release filling the quiet room.

After a moment she leaned forward, both hands hitting the bed beside him as her hair spilled around his head. She smiled and leaned on one hand to brush it out of his face. "Sorry."

The flush of her cheeks and wide eyes made his spent erection twitch inside of her. "You're amazing, you know that?" He swiped his hand across her temple, pulling the hair from her face.

She didn't respond, and when she attempted to shift off him he held her steady, grabbing her face with both hands to bring her lips to his. She allowed him to nip lightly at her mouth but didn't respond. "Kiss me, Anne."

"I have morning breath."

"So what? I do, too."

She smiled and he took advantage of the parting to suck her bottom lip into his mouth. She moaned against him, instinctively rocking her pelvis against his. The slickness that engulfed him almost brought him back to life, but he wasn't eighteen any longer; they'd need a little time.

She finally reached over his head, dragged a short robe off the headboard, and wrapped it around her before standing. He'd be happy when he could convince her to walk around the house buck naked; just the thought of Perfect Anne bending over to load the dishwasher, giving him a spectacular view, made him smile. Luckily she was turned the other way so he didn't have to explain the reason for his grin.

"Want some coffee?" She ran a hand through her hair as she dug in a dresser drawer and pulled out some clothing.

"Sure." He threw the covers off his body and stood up. Her eyes flicked over her shoulder and quickly back to the drawer. He vaguely recalled taking his shirt off and dropping it in her hallway so he went to find it, knowing full well she'd watch him, thinking he wouldn't know. Having her look at him did ridiculous things to his insides. He'd never wanted anyone to want him the way he did her. It was like an addiction; she kept reeling him in for more and didn't even know it.

Anne watched Mike walk out of her bedroom. His body was exquisite, and she noticed another tattoo on his muscular back that she hadn't seen the night before. It was an odd symbol: V-shaped, with some script below it. Whatever it was, it was a major turn-on, and so was the way the sides of his ass indented. Was he flexing? She remembered the feel of it under her fingers; it gave her the perfect place to grab as she pulled him into her. Just the quick look over her shoulder reminded her that all of his body put others to shame. How had this happened to her? One of the hottest men she'd ever laid eyes on was in her house—and naked for goodness' sake—after giving her the most amazing night and morning of her life.

When she heard him shut the hall bathroom door, she went into her own master bath to pull on some yoga pants and a tank top. After putting her hair into a loose ponytail and freshening up, she met him downstairs. He was already eating another brownie while he looked out the kitchen window, and she could smell coffee brewing; the wonderful tinkling of it falling into the pot was one of her favorite sounds.

"You didn't have to start the coffee. I could've done it," she said. She'd forgotten to set it up last night. Apparently rushing into her bed with sexy Mike trumped thoughts of the following morning's caffeine fix.

"Yes, you could've, but I'm capable." He put the rest of the brownie in his mouth and pulled her into his arms. "Hope you don't mind I ate one for breakfast."

"Of course not, but I could have found something more breakfasty if you like."

He laughed. "Anne, I'm a man who lives alone. If it's edible, and it's morning, then it's breakfast. And your brownies are delicious. Now sit down and I'll make you a cup." He gave her a quick kiss on the cheek and left her to open the fridge and retrieve the creamer.

He seemed so at home in her space, not asking permission, just doing what he wanted. She would have thought it annoying, but it wasn't. She actually enjoyed knowing that he felt so comfortable. It was kind of sexy watching him fish around Claire's pink princess cups and pull out two mugs. No one had made her coffee in a long time.

"So even though it's Saturday, I'm still behind with the Monser car. I have a lot of work to do today."

Oh boy, here it came. He was priming her for the efficient thank-you and good-bye. "That's no problem. This was fun."

He turned to face her, creamer dripping from the bottle onto the counter. His stare was unsure. "*Yeah*, it was fun. Which is why . . ." He turned and handed her a steaming mug before he continued. "Which is why I want to come back tonight. See you again. We can go somewhere for dinner, or whatever. But it won't be till late."

Her eyes widened. Thank goodness she hadn't yet taken a sip of the hot liquid.

"Did you have plans . . . If you do that's—"

"No. I didn't have plans," she interjected, not wanting to miss the opportunity. "Of course you can come back . . . whenever you're done."

He sat down across from her, a slow grin creeping up his face. "You sure?"

"Yes. I'm sure."

"Good." He looked pleased. He took a drink of his coffee so she did the same. He'd nailed the creamer-to-coffee ratio so she told him so.

"I just made it the same as mine and hoped you would like it."

"I do . . . like it," she replied.

"I'm glad." He stared at her, and she wondered what he was thinking. It felt like the conversation was about more than how they liked their coffee.

When they finished their drinks he got up to leave. She followed him to the front door, nervous and unsure of how the morning-after parting would go. Should they kiss, just say good-bye?

He took the worry away when he pulled her against his body and kissed her. Before leaving he whispered into her ear, "I was going to tell you to *think* of me today . . . but I changed my mind. The only person getting you off today is me." He leaned in and kissed her once more, hard on the mouth, before he walked out.

She shut the door and stood there completely dumbstruck. What did she do with this? Ride it out and have fun while it lasted? She was afraid to hope that what they had was something more, and when had she decided she wanted something more? Not long ago the best choice seemed to be fun only. But now . . . now she wasn't sure what she wanted.

She quickly decided the best policy was not to create or have any expectations, just take it one day at a time. Even though his words about her mother had made her feel like he really cared. The feeling of their blissful morning settled low in her chest, and the fact that she could still faintly smell him on her skin allowed her to decide she would give herself to the possibility that maybe, just maybe, Mike Everett was in it for more than a night. Maybe he was in it for the long haul.

He'd only been gone four hours, but for Anne it felt like an eternity. She hadn't pined for a man since she'd met Scott that day at the community college, and this was even more intense. She tried not to overanalyze that thought as she sat in front of her laptop. The cursor teased her, like a finger tapping in irritation as she considered her words for this blog post. She'd ignored the comments from last Saturday's date and gone on about her business despite the private emails, tweets, and Facebook messages from her followers. They were all happy for her, she knew that, but publicly acknowledging that she was seeing someone made it *something*, and that was a big step. When—or if—it ended, she'd have to publicly acknowledge that also, and that just flat-out sucked.

Part of her brain liked to think *Maybe it won't end*, but that wasn't very realistic. Most relationships ended for whatever reason, and between her and Mike, there were plenty of factors working against them. Age, children, life plans, her irrational tendency to push good things away out of fear. She was really trying to avoid that last one.

Something had changed today. She felt the need to share this. All through her journey she'd been open on her blog, never oversharing, but telling enough to be relatable to her readers. It was what made the blog real, the relationships meaningful, and she knew it was why people came back. She, Callie, and Lindsey put themselves out there, connected with people, and this was the first time something major was taking place in her life that she hadn't acknowledged. It was beginning to feel disingenuous, and she didn't want that. It was time, although she struggled with how much information to give to be honest without being annoying or elusive. Her readers were too smart for that, and she didn't want to insult the people who were repeatedly there to support her when she needed it.

Stuffing the last bite of her brownie in her mouth, she closed her eyes and let the chocolate melt over her tongue. She really could make a mean brownie, thanks to her mother. It was all about the imported 60 percent cacao chocolate she used, and the two sticks of butter, but that was another thing she wouldn't think about. As she wiped her hands, brilliance struck. She could talk about what was going on, give her readers what they wanted, and still be true to her blog and make it "normal." Maybe.

Fingers flew over the keyboard now that she had her angle, and it felt good to get it out, share the joy that had been filling her days the past couple weeks. She would need to brace herself for the comments on this post. She considered closing comments on it, but her readers wouldn't rest, they'd reach out in other ways, better to just deal with it now and move on. This blog was part of her life now, supported her livelihood. It was a safe place to share, just a little, about the man who was driving her crazy in the best possible way.

Nineteen

A day full of work and Mike had made great strides on the Mustang. After today he might actually end up ahead of schedule, which he considered a miracle. He was proud of how it was turning out. He usually didn't have any reservations about his restoration work, but this one had concerned him a little. However, now even Manuel's amazing pink paint job was growing on him.

It was a beautiful machine, and he had to keep telling himself that surely Dan Monser would have instilled a deep respect for a classic car in his sixteen-year-old daughter. It wasn't really convincing him. It still blew his mind that his hard work would be enjoyed by a group of girls while they giggled all the way to the mall, but that didn't stop him from doing his best. He would make sure that this would be the most badass pink fastback on the road.

After a while he switched projects and focused on Aiden's truck, fulfilling his end of their unwritten bargain. Cheap drinks for tune-ups. It was no big deal—it didn't take Mike long to change the oil and rotate his tires every few months.

Mike hadn't showered yet since he knew he'd get dirty working, and every once in a while he would catch a hint of the floral scent that permeated Anne's house, and her body. It wasn't as if he needed the reminder. All he'd done while he worked was think about being with her, how amazing touching her had been, and the way she'd opened up to him. There was still a lot he didn't know about Anne Edmond, but he knew what had happened between them in the past twenty-four hours was special. Every time his mind went to the vision of her sitting on top of him he worked faster, wanting nothing more than to get back so they could do it all over again.

After finishing up with the truck, he cut through the office to the small bathroom and washed the grease from his fingers the best he could. It was nearly seven and he still needed to order a couple of parts online, shower, and then drop off Aiden's key's next door at the bar before he could see Anne again. He sat down at his desk and picked up his cell phone, hoping she might have texted or called. She hadn't.

He hesitated for a minute and then sent her a message.

MIKE: Be ready for me. Naked.
ANNE: Who would let you in?
MIKE: Your neighbors would love it if you did.
ANNE: NO way. And they're all old!
MIKE: No one is too old to enjoy the sight of a
   hot naked woman.
ANNE: I wouldn't do that for anyone!

MIKE: But I'm not just anyone. Do it for me.
MIKE: Please.

He loved goading her, and he could imagine her sexy
blush when she read his text. Anne Edmond was a crazy
hot woman, even if she didn't seem to realize it, and convincing her to release some of these inhibitions gave him
immense satisfaction.

She still hadn't responded five minutes later and he
started to get nervous. He'd made a habit of revealing
himself and his feelings through texts to her because it
was easier, but not being able to gauge her reaction was
unnerving.

He started to type again—let her know that he'd
been teasing—but as he was typing another message
dinged in.

ANNE: Just show up, and then you get what you
    get and you don't throw a fit.

He grinned, recognizing the phrase from his sister's
house; Erin learned it from Bailey's preschool and now
used it all the time with his niece.

MIKE: I like it when you talk dirty, babe. You
    can play the naughty teacher.
ANNE: Just hurry and get here!
MIKE: Okay, Perfect.

He set his phone down and started up his computer
to put in his parts order. Out of recent habit he opened
the *My Perfect Little Life* blog first and was shocked to

see a new post from Anne from earlier that day. It was titled "Breaking the Silence Triple-Chocolate Brownies," and he began to read with a smile on his face.

I know you've all been waiting for me to respond to the comments from last weekend about my "date." I've debated how to handle it online, if I should ignore it, lie (I know, yuck, not an option), or give details (sorry, also not an option).

Well, I decided on giving a little info, as I love you all and know you want the best for me. Your support of me and Bug over the past few years has been amazing and warmed my heart. I think of you as friends—some of you longtime readers are even like family to me—and I thank you for your kind words. I know you are curious so I thought it right to set the record straight. So, YES, I was on a date last Saturday! And the ladies were correct: He is quite amazing to look at. In fact, I don't know how this happened, but I'm glad it did. He is sweet and funny and best of all he makes Bug laugh.

I won't say too much because right now it's not serious, we're having fun getting to know each other, and I want to protect our privacy. I hope you all understand. But I will tell you this: I made him brownies (yes, I can bake, too!) and they were a hit if I do say so myself. So make them for the sexy man in your life today!

She'd taken a picture of the brownies, which, as she said, were amazing, on a plate. She'd made it look pretty, covered in powder sugar and sitting next to a glass of milk. She'd obviously taken it before he got to her house the day before. The recipe followed, and then the comments started. He wasn't sure if he even wanted to read them. He'd read enough of her blog to know they'd be happy and encouraging, but he couldn't get her words out of his head.

Most of it made him insanely happy, because she sounded happy. But he still felt a little off about the whole thing. He was pretty sure it was the part about it not being serious. He'd never made a conscious decision to call this a serious relationship, but he knew what he felt for Anne was more than *having fun*, which in his mind meant just sex. This was more, much more.

Was she just keeping that to herself because it was too personal for the Internet, or did she really not feel what was happening between them the way he did? He ran a hand down his face and cursed under his breath. Finally she'd done what he wanted, acknowledged them on the blog, and he still wasn't satisfied. Maybe he was being an asshole. He couldn't be irritated, it was her site and she deserved to handle it the way she saw fit. And he wasn't even sure what he wished she would have said. He just felt . . . unsettled.

He stood up and headed for the shower. Fifteen minutes later and he was ready to go in jeans and a navy T-shirt. He grabbed his and Aiden's keys, his wallet, and headed for Smokey's.

It was a Saturday so the back lot was full of cars. Mike could hear the bass of the music pounding through the old brick walls the minute he stepped outside of Aiden's truck and headed up the stairs to the front door.

His thoughts traveled back to the not-so-distant Saturday when he'd pulled Anne's curves against him on the dance floor. Now he knew what they looked and felt like naked against him. He couldn't wait to get back to her.

Mike nodded at the doorman and entered the throng of bodies. He really hated the crowd on Saturdays, which was why he usually avoided it. He knew it wasn't Aiden's favorite night, either, but although the club crowds weren't the best tippers, they made up for it by sheer quantity so his friend dealt with the crazy weekends.

Mike found his way to the bar and jerked to the side as a hand closed around his biceps. Katie was beside him, dressed in tiny shorts and a flowery top, her hair big and makeup heavy. *Shit.* He really would have liked to get in and out. Anne was waiting for him.

"Hey." Katie managed to make it a purr although she had to speak loudly to be heard over the noise. "Come to see me?"

"Well, actually . . ."

Katie turned, cutting him off to chat with a group of women sitting at the end of the bar. Mike quickly looked around for Aiden, who was nowhere in sight. The other bartender who worked weekends was close, and Mike tried desperately to get his attention.

Katie pressed into his side again, one arm flinging around his neck. He looked down at her warily. Needing to get out of this situation as soon as possible, he leaned a little closer to speak into her ear and practically shouted over the music, "I'm actually not staying, Katie. Sorry." He pealed her arm away from his body and started to make his escape.

She gave him a pouty face and re-insinuated herself on his person by leaning her head on his shoulder. Good God, he needed to get out of here, Katie was trashed. Looking back at the bar he finally saw Aiden, coming out of the back with a keg over his shoulder. He set it down, his eyes darting between Mike and Katie.

"Hey man, you okay?" Aiden asked.

"Not really, I'm kind of in a rush. Truck's good for a few more months. I'll see you later this week." He handed him the keys.

"Thanks."

Mike again gently pushed Katie away from him, and when Aiden pushed a glass of water in front of her, Mike took the opportunity to haul ass for the door. His victorious escape was sweet, but also short-lived. He intended to walk back to his shop—which wasn't far—when he heard footsteps. Not just any footsteps, of course, but heels precariously making their way down the flight of wooden stairs. Fuck.

"Don't leave yet, Mike. Just give me a second. Please? I've missed you." Katie's heels now wobbled on the gravel lot, the sharp tang of alcohol clinging to her body as she edged closer. "I haven't seen you lately."

"Katie, you're going to fall out here, and I really do need to get going." He pulled his keys from his pocket.

"Where to? It's Saturday night?"

He froze, completely unsure of what to say. He didn't feel he owed Katie any explanation about what he did. Seriously, they'd only gone out the one time.

"Oh, do you have a date? With someone else?" She looked so shocked and distressed all at the same time. Shit.

"Katie, I'm not sure what you want me to say. I'm sorry things didn't work out between us. You're a really ni—"

"Don't." She put a hand against his lips to shush him and he clamped his mouth shut. "Don't tell me I'm nice, beautiful, or sweet, or any other stupid bullshit."

He gently removed her hand from his face. "Okay. Then what do you want me to say?"

Her body sagged and her face took on a pitiful look, her head tilting to the side. "I really liked you, Mike, for a long time. When my roommate and I moved into the duplex behind your shop last fall I watched you working on those cars all the time when you had the garage doors open, wishing that you would see me and ask me out."

He really didn't like where this was going. Her voice was escalating and her words slurring. It also made him feel like shit. He never wanted to hurt anyone, but clearly he had, and he regretted it, immensely.

"And then you did ask me out." She inched closer to him, her eyes pleading—and yes, there was definitely vodka coming out of her pores. "I know our date wasn't perfect, but you must have liked me enough to ask me . . . and then . . . and then *she* . . ."

"Katie, stop. I think you've had a little too much to drink, and Anne has nothing to do with me and you." At this point he didn't know if he was disgusted with her behavior or felt sorry for her. A little of both if he was being truthful. He also just wanted to leave.

"That's crap, Mike, and you know it. You flirted with me at the bar for weeks and then asked me out. Then you met her. She has everything to do with it."

He glanced around. Her theatrics were drawing attention from the people milling around in the parking lot smoking. With every word she moved closer until he had his back up against someone's pickup. "Katie, I'm sorry. I never wanted to hurt you. Why don't I walk you home?"

And then she lunged for him, her lips hitting his, the stickiness of her lip gloss moving across his mouth for a second before he pushed her away.

"Okay, now stop." He put both hands up to block her, and a tear ran down her cheek. She gasped and put a hand over her mouth. He watched her for a moment, wondering what the next best move would be, but she continued on.

"I really thought you liked *me*. I know she's totally perfect and pretty for someone who's, like, in their thirties. But she has a kid. And a mommy business. Do you really think she wants to marry a mechanic? She even said you all weren't serious! But I like you a lot, Mike! I don't even care that you work on cars for a living."

Wow. That struck him speechless. He wanted to ignore her words; she was hurt, drunk, and completely irrational. But her comments about his work hit home. Obviously Katie had read Anne's blog post, too, which pissed him off, but she'd had the same thought he did. Was Anne just testing the waters? This wasn't for keeps, only for fun with her? He didn't want to believe it but . . .

"Katie, you need to go home. Or back inside the bar."

She sucked in a deep breath and stared at him for a second before she spoke again. "This won't last, Mike."

"Thank you for your brutal yet unwanted opinion." He was barely able to hold in his fury. At what, he wasn't sure—her definitely, but more at the doubts that her words had unleashed in his mind. "I'm leaving, you need to go, too."

She looked at him, a whiny sigh emitting from her mouth. At this point he couldn't muster a bit of pity for her. Finally she stumbled back to the steps and headed up to the front door. He wanted to just turn and go, but he couldn't. With a sigh he followed her up and made sure she not only didn't fall, but also got back inside. Aiden would hopefully help her sober up.

After watching her shove past the doorman, Mike made the short trek back to his shop and sat down in his Camaro, parked in the alley. He slammed the door and leaned his head back on the leather headrest. He wasn't entirely sure what he was thinking, what he wanted, or what he was feeling. He knew he wanted Anne and for more than a little while. Was it possible that she didn't want to share the details of their relationship because of who he was or what he did? She didn't make him feel beneath her because he didn't have a college degree or a white-collar job. But was she thinking it?

He could shake off the opinion of Katie, but Anne . . . he needed to feel something from her, something more than lust. He'd always been proud of his work, happy with his place in life, and satisfied with his future prospects. But now . . . something was missing. A new void had appeared in his life, one he hadn't even been aware of.

He'd been with his fair share of women over the years. He'd had some good times. Sure, some of them had wanted more, but one thing had been consistent: He'd remained uncommitted and liked it that way. Alone was safe, alone was easy, and alone didn't hurt. He'd had enough of pain and loss, but just the thought of *not* having Anne threatened feelings he'd rather not experience. That realization alone made him feel a little suffocated, and how the hell had it happened?

He picked up his phone, his body humming with frustration of every kind. He wanted to get his hands on Anne, touch her, taste her, and smell her. He wanted to know what was in her head. And that she felt for him what he felt for her. He sent her one more text.

MIKE: I decided I will throw a fit if you're not naked. I need you, Anne. Right now.

He switched the sound to off and started the engine. He didn't want her to reply, he just wanted her to do this for him, get out of her comfort zone because he'd asked her. Was he testing her? No, that wasn't his style, but he still wished she would do something to let him know this was more than just a physical thing. If it wasn't, he didn't know if he'd be able to stand it. He had a really good feeling he couldn't. Soon they would talk and he would get inside her pretty little head and find out how deep this ran on her side. He wanted all of her.

Twenty

Anne leaned forward on the edge of her bed, one arm covering her naked breasts, which was silly since she was alone in the house. She'd already prepared for Mike's return by lighting several candles in her bedroom and removing all of her clothing. The front door had a note — *Come upstairs and lock the door behind you*—that she'd just placed there after receiving his text. Hopefully no strangers would come by, which she figured unlikely at this hour.

She'd wanted to surprise him—and herself—by taking a chance, letting herself feel and act sexy, but this last message had confused her. Something about it felt . . . angry. She wasn't really sure what to make of it.

She bit at her bottom lip and glanced around the room. Luckily darkness had fallen outside so the candlelight created soft golden warmth—as flattering as light could be, she figured. She envied women like Callie who felt comfortable with their bodies. Anne wished she was one of those women who could strut around in the nude for a man. She would probably never be that way, she hadn't been even before pregnancy, but she wanted to. She wanted to do that for Mike, because no one had ever made her feel as wanted as he did, and that realization shook her to her core.

They weren't in love with each other, but she couldn't deny the pull she felt to him and it was more than skin-deep.

A soft knocking on her bedroom door startled her—she hadn't heard him arrive, much less come up the stairs. She took a deep breath and stood in front of the bed as he opened the door. Her heart pounded as she fought the instinct to grab her robe and cover her body. The hall was dark, but the candlelight was just bright enough to highlight Mike's face. He stood completely still for a moment, hands at his sides, just staring with hooded eyes.

"Hi," she said, trying to sound seductive and failing miserably when her voice shook. Yet he didn't even seem to hear her. From the tone of his text, and now his silence, she sensed something wasn't right. Her shoulders fell with concern and she shifted from one foot to the other. "Is everything . . . okay?"

He nodded, seeming to snap out of his haze. "God, yes, now it is."

She couldn't help a weak smile as he walked into the room, his gaze locking onto hers. She waited for his eyes to travel south, and when they finally did she managed to keep her arms still and let him peruse every inch of her. Every nerve seemed to react to the touch of his eyes; her arms tingled and her breasts felt heavy. She was amazed at how empowering it felt. When he finally looked back at her face, her entire body was hot and languid.

"You're so beautiful," he whispered. Those three words made it all worth it.

He stepped toward her slowly. His hands settled on her bare hips and slid up the sides of her waist while at the same time his mouth crushed into hers. The impact of their bodies joining made her weak, her skin soft against his jeans and shirt. Combined with the masculine scent coming off his skin, she was worked up to the point of frustration. His fingers were rough and she felt every stroke as he ran them over her back and bottom.

Wet lips ran along her jaw as he backed her into the mattress. He stopped right before she slid down to the comforter, her body thrumming with anticipation.

"I need you, Anne, more than I've ever needed anything in my life." He swallowed hard and leaned forward to her ear, his tongue running against her lobe before he spoke softly. "I want you to need me, too."

Her eyes focused on a candle behind him, and between the words and the touch of his mouth she thought she might be dreaming. She knew what he said, and what she thought that meant, but she wasn't sure so she took the safe route. With both hands she grabbed onto his face and made him look at her. "I do need you."

"Are you sure?"

She reached one hand down and ran her palm over the bulge in his jeans. "Yes, I'm sure."

He put his hand over her fingers and stilled her stroking. "No. I don't mean I want you to need this. I want you to need *me*."

Silence enveloped them as they stared at each other. He'd been so playful this morning and in his earlier texts. She wondered if something had happened but didn't want to ask, so she said exactly what her heart told her to. "I knew what you meant, and my answer is the same. I need *you*, Mike Everett. Now please touch me or I'm gonna die."

His lips curled at one side, a small dimple showing in his cheek. He grabbed her arms and pulled their bodies together as they tumbled onto the bed, the sounds of urgent kissing filling the room.

He stopped, gasping for breath as he brushed her hair from her face. The emotion in his eyes made her want to say something she shouldn't. Something that couldn't be unsaid, so instead she squeezed her lips shut and let her fingernails run down his sides until she could grab a fistful of fabric. He pushed his body up, hands dipping into the bed beside her so she could pull the shirt up and then over his head. She was breathless as she took in the sight of his beautiful body.

"Am I hurting you?" he asked.

"No," she whispered, squeezing his shoulders because he hadn't waited for an answer, he just tucked his mouth into her neck and began kissing her shoulder, then her breasts. One and then the other, his tongue wet and firm. He sucked one nipple into his mouth and she arched against him, the pleasure too intense. Denim scratched at her inner thighs where she only wanted to feel the warmth of his skin.

"Mike, I want all this off. I need you naked."

She felt his chest rumble against hers before he pushed off the bed and stood beside it. "Yes ma'am."

His boots, jeans, underwear, and socks were gone in a hurry and he was back on her resuming the seductive ministrations to her body. She spread her legs wide, allowing all of him to settle against all of her. Everything about touching him felt right and natural, and when he began to move up and down, his erection slipping through her folds, she accidentally released a small moan.

"I love the sounds you make," he whispered, continuing to grind against her.

A severe blush broke out across her face and radiated through her entire body. He continued the kissing, licking, and caressing all over her torso as she tried to return the favor. He was nearly frantic with the way he devoured her body, moving over her face, chest, and stomach while his fingers stroked between her thighs. Every few seconds he would tell her how good her skin tasted, how much he wanted her, and what he was going to do to her. Her body was humming, on edge, and begging for release.

Finally he went to his knees and rolled on a condom before he resettled himself and entered her slowly. She lifted her legs and wrapped them around his waist, pulling him closer. She knew she'd succeeded in garnering his full attention when he grabbed both of her hands and held them above her head. The intensity of his thrusts increased, bringing her closer and closer.

Right before her body flooded with the sensation he let one hand travel down to her center once again, teasing until she went over the edge. He followed right after her, his thrusts slowing and his breaths becoming ragged until he cursed quietly and sagged against her.

After a moment they were both spent and panting and he rolled over onto the pillow, one arm flung across his face. "Good Lord, Perfect. You're amazing."

Anne pulled up the sheets and covered them both before snuggling in beside him, one arm across his torso. "You're more amazing."

His arm dropped from his face and he twined his fingers with hers on his chest. "We're amazing together."

The comment had her heart blooming and her brain venturing into dangerous territory. But she had to agree, something special happened between them, something that scared the bejeezus out of her. So instead of a reply she just ran her fingers across his chest and molded her body against his. Hopefully he could feel the things that she didn't have the nerve to say.

The next morning Anne carefully rolled out of bed, hoping not to wake the giant mass of man sprawled stomach-down across her yellow houndstooth sheets, the same sheets that were now just barely concealing a very perfect behind. She stood staring for a moment as she slipped on her robe. She tilted her head to one side, then the other, taking in a nice long look.

A month ago she would have bet she had a better chance at being asked to plan a party for the president than to sleep with a man like Mike, young, firm, and sexy. She smiled at the turn of her good luck and continued her perusal.

One naked leg peeked out and she admired the dark hairs and corded muscle running up his calf and into his thigh. His face was turned toward the opposite wall and she wished she could see it. She had yet to see his handsome features relaxed in slumber. She considered tiptoeing to the other side of the bed.

"You got your fill yet, Perfect?"

"Oh . . . shit," Anne hissed as soon as he started speaking. She held a hand up to her forehead as he rolled over to face her, a massive grin on his face. "You scared me to death," Anne said.

"Well, how do you think I feel. I was the one being ogled." His hand reached over his head and he stretched hard, his pectoral muscles lengthening and driving her mad.

She put a hand on her hip. "I *just* got up. And I wasn't ogling you."

He lifted a brow and let his arm drop back against the bed beside him. It caught at the sheet and yanked it a little to the side, giving her a good idea of something else she'd like to ogle. As if he could read her mind, he let out a laugh.

"Okay, fine." She crossed her arms against her chest. "There may have been some ogling. Like I can help it. You're naked. In *my* bed."

"That I am, and it's a very comfortable bed. Even more so when you're in it with me, so why don't you make that happen." He stretched his arm out to her and crooked a finger.

"First, I need coffee, and this morning it's my treat. Oh, and I went by Callie's yesterday and picked up some of her pecan rolls."

Anne tightened her robe around her waist and headed for the hall. She heard the bed squeak behind her and then the rustle of clothes, so she knew Mike was going to follow. Downstairs she started pulling out everything she needed and got to work with the coffee. Just as she pulled the plate of rolls from the microwave, strong arms grasped her from behind, followed by a warm mouth on her neck.

"Hmmm, you smell like a woman who got lucky last night," Mike said.

"Oh jeez, is that a good smell? Because I'm not sure."

He ran his tongue along the skin just below her ear. "Yep, it's my second favorite. The first being whatever that flowery stuff is that I can smell every time I'm around you."

Anne's stomach dipped at that compliment, and also at the implication. He noticed her, even the little things, and they were his favorite. She pulled gently from his arms and set the plate on the table. "That scent is lilac. I've always really liked it so I have it in candles, body products, fabric softener—you name it, I probably have it in lilac. I might go a little overboard."

"No way, don't stop. It's you." Mike sat down across from her at the table, took a bite of his cinnamon roll, and winked at her.

For the second time in thirty minutes Anne nearly jumped out of her skin when she heard a voice call out from the living room. "Hey sweetie. Thank goodness I can smell coffee—"

"Oh shit, it's my mother," Anne whispered in a panic, looking from left to right. There was absolutely no avoiding what was about to happen. She froze as said woman appeared in the kitchen doorway. Marie shot a glance at Mike and then Mike's lower half, which thank heavens was sporting jeans. Meanwhile his upper body was sinfully bare and Marie's eyes were glued to it.

"Well my goodness, sweetie, I'm sorry. I obviously should have called to see if you'd have company at eight a.m. on the *Sabbath*."

Mike stood up and lifted his hand. "Hello Mrs . . ."

"Please call me Marie," she said as she stepped over and took Mike's hand. Anne didn't miss the way her mother looked him up and down.

"Nice to meet you, Marie. I'm Michael Everett."

Anne stifled a laugh at his use of the proper name. She knew her mother well enough to know that she was teasing with the holier-than-thou act, but Anne still wasn't thrilled about being caught. She felt like a teenager being found making out on the couch—not that she'd ever actually made out on a couch when she lived with her parents. How had she not heard her mom put the key in the door? Oh yeah, she was mooning over the sexy half-naked man's romantic words about how she smelled.

Anne tried not to be overly concerned about her mother's noticeably labored breathing. Was she feeling okay? Should she be resting? Anne feared that her mother's days of going about life carefree were seriously numbered, but right now Marie appeared to care less about her health than her appreciation of Mike's form. Anne could understand that; Mike's form was a sight to behold for any woman.

"I, uh . . . apologize for being indisposed," Mike said. He glanced at Anne nervously and started to move toward the door. Her mother had other ideas. She placed both hands on his broad shoulders and shoved his body—nearly double her size—back down into the chair.

"Don't you dare apologize and don't you dare

move . . . a muscle." On that last word Marie gave each deltoid a firm squeeze. Anne rolled her eyes as her mother headed for the kitchen cabinet. "Well. I guess I'll take my brew to go and be out of your hair."

"Mom, I'm sorry, did you need something? Are you doing okay?" Anne's thoughts were pinging back and forth between worry and embarrassment.

"Oh I'm fine, in fact I'm wonderful." She smiled at Mike over her shoulder before pouring her coffee into one of Anne's thermal travel mugs. Luckily she took it black, so no sugar, but Anne knew the caffeine was going to have to go with her mother's high blood pressure. But no one told Marie what-for. Obviously, and Anne wasn't really in a position to cast judgment.

Anne turned her head to Mike; his smile was nearly boyish. The same kind you give to your best friend when you realize you've gotten out of trouble by the skin of your teeth. She widened her eyes in question and he wagged his brows at her. Even in such an awkward situation, he managed to look relaxed and smug; it irritated her and made her want to kiss him at the same time.

"So *Michael Everett*, may I assume that since I've already seen you half naked, and my daughter has seen . . . more than half . . ."

Anne groaned. "Mom, please."

Marie waved a hand at Anne to shut her up as she continued her question. "As I was saying, can I expect you tomorrow at my house for Monday-night dinner at Grandma's?"

"*Mom*—"

"Sounds great," Mike said at the same time.

Anne fought dueling emotions of thrill and dread. She

could have sworn that Monday night at Grandma's was definitely not something he would be into, but he was too kind to turn an old woman down. When her mother left she'd have to tell him it was fine to bow out. She'd cover for him.

"Well, good, it's a date. I'll just see you two kids tomorrow then." Marie walked into the living room to leave, and Anne knew better than to let her go without following. When they made it to the front door she braced herself for the real reaction.

"You know," her mother said as she turned, one hand on the door. "When I pulled up and saw that fancy car, I hoped it wasn't just one of the girls, honey . . . gracious, what a man."

"If you saw the car, Mom, why didn't you knock?" Anne scolded under her breath.

"I did, it was just quiet, in case you were sleeping." Marie winked and then laughed as she opened the door.

Anne rolled her eyes and sighed.

"So this *is* Uncle Mike, right?" Marie asked quietly.

"Yes, Mother, it is, but I'm not sure if it's super serious right now so don't get any ideas. I wish you didn't invite him over for dinner. How awkward."

"Well, he could have said no," Marie said matter-of-factly.

"Oh yeah, right." Anne lifted her arms and whispered, "Some partially dressed guy meets the mother of the woman he *stayed with*, and then turns down her invitation for dinner. He's not a jerk."

"I think he wanted to come. Did you see his face light up? And please tell him shirts are optional." Marie pulled the door closed behind her.

* * *

The next day came quickly, and it didn't take long sitting at Marie's dining table for Mike's nerves to evaporate. She was funny and kind, just like her daughter. He was enjoying himself despite their awkward first meeting.

Of course she'd made the obvious—and correct—assumption that he'd spent the night with Anne the day before, which was never the first impression one was going for. But there was really no other way to explain his bare torso and bedhead. Yes, he'd been embarrassed, but he'd liked her immediately. She had a quick wit and a sparkle in her eye. And she loved Anne and Claire fiercely, that was obvious and definitely her best feature.

"This meat loaf is amazing, Marie," he said genuinely as he helped himself to his third helping. "I'm not used to eating so well."

"That's a shame, Michael," Marie said with a click of her tongue. "Sadly, that's a symptom of bachelorhood, and from what I hear there's only one proven remedy."

"Oh my God, Mom, are you serious right now?" Anne looked adorably horrified at the end of the table, unable even to meet his eyes.

"What's a bachelorhood?" Claire asked across the table. She wasn't fond of meat loaf so Marie had made her a plate of cucumbers and ranch—her favorite, he learned—and mashed potatoes. Her question was so innocent, yet Anne ignored it so Claire grew louder. A tactic he was familiar with from his niece. "What's a bachelorhood, Grandma Ree?"

"It's a horrible disease that makes nice boys lonely and malnourished—"

"Oh my gosh, Claire, eat your dinner," Anne said, shooting her mother a glare. "It's not a disease. Grandma Ree is pulling your leg."

Mike smiled around his fork and grabbed Anne's knee under the table. Finally she looked up and he winked at her. She managed to sag a little in her chair; he hoped it was from the release of stress. He didn't want her to be uncomfortable. He was enjoying himself, and he wanted her to enjoy herself also.

"So, Michael, Anne says you work on old cars? My late husband used to drive a classic car when we were first dating. Well, at the time it wasn't yet a classic, but he kept it running. Sold it and made a tidy little profit in '89, I think. We had some good times and made some great memories in that car."

Mike smiled at the wistfulness in her expression. He loved stories like that; it always made a reno job more rewarding when the owner had a story to go with the vehicle. "You recall what kind it was?"

"I know it was a Ford, but other than that I don't know. Although I bet . . ." She stood up and turned to the wooden buffet that was nestled along the wall in the tiny apartment. From a drawer she pulled a small frame. "Here we go."

Mike took the photo as she sat back down and examined the car that stood behind a young couple in the faded image. "No way, a '40 Ford. My father had one of these. This was the car I learned to 'wrench' on. In fact, this odd-shaped taillight was my first tattoo."

"You have a tattoo? Does that mean you're bad?" Claire's eyes were wide, and she had ranch on her upper lip. "Can I see it?"

He was instantly a little embarrassed he'd brought it up. He'd gotten the ink right after his father passed, and although he loved it, he wasn't sure if he would do it again at this point in his life. He also wasn't sure about flashing his naked back for three women, one of whom was six and impressionable, over meat loaf.

He glanced at Anne and she raised an eyebrow as he spoke. "I'd better not—"

"Well of course you should," Marie interjected. "I *have* to see it if it's a '40 Ford. My husband really loved that car, and well . . . since I've already seen you without a shirt it just makes sense now, doesn't it?"

Anne rolled her eyes, and he cleared his throat. "Okay, if you insist."

He stood up from his chair. Of course he'd chosen to dress up a little for Anne's mother so he had on a button-up shirt, tucked in, over a T-shirt. *Shit.* This was going to feel like a gosh damn striptease. He tried not to meet eyes with Claire—she was a little girl, for heaven's sake—so he looked at Anne as he unbuttoned the top few buttons, but the warmth in her eyes was going to be a problem. Nope. He glanced at Marie, and her smirk undid him. No way. His eyes landed back at Claire. She giggled, her ranch mustache still firmly in place, and he lifted his gaze to the ceiling. He couldn't look at these three women as he pulled his shirt off. What the hell had he gotten himself into?

Finally he turned around, grabbed the hem of his T-shirt, and hiked it up his back. The tattoo was dead center between his shoulder blades, and it sort of looked like a double red V, one on top of the other, with a thick black outline. His dad's initials and the date of his death were scripted across the bottom.

"You should have gotten a unicorn." Claire said, and thank goodness for six-year-olds, because it released the awkward tension in the air. After a minute he turned back around, tugging his T-shirt back down.

"I love it," Marie said. "I remember that taillight. They were unusual, on those big rear fenders. That's a good-looking tattoo."

"Thank you. I used to like sitting on that fender when I was a kid, made my dad so mad. It was the first thing I thought of when I wanted to get something to remember him. We spent a lot of time working on that car together." Mike pulled his shirt back on and buttoned it up, but he didn't bother tucking it in before he sat down.

He looked at Anne, who finally appeared to be enjoying the moment, and he warmed inside when she reached for him under the table. He squeezed her hand and then turned back to her mother, who obviously hadn't missed the interaction between Mike and her daughter. "Thank you for sharing that photo, Marie, it's really great. Too bad you don't still have that car. I'd have bought it from you."

"It is. I miss it. If I'd have known Anne was going to meet a man who restores classic cars and has a thing for '40 Fords then I would have made Wade hang on to it." She sighed and then grabbed a few dishes. "Who wants banana pudding?"

"Meeeeee," Claire shrieked.

Anne released his hand and stood up. "Sit down, Mom. I'll get the dishes and dessert."

"I'll help," Mike said as he stood. He grabbed his plate and Marie's.

"Well, I won't argue with you there." Marie settled back into her seat and started talking with Claire.

Mike followed Anne into the small kitchen and immediately put the plates in the sink so he could get his hands on her, turning her around from the refrigerator and pulling her into his arms. He whispered into her ear, "I'm dying to make out with you."

She laughed quietly and cupped his jaw with her soft hand. "You need to be a good boy, Uncle Mike."

"Didn't you hear? I can't be good, I have tattoos. Plus it's so hard when I can almost see down your shirt." He put a finger into the low neckline of her top and pulled far enough so he could peek in.

"Hey!" She slapped his hand away, laughing, and turned to the cabinet. She pulled some bowls down and began scooping out servings of banana pudding. He wrapped his arms around her waist and glanced over her shoulder.

"I'd like to lick banana pudding off your body," he whispered, her floral scent filling his nose.

She giggled and whispered, "I'd like to lick it off your tattoo. Among other places."

God how he loved it when she played back. "You would, would you? You like my tattoo, Perfect? You should have said so before. You can lick any part of me you want."

She leaned back into his arms and for a moment they were silent, only the sounds of their shared breathing filling the air in the kitchen. The playful laughter of grandmother and child came from the dining room, and Mike felt at peace. He had Erin's family, but something about being with a woman he enjoyed—in this context of family togetherness—just felt good.

"Anne, thank you for bringing me tonight. I've had a good time."

She turned in his arms and looked in his eyes. "I'm glad you're here, too, even if my mother enjoys humiliating me."

He grinned. "She loves you. It makes her happy to joke around."

"I'm glad it makes someone happy."

He threaded their fingers and leaned his forehead against hers. Touching Anne was the simplest pleasure, but he craved it. This kind of small intimacy felt amazing, and also terrifying. He wanted something he'd never wanted before, and he wasn't sure what she was thinking. He pushed those thoughts away. "You make *me* happy, Anne."

She just stared into his eyes for a moment, and then she finally whispered back, "You make me happy, too, Mike."

Twenty-One

Watching Callie coach the dance team was exciting. Anne sat in the bleachers, Claire next to her coloring, as the music pounded through the Preston High School gymnasium. The girls looked amazing, but the best part was watching Callie in action because she definitely knew her stuff and took it very seriously. It was fun to see this intense side of her.

"No, no, no, Caitlin." Callie killed the music and yelled through the expansive room, her voice echoing over all the shiny surfaces. "The back leg in attitude, not straight. Don't let me see that straight leg again."

The teenager nodded and bent her outstretched leg, wobbling only slightly.

"More, more, a little too much." Callie tilted her head. "Good, now lift your chin and don't forget to smile." All sixteen girls beamed, their smiles fake, but Callie's was real. She'd invited Anne over to watch the fourth practice, and Anne had been more than happy to accept. She'd never been a girl like the ones before her, beautiful and popular. Jessica Monser was one of the sixteen dancers, of course, so Anne had decided to kill two birds and meet with her and her mother, Jill, before practice to go over some final details for the weekend.

"Okay, girls, amazing job. I'll see you tomorrow for conditioning day and please be on time. We have less than a month before camp and I'm planning on us coming home with Best Overall award."

The girls cheered and clapped before dispersing to gather their stuff. Callie walked over to the bleacher where Anne sat and took a deep breath. "How do they look?"

"Incredible. I'm so impressed," Anne said, and it was true.

Callie smiled. "Thanks, can't take the credit. It's only my fourth day. The previous coach did a good job. I heard rumors that the she was fired due to some inappropriate texts with one of the administrators, but who knows and who cares, I'm just glad to take her place."

Anne laughed. "I'm proud of you." She glanced around for Jill and saw her talking with her daughter in the corner. Anne stood and waved, and they headed over to say goodbye.

"The girls are looking fantastic, Callie. I'm really pleased you took over," Jill said. "I don't know how you do it and run the bakery."

Callie smiled. "Thank you, Jill, I'm thrilled to be coaching, and I'm lucky to have a very dedicated employee who's willing to put up with me coming and going."

"Oh yes, Eric. He sure is a cutie, it's a shame he's . . ." Jill said, waving a hand around like she couldn't find the word.

"*Gay*?" Callie finished for her. Anne tried to hold back her smile.

"Yes, that." Jill smiled awkwardly.

Callie leaned over to stuff her notebook in the bag. "Well, I assure you, he's not missing out on anything."

Jill laughed but it sounded strained. Callie was good at casually defending her friend, who shouldn't need defending. It never ceased to amaze Anne that people still had trouble discussing such things, but she shrugged it off, which is what Eric always did.

Another mom, sporting an unfortunate haircut, approached. Jill introduced Callie as the new coach and then Anne.

"Are you the Anne of the *My Perfect Little Life* blog?" the woman said with her mouth agape. "I knew you lived around here, but we've never met."

Anne smiled. "Yes, that's me. Do you read it?"

"Of course, I love it, and Callie your recipes are amazing, I also made Lindsey's altered Christmas wreath this past December." She made an odd face and glanced around toward Claire before she lowered her voice. "It's too bad about what happened today, Anne, with that video on Facebook. I don't know why someone would want to embarrass you like that."

Anne's heart sank like a lead ball, but she held on to her smile as she cast a quick questioning glance at Callie. Her friend's eyes were wide and she shrugged, her own plastic smile firmly in place.

"Oh it's no big deal. These things happen," Anne lied, because she had no idea what the woman was talking about. She just went on to shake her head, her eyes full of pity as she looked at her and Callie. Anne thought she might vomit, and she didn't even know what this woman was talking about.

Jill Monser's face scrunched in question. "What kind of video?"

Anne froze and luckily, or not, the woman butted in and continued. As the words poured from her mouth it was confirmed. Anne was going to be ill.

"Well, Anne's dancing . . . with some guy. I have to say, Anne, it kind of looked like fun, so don't you feel bad. We've all gotten a wee bit tipsy before."

Jill shot Anne a concerned look. "Anne, is everything okay? Why would someone post something like that? It doesn't sound very appropriate."

Anne took a deep breath and looked sheepish. "I'm not sure. Someone was clearly just trying to be mean. You know how people can be on the Internet. Wanting to share every detail, but don't worry about it, we'll get them to take it down." But even as she spoke she felt more and more light-headed. She couldn't even imagine what or who or why this had happened.

"Oh I hope so," Jill said. "We're inviting a lot of Dan's colleagues Saturday, and I plan to give your name out. You know how important an online image is these days."

She certainly did know, better than anyone. But what did Jill's words imply? Was it a warning? Was she concerned that Anne couldn't handle it? Was she judging her? Any of those was enough to make her feel sick.

"No worries there, Jill, Saturday is going to be wonderful. We can't wait," Callie said and picked up her purse and gym bag. "Anne and I have a busy day ahead of us so we'll plan on seeing you all soon."

Anne collected Claire and her coloring books and

then followed Callie through the gym and out the door. When they hit the fresh air Anne gasped and covered her mouth with her hand. "Callie, what just happened?"

"I don't know, sweetie. Let's just get in the car and we'll find out."

Anne followed like a robot, her mind shutting down. She didn't even want to consider the possibilities, only rewind time to ten minutes ago before the humiliation occurred. She hadn't looked at the blog or anything on her computer since late last night. What time did this video go up? Was it on the *Perfect Little Life* Facebook page, and how many people had seen it? They walked straight to Anne's car and Callie—bless her—dealt with making sure Claire was situated while Anne sat down in the front seat stunned and wide-eyed.

When Callie finally joined her in the front seat she pulled her cell phone from her bag. "Oh gosh, eight missed calls from Eric."

"I don't know if I can look," Anne said, nearing hysteria. She hadn't done anything truly scandalous, but her mind reeled with possibilities. This was her worst nightmare come to life—becoming an embarrassment to herself and her family. Looking like a fool, a fraud, or, even worse, a horrible mother. Shame coiled inside her stomach.

"What's wrong, Mommy?" Claire called out. Anne ignored her, knowing if she responded to or looked at her daughter she'd lose it.

"Nothing is wrong with Mommy, Claire. Don't you worry," Callie said calmly, shoving her purse in the backseat. "Why don't you look through my purse, all kinds of goodies in there."

"Yay!"

"Just take a deep breath, Anne. Nothing can be that bad," Callie said.

Anne felt tears pushing against her eyelids as she stared in front of her.

"The same post is up from last night on the blog, the one about Mike going to your mom's for dinner. I don't know what they're talking about, how would we be linked to Facebook . . . oh wait." Callie got quiet.

"Oh God, is it hot in here or is it just me? Perhaps I need to turn the air on." Anne started the engine and cranked up the AC as Callie pushed at buttons on her phone. Suddenly music started playing from the phone, music that Anne recognized all too well: It was the same "pony riding" song she'd heard at Smokey's while she danced like a drunken hooker. She couldn't even look in Callie's direction, let alone watch the video. She knew exactly what it was.

After a moment that felt like an eternity they both sat without speaking. Callie continued to stare down at her phone, scrolling, and scrolling, and scrolling. Anne couldn't take it anymore.

"I can't believe this, Cal, I really can't believe it."

"It's going to be okay, sweetie. We're going to get to the bottom of this, and when we do I'm gonna be kicking some butt and piling their body parts into a pink pastry box. But first you need to get Claire home and I'll come over soon. But, Anne, you need to look at Facebook, there are a couple of things you need to see."

She finally looked and it was bad, as bad as it could be. Some asshole had left an anonymous comment on the most recent blog post filled with links to Facebook. The Smokey's Facebook page, to be exact, and the most humiliating one linked to the video of Anne and all her drunken glory dancing with a stranger. She was humiliated, ashamed, and deeply saddened.

She'd let her readers down, proven herself a fraud. She was supposed to be a wholesome, single mother who taught people how to make party favors. This video made her look like trash.

But as awful as that video was, it wasn't the worst of it. The other links to the Smokey's Facebook page were of photos, photos that included Mike and the blond girl that she'd seen at his shop previously. They were standing at the bar, heads close, her hands on his body. And they were dated exactly four days ago, the same night he came over and demanded Anne be waiting naked and ready. The night he'd texted that he needed her. The night had felt different and like more than just sex. The night she'd been so, so stupid.

And she was stupid still, because all she wanted to do was call him, but obviously that was no longer an option. Anne stared at the wall of her kitchen, her feelings a mass of confusion in her brain. She'd even told Claire to go play at the neighbors, which she rarely did.

She could no longer stomach reading the comments. They were—for the most part—loyal and coming to her defense. Things like "Everyone makes mistakes," or "Anne deserves to have fun," a few "You look great, Anne," and all the more surprising, some threatening bodily harm on Anne's "new boyfriend." But as there always are, some people were looking to cast the first stone and loved to watch the mighty fall. How could a hundred "we support yous" get maligned by one "A good mother wouldn't go out and get drunk like that." Anne felt like crawling in to bed and staying for days.

She'd been able to track the IP address of the anonymous commenter, and found it to be local, but that didn't help. It could be anyone in the Greater Kansas City region. She hadn't known anyone at Smokey's that night besides her friends and Mike.

She laid her head down on the kitchen table and took a deep breath. She had already deleted the comment with the links, and closed the post to new comments, but they'd moved over to Facebook and Twitter, places she couldn't control. She did delete the shared video on the *My Perfect Little Life* Facebook page, but what good did it do? The original video said it had been shared twenty-six times already and had over two thousand comments. It was out there—viral—forever and ever.

The Internet, the place Anne had turned to for years for love and support, had brought her to her knees in more ways than one. With a few clicks someone had not only threatened her reputation and her career, but destroyed her heart as well. How could she have ever underestimated the power of an online community? She should've known a good thing couldn't last forever, whether professionally or in love.

But no, no, she didn't love Mike. She couldn't have. She hadn't even really cried yet, because what for? She'd known this was coming, it wasn't a forever thing. Mike was young, hot, and way out of her league. Why wouldn't he be seeing someone else, some hot young blonde in particular? But she was still numb, in shock.

A loud knock came from the front door and Anne

jumped up to make her way to the living room. She saw Callie's car out the window and her and Eric making their way to the front door. Apparently they assumed that Anne was currently a mess and needed to be checked on. They probably had assumed correctly, much to her humiliation. Anne opened the door and gave them a weak smile.

"Oh sweetie, how are you?" Eric threw his arms around Anne, and she hung on tight. It felt good to be held by someone big and strong, although he was the wrong big and strong she craved.

"I'm better," she said into his chest. "Please tell me this was all a dream."

"I wish," Callie said as she pushed her way past them and sat down on the couch. Anne slowly pulled herself from Eric's arms and turned to Callie. "I've had three customers ask me about it today at the shop."

"Oh fuuuhhhhit." Anne sat down and put her head in her hands. She should have just let the nasty words fly; Claire wasn't home yet and she had every right to be flinging obscenities around.

"Anne, Eric and I have been assuring everyone that it's no biggie, and everyone is supporting you. A lot of people have even laughed about it. You're going to show whoever did this that this shit doesn't faze you, got it?"

"Callie, this blog has been the lifeblood of my business and my life for the past three years. It puts food in my daughter's mouth, and I'm proud of it. If people think I'm a horrible person . . ." She groaned. "Oh God, that video, I look like such a skank, and I didn't even like that jerk."

Nope, instead she'd brought another man home, and

that turned out to also be a giant mistake. She couldn't even bring herself to discuss the worst of it with Callie and Eric, although she knew they'd clicked on all the links and seen the photos of Mike. She was grateful to them for not mentioning it. She hadn't spoken to Mike since he'd dropped her and Claire off at her house last night after dinner at Grandma Ree's, and the thought that everything they'd said and done in the past few days had been a lie was destroying her.

"Look at the bright side, Anne," Eric said. "You look hot as hell in that video."

"Right? I still stand by that outfit." Callie said with a weak smile.

Anne managed to laugh a little, a giggle that despite her best efforts turned right into pitiful tears. Uncontrollable sobs racked her body, and immediately Callie jumped from the chair and sat beside her on the couch to wrap her arms around Anne's neck.

"Oh sweetie, don't let this bitch get you down. So what, you had a couple of drinks at a club and danced like a stripper. We've all been there."

"No lie," Eric added.

Anne looked horrified, and Callie shrugged. It didn't help even if they were teasing, although more than likely they were being completely honest. Anne was humiliated, ashamed, and devastated. "It's more than that, Cal."

"I know. It's about Mike, too, we saw the photos. And damn it, he doesn't deserve you. And you better believe that I'm gonna beat his ass."

Anne loved Callie's loyalty, but they both knew Mike could lay tiny Callie out with his pinkie—not that he would, because he was not that kind of guy. But why should she give Mike any credit? Clearly he was not as nice a guy as she had thought. At least not honest. But was that even fair? They'd never *specifically* discussed exclusivity, was she just an idiot for assuming it was implied? An idiot for thinking he wanted only her? She had to have known the hot girl wasn't delivering pizza that day she came to his shop. All the warning signs were there, she'd seen them, and chosen to ignore them. Her mistake.

She felt the tears burn at the corner of her eyes again when there was a commotion at the door. "Mommy," said a muffled voice from the other side and Claire entered.

"Hi, baby." Anne stood up and opened her arms to her daughter. "Did you have a good time with Veronica?"

"Yep, what's wrong, Mommy?"

"Oh nothing, Eric just told me a sad story." Anne smiled and waved her hand dismissively, not liking all this lying to Claire. "You know how Mommy cries at silly things sometimes. Now why don't you run upstairs and get ready for gymnastics."

Anne glanced at her watch. "Oh crap, gymnastics. Mike and Bailey were going to come by and get Claire and me? What am I gonna do?" In the stress of the day she'd completely forgotten they'd made those arrangements.

"When will he be here?" Callie asked.

"Twenty minutes maybe?" Anne answered.

"Well, leave now."

"But he'll still be there, even if I don't ride with him."

"Skip gymnastics tonight," Eric said.

Anne nodded. That's what would have to happen. She couldn't spend a minute with him, much less an hour; she wasn't ready. "Well, I need to text him now and tell him we're not going."

"Ooh yeah, good idea," Callie said. "Before he gets here."

Anne grabbed her phone and opened her text thread with Mike. It broke her heart to see his last text to her. It was just a random *On my way, Perfect* from yesterday before he picked her up to go to her mother's. Damn him. Yesterday had been such a good day, and she'd felt such promise in the words he'd said. *You make me happy, Anne.*

She typed in a vague message saying something had come up, sorry but they were going to have to miss class tonight, and hit SEND. They were all sitting in silence when she heard the telltale rumble of his Camaro. "Shit!" she whispered loudly.

"Is that what I think it is?" Callie whispered.

"Damn, even his ride is hot," Eric said, peeking out the front window.

"Eric! We hate him now," Callie said.

"Doesn't change the fact that he's hot as hell," Eric said.

Anne locked eyes with Callie. "He's early. What do I say?"

Callie's eyes were panicked. "I don't know, keep it short. You can't do this right now." She angled her head toward the stairs where Claire was ascending.

There was a knock on the door and for a moment they all froze. Anne's heart worked overtime in her chest and a pain shot through her at the thought of seeing Mike and not being able to touch him. Knowing that he didn't feel what she thought he'd felt, or want her like she wanted him.

"We're here for you." Callie said quietly. "Just keep it cool."

Anne nodded, ran her hands down her skirt, swiped under her eyes, and opened the front door. Immediately the air left her lungs. Of course he just had to look amazing in jeans and a baseball cap. He held Bailey's hand but let it go gently to remove his sunglasses the minute he saw her. Oh gosh, she must look like she'd been crying.

"Anne? What's wrong, babe? Is your mother okay?"

The sweet sound of his voice and the caring in his eyes was so painful. Of course it was just like him to immediately worry about her sick mother. Then again, she really didn't know what was *just like him* apparently. She swallowed and did what she had to do.

"No, Mom's fine," she said with a shake of her head. "I'm sorry, you're a little early. I sent you a text but you must have been driving. There's been a change in plans. Claire and I are going to have to skip gymnastics tonight so you better go on without us."

He was still for a moment, but then he shifted his weight to the opposite leg and put his hands in his pockets. If she was a body language expert she might know exactly what that meant, but her uneducated guess was that it was a symbol of pulling away, putting up a defensive wall. That was certainly how it felt.

"Okay." His tone was quiet, his words drawn out and searching. "You wanna tell me why?"

"Ummm." She heard commotion behind her and

suddenly Claire pushed her skirt aside and peeked out the door.

"Hi, Bailey and Uncle Mike. We're ready." She stepped onto the porch, her purple leotard on, gym bag in her hand. She'd even put a matching bow in her now lopsided ponytail. "Let's go, Mom."

Anne managed to meet Mike's eyes. His face was blank, his eyes assessing her, and jaw hard. They both ignored Claire tugging on Anne's skirt.

"What's going on, Anne?" he said under his breath, all kinds of angry warning in his voice. He was not happy and wanted her to know it without alerting the girls. Well, that made two of them. She wasn't so happy herself.

"I'm sorry, Mike. It's been a bad day, but not now. We'll have to talk later." Anne brushed her hair from her face and looked at the ground, unable to watch his narrowed eyes boring into her.

"Come on, are we driving in your cool car, Uncle Mike?" Claire asked. Anne wished Eric and Callie had been able to cut Claire off at the pass. Maybe they'd tried, but the way this was playing out was breaking Anne's heart.

"No, baby, not this time." Anne looked up to see Mike's jaw clench at her words. Then he took a step toward her.

Panicked, Anne glanced over her shoulder at her friends. Callie sat on the couch and gave Anne an encouraging nod. So much for beating his ass. Anne pulled the front door shut a little more behind her.

"Anne, what's wrong? Is someone in there with you? Is everything okay?" His voice had suddenly gentled, and she hated that she loved the sound of it so much. But it was the same voice he'd obviously used on some other woman Saturday night before he came over to her house. Just the thought reminded her of what she must do.

"Just Eric and Callie, and we can talk later, Mike. Claire, come inside, sweetie."

He grabbed her arm and squeezed gently. "Anne, talk to me. Please."

She painstakingly freed herself from his grasp. "Later, okay?"

She hated the tears in her voice and the moisture she knew formed in her eyes. Mike's eyes rapidly scanned her face. He looked bewildered, panic-stricken. But most of all he looked hurt. It was all she could do not to reach out for him, comfort him and have him comfort her. Beg him to want her— only her—because she needed him to need her. Hadn't those been his words the other night? Why had he said that after he'd obviously just left the arms of another woman? She couldn't go there right now, she was barely holding it together. The girls were both standing on the walkway chatting, and they couldn't have this discussion in front of them.

"I don't know what to think right now, Anne. You have to give me something."

"I've just been thinking Mike, and we need to talk, but not here. Not right now. Alone."

For a moment he didn't move a muscle. Then finally he took a step back and put on his sunglasses. "Fine. I get it."

He turned suddenly and called to Bailey.

The girls started spouting words of confusion over the

situation and when Anne clarified that she and Claire weren't going to gymnastics, Claire started crying. She loved going and they'd never missed. "Just this time, Claire. Please don't cry."

"But I want to ride with Uncle Mike." Her tears were real and her wails loud. Thankfully Eric rushed outside and scooped Claire up into his arms.

Mike turned to her one more time after pulling the front seat forward for Bailey to get in the backseat. "I don't know what just happened, Anne, but I hope you're sure it's what you want."

Twenty-Two

Mike sat in the upstairs viewing balcony at gymnastics and stared at his phone. Just as she'd said, he had been driving when he felt the text come through in his pocket, and not in a million years would he have guessed it was Anne blowing him off. He still couldn't believe that she'd done it. He read her text again.

> ANNE: I'm sorry, something has come up and
> we're going to have to skip gymnastics. I'll
> talk to you later.

He'd been happy on the way over, excited, the way he felt every time he was about to see her. Something was going on and he needed to understand. He circled back to what the hell possibly could have caused Anne to pull away from him. He'd instantly assumed it was her mother's health since she'd just shared the situation with him, but she'd said no. Plus, Marie had seemed okay the night before.

He glanced down the length of the empty wooden

bench, remembering the look of pleasure on Anne's beautiful face when he'd touched her right here. He'd do anything to go back in time and experience that moment once more. The fear that he'd never see or touch her like that again made him ache inside. He leaned forward and held his head in his palms.

He thought back to last night when he'd told her she made him happy. It had in fact been one of the most purely perfect moments of his entire life. He wasn't ready to let that go. He tried texting her.

MIKE: Anne I need you to talk to me.

He waited for five minutes, knowing that she probably wouldn't respond, and sure enough she didn't.

After practice was over he took Bailey home, avoided any conversation with Erin, and went back to his shop. He focused on the Mustang until late, and before he went to sleep he tried to call her. She didn't answer.

The next morning he got up early, worked some more, and prayed she would reach out. Of course she didn't. No text, no call, no new blog post—because he'd checked several times throughout the morning. She had just up and decided to pull away. He'd never experienced anything like this. It made him furious and more than anything, it hurt.

God, did he miss her already. Their weekend had been great; they'd gotten close. Had they gotten too close? He knew that Saturday night had been intense, but Sunday morning had been good—more than good, it'd been perfect. They'd laughed and when he left they'd been happy. Or so he thought. Then the dinner at her mother's—

everything had seemed amazing, more than amazing. It had all felt right. The last post on her blog was the one where she mentioned taking him to her mother's from Monday night. He'd loved that post so much, it had felt like a big step for her, and instead of scaring him like it might have in the past, it made him smile. Something had happened yesterday.

By ten o'clock he was starting to get pissed all over again so he sent her another message.

MIKE: Talk to me Anne, what the hell is going on?

When she once again didn't respond he sat back in his desk chair and took a deep breath. He rubbed his eyes and pulled his hands down his face, as if he were trying to erase the image of Anne's last text and lack of response to him now. He needed to stop thinking like a fucking girl. He was going to get his shit together and sort things out with Anne.

He had a job due that afternoon so he couldn't go over there now, but when she hadn't responded by noon he was a mess. Mike had never been in this position. He felt like he was losing a part of himself he didn't know existed, and it wasn't fun. Jesus, the thought that things could truly be over was like a punch to the gut. Right then and there he decided he was willing to do whatever it took to bring Anne back into his life.

His client arrived around two to pick up his Chevelle, and then Mike headed to Callie's Confections down Main Street, hoping maybe she'd be willing to help, or at the very least explain what the fuck was going on.

Being left in the dark was starting to piss him off. It was close enough to walk, and he was determined to get to the bottom of this.

The bell jingled as he entered, and the smell of cinnamon and buttercream filled his nose. Any other day he would be tempted, but today he couldn't care less about food. Eric stood behind the counter and turned, his eyes widening when he saw Mike.

"I wondered when you'd come by. Someone has been a very bad boy." Eric tilted his head. Mike wondered what the hell he was talking about, but he went on. "Normally I would approve of being a bad boy, but not this time, buster. Anne's too good for that."

Okay, now Mike was fuming. "I'm fully aware of how wonderful Anne is. What's pissing me off is not knowing what I did wrong. What happened last night?"

Eric jerked his head back in confusion. "How do you not know?"

"Where's Callie?"

"Dance team practice. Don't act dumb, playboy, the witch you're seeing and her video have leveled Anne. Whoever she is, she needs to be drawn and quartered." Eric cringed slightly at his own words. "I've clearly been watching too many cable historical dramas, but who can help it with all those men in tights?"

Mike was still processing what Eric had said and trying to ignore the other images. "What the hell are you talking about? I'm not seeing anyone else."

"Yeah, well, after that bullshit on her site and Facebook yesterday, what else would she think?"

"I don't do Facebook, so how about you tell me exactly what's happened."

"You really have no idea? And who doesn't do Face-book?"

Mike shot Eric a don't-mess-with-me look and the guy finally got to talking. When he pulled out his iPhone and showed Mike the video—and the fucking pictures—he was speechless. And also boiling with anger at whoever had done this, although he had a pretty good idea, and he wanted to strangle her. To add insult to injury he had to relive seeing that douchebag's slimy hands on Anne. He'd seen it the first time, but watching it again—after he considered her his—that was torturous.

The worst part was Anne *was* his, or at least she had been, and she was hurting. He couldn't blame her for being upset. He lifted his ball cap from his head and set it back down. "Goddamn, I can't believe this."

"One commenter even said they saw you and Katie having a lovers' quarrel in the parking lot, and then kiss and make up."

"Damn it, that's not how it is at all. Did Anne read that comment?"

"What do you think?"

"Shit. I can't believe this." Mike pulled the hat off again and ran his fingers through his hair. He didn't even know what to do with himself he was so angry, but—more important—he was worried about Anne. He had to talk to her.

"Sooo . . . you're not seeing someone else?" Eric asked.

"Hell no!" His reply was short and showed just how pissed he was getting, but after a moment's pause he continued. "But *technically* the events aren't a complete lie. I did go to the bar, obviously, but not to see her, and we didn't have a fucking lovers' quarrel. Katie did try to kiss me, but I didn't kiss her back—I pushed her away—and that was it. I left and went straight to Anne. Obviously Katie is pissed and wants to come between Anne and me, and it's fucking working. I can't believe she'd do something this crazy."

And he couldn't believe it might cost him everything.

"Well, if you say that's the truth then I believe you, but Anne is heartbroken," Eric said quietly.

"And that kills me. Shit, I never meant to hurt her, she's . . . God, she's fucking perfect. I want her . . . all the time." Mike squeezed his fists together and turned to face the window. He couldn't even wrap his head around what he'd just learned.

"Dude. You have to pull your shit together," Eric said. "You can fix this, it's just going to take some time. Anne has trouble believing that she's as wonderful as everyone knows she is. She's hard as hell on herself, and it took nothing for her to believe this thing with Katie and you was exactly what it appeared to be. You being with a younger, hot woman made complete sense to her. You just have to convince her of what you just told me."

Mike turned and stared at Eric. "Then that's exactly what I'm gonna do."

That afternoon Anne lay in bed staring at the painting on her wall. It was a self-inflicted torture at this point, remembering the conversation's they'd shared in her bed as they looked at the wildflower scene together. It was now nearing the twenty-four-hour mark since she'd seen the hurt and anger in Mike's face on her porch.

She had never planned on feeling such pain again.

Early parts of her life had been horrible; some memories were so bad she'd locked them deep inside her never to surface again. She wished she could lock this hurt away, because it was consuming her. Why did it take losing something to realize how critical it had become to your happiness? And when had that happened with Mike?

She had tried so hard to take it slow, protect her heart, and tell herself that it was no big deal. Instead she now knew it was a huge deal, and realizing it wasn't reciprocated was worse. Her heart had been breaking for the past twenty-four hours. She'd barely been functional.

After Callie and Eric had left last night Anne had called her mother and asked if Claire could spend the night. She'd needed the space for two reasons: One, because she wanted to cry freely, and two, because she was trying to make Claire happy after the mess with missing her gymnastics class. An impromptu overnight to Grandma Ree's had done the trick.

Evading questions from her mother had been stressful, but finally Anne just said she couldn't talk about it quite yet. She knew her mom was concerned, but she would give her space. Marie Harris knew how to give Anne what she needed; she always had, whether it was a new life, or a shoulder to cry on. Right now what she needed was to wallow in her misery for a while.

The clock on her nightstand read 3:05 p.m., and Anne's stomach growled. She hadn't really eaten all day. If a breakup was good for one thing, it was making your pants fit a little better. Eric always said it was nature's way of preparing your body to go back on the market. Except Anne was never going back. Relationships were not worth this; the gnawing in her stomach matched the emptiness of her heart. And she hadn't knowingly allowed him access in the first place.

A knock at her front door had her sitting up. She ran to the bathroom and looked at herself. She was a hot mess, her hair in a ratty ponytail, mascara masking her eyes.

Another knock, this one louder. "Shit."

Her phone vibrated on her dresser. She'd ignored it all day but she finally went and picked it up. It was full of missed calls and texts. The most recent stopped her heart.

> MIKE: I'll stand here all night, Perfect. Open
>   the door.

Oh God. She scanned through the texts quickly and saw one from Eric that had words like *Mike*, *bakery*, and *told*. She groaned and ran back to the bathroom and grabbed her toothbrush. She rearranged her ponytail, wiped at her eyes, and gave herself a quick splash of body spray. She remembered she wasn't wearing a bra under her tank so she grabbed her robe and threw it around her shoulders. There was no hiding that she was a wreck; she'd have to own it.

She ran down the stairs, her pulse rapid and beating out of control when she saw Mike's Camaro out the front window in her driveway. Why did everything make her want him? She opened the door and met his eyes—they were shadowed and his mouth was grim, one hand resting on the door frame. After just a beat his expression softened.

"Anne, I'm so sorry."

His words were quiet, and damn her stupid emotions for instantly succumbing to the apology in his voice and the sadness in his eyes. The sight of him made her heart pound in fury but also break from the pain of it all. Of course he was sorry, he'd been caught. He could never be as regretful as she was.

"There's nothing to be sorry for." She swallowed hard, trying to keep her tears from making an unwanted appearance. She knew if she started she wouldn't be able to stop, and this conversation required her to be strong. It was bad enough that she looked like a woman who'd been sobbing in bed all day. She whispered, knowing her voice would break if she didn't. "We never made anything official. It's okay."

"Damn it, Anne! It's not okay, and it's not what you think." He reached for her face and she pulled back. He flinched, the shock in his eyes obvious, and even when she was this angry, it killed her to see the pain of rejection in his face. He put his hands in his pockets. Despite the heat of June, a light breeze caught the tips of his hair and he looked away from her as he continued to speak. "I didn't think *official* had to be said. Couldn't you tell how much I wanted you? Wanted to be with you, only you?" He stared at her once more. "Did it *feel* like I was seeing anyone else? Because I'm not. I wasn't."

No, it hadn't felt like it. That had been a complete shock. But it also hadn't felt like her husband was banging his cousin's wife on the side. Clearly she was oblivious to such things; certain realizations were obviously better served up as a slap in the face. They really got their point across that way.

"If you're not seeing someone . . . then . . . I don't understand . . ." Her voice hiccuped. Rather than try to continue she looked down, willing herself to regroup. She couldn't cry in front of him.

He took a deep breath, and the hesitation made her knees threaten to give out.

"So, yes, I stopped in to Smokey's before I came here that night. I had to give Aiden the bartender the keys to his truck. I'd worked on it earlier that evening. Katie was at the bar and before I could get Aiden his keys she came up to me, she wanted to talk, but I only wanted to get to you. I left her at the bar, hopefully to sober up, but she followed me when I left to walk back to my car. Yes, she did try to kiss me. She was really drunk. That's not an excuse for her or for what happened, but you must know I wanted nothing to do with her. I just wanted to get here, to you. I should've told you, but I just wanted to forget it. I didn't want anything to mess up what we have, and when I got here I did forget about it. You're all I think about when I'm with you."

He stepped into the house without her permission and moved close, his front brushing hers. She didn't stop him, just like she hadn't stopped him at gymnastics, or that night at Smokey's, or even that day against the Chevelle in his shop. When his body was close, hers responded like there was no other option but to lean into his touch. Except now when she thought about that first day she'd gone to his shop she remembered Katie coming in like she owned the place. He'd never explained that, and Anne had chosen to let it go. At the time he had every right to be seeing someone, and that blond big-boobed sorority girl had made perfect sense.

He lifted his palm once again, and this time she let it settle on her jaw. His thumb ran across her bottom lip, and sparks traveled through her body. She closed her eyes. Apparently the power of Mike's touch was more potent than anger, stronger than confusion, and as instinctual as self-preservation.

"I knew from the beginning this was a bad idea. We're so different," she whispered.

"We're not supposed to be the same, Anne. I'm a man and you're a woman." She could hear the smile in his voice and feel his warm breath on her cheek.

"But I'm a mother, divorced, and let's face it, I'm older than you."

He scoffed and tugged at her hair from behind, forcing her to meet his gaze. "Will you get over that? How old are you exactly? Or have you noticed that I care so little that I never asked you?"

"Almost thirty three."

He grinned. "Ooh you are—umph." He held on to his stomach where she'd shoved. "Anne, I was kidding. So you're thirty-two, who gives a shit? I sure as hell don't. And we're not that far away. I'm twenty-nine almost thirty."

"It's more than that, though. I can't have this kind of drama in my life. It's exhausting, painful, and embarrassing. That video of me . . . people saw it, clients, friends, and people here in town. I've had my website and blog for years now. It's my job, and never has anything like this happened. I wasn't completely honest with you about it. The site is important to me. Very important."

He nodded his head. "I understand, I do. But it's still

just a *blog*, Anne. Don't let stuff out on the Internet come between us."

She sucked in a breath—the words were so familiar—and instantly she shut down. Any warmth that had begun to radiate inside was threatened with that sentence. It was so much more than a blog to her. Why didn't anyone understand that?

"Mike, right now I just need to be alone. Please."

"So you are. You're going to let something that happened on the Internet break us apart, is that what you're saying?"

Anne couldn't think. The sad truth was, she was a complete wreck inside. A fearful woman sure she was one thread from unraveling altogether. She was a sham, and the thing he liked about her, the perfection: Well, it wasn't real. Sooner or later she would be a disappointment to him and herself.

"Honestly Mike, I don't know what to think right now. The past few days, shit, the past couple of weeks have been a whirlwind. I just need to reevaluate. I thought I knew who I was and what my goals are in life. And now . . . I just. I just need some time."

He was quiet for a long moment, his eyes never leaving hers.

"Okay, fine." Mike turned toward the door. "But you remember, Anne, this is your decision, you chose this. I don't want time away from you, I don't need to plan out my goals or reevaluate. I know what I feel and I want you, *only* you. But you have to want me back."

And then he was gone.

Twenty-Three

Thursday morning Anne lost herself in the final details of Jessica Monser's sweet sixteen party. If she had known the extent of the work this party would require, she'd have charged them double, but she was enjoying the creative process and hopefully she'd get some great exposure. She dreaded for the weekend to pass and leave her with empty hours to think about Mike. He hadn't texted or called since he'd left the previous evening, and she didn't blame him.

She pushed thoughts of him away and set down the last of the boxes full of decorations in the barn, which was breathtaking. It was now clean, the old cement slab floor power-washed and wooden walls swept clear of dirt and cobwebs that had accumulated over years of being a barn. The tables were arranged and waiting to be covered with black tablecloths and mismatched vintage lanterns that Anne had painted pink. The walls were lined with strings of white Christmas lights just waiting to be plugged in and sparkle. Soon the space would be completely transformed into a pink-and-black fairy tale.

With the owner's consent the Monsers had paid for a new cement pad to be poured on the backside of the barn, which would be the location of the Mustang's big reveal. It overlooked a serene wheat field that would be gorgeous the evening of the party as the sun set. Even the old farmhouse at the front of the property was beautiful, the outside also freshly power-washed and the walkways neatly trimmed. She almost wished she could move in it was so gorgeous, but Anne's favorite part was the flower garden off the side of the main house, which was now in full bloom. It reminded her of her mother's painting in the bedroom, which of course now reminded her of Mike. He was the only man who'd ever shared that space with her, and now every morning she was reminded of his presence and subsequent absence.

Anne took a deep breath and got back to work. Claire's laughter caught her attention from the corner of the barn where she sat watching a cartoon on Anne's phone. Thank goodness for electronic devices and a roaming cellular connection. Anne turned a circle and took in the full space. She'd made sketch after sketch of how this would all go down, and she was excited. It was going to be beautiful.

Jessica had desperately wanted a "white" party, which at one time had been all the rage in the celebrity world, but Anne had quickly shown her how unrealistic it would be to ask teenage boys to wear white clothes and convinced her to do pink and black. She'd put together a design board of ideas, and both Jill and Jessica had swooned. So the girls' invitations had requested they wear pink and the boys wear black.

After a few hours of arranging chairs, unpacking centerpieces, and spray-painting a few odds and ends, Anne was exhausted. She decided to check in on the blog. She, Lindsey, and Callie had discussed how they would handle the damage control and decided not to make a huge deal of it. Last night Anne had called Jill Monser and once again assured her everything was well, then she'd done a quick post that said she was sorry someone had done what they'd done, and she was trying to deal with it quietly. She hoped everyone would respect her privacy at this time. She again thanked them all for their friendship over the past few years and made sure to close it so no one could comment. She'd been too chicken to even log onto Facebook or Twitter for the past forty-eight hours.

Lindsey, who was thankfully back in town and caught up on the details, was to follow up this morning with the first post of a series of projects. She was decorating a nursery for her pregnant sister on a budget of three hundred dollars using found and secondhand objects. Their readers had been looking forward to it and Anne was curious herself and looked forward to showing the readers that they were going to be business as usual.

Anne booted up her laptop and pulled up the blog. She couldn't believe what she saw; the post was titled "No Glass Houses" and the author listed was Callie. *Oh crap.*

Anne clicked on a video. It was a darkly lit bar; the video was shaky and girls giggled off camera. Finally it panned to a mechanical bull and on it sat Callie herself, her hair much shorter so it obviously wasn't recent. Anne gasped but couldn't help smiling. Callie was clearly drunk, her arms waving in the air to a suggestive country song as her friends videotaping the affair cheered her on, one yelling, "You're a sexy bitch!"

As the bull started up, Callie's legs wide and gripping, her skirt rode up her backside, revealing a hint of her butt and what appeared to be a thong. Guys circled the bull pit, enjoying the show of tipsy Callie eating up the attention and rocking her body on top of the bull. Every jerk of the machine lifted her tight skirt a little higher, and she leaned forward as she tried desperately to hold on,

"Oh my God," Anne whispered to herself. "Callie, why did you do this?"

Anne knew the next time the bull circled and Callie's backside came into view it was going to be indecent, but suddenly the video stopped. She let out a sigh of relief. The text below was short but sweet.

> *Who hasn't done something embarrassing? I think we all have, but having it made public sucks. We couldn't have our Anne suffer alone.*
>   *We love you Anne!*
>   *(And can I ride a bull or what?)*

There were already over twelve hundred comments. She skimmed through a few and realized almost all were readers sharing their own humiliating stories. Thirty minutes later Anne was wiping tears from her eyes. No one had ever done anything so sweet for her before, willingly making a fool of themselves. Another thing she could thank her site for . . . bringing these women into her life. How could Mike ever suggest it was just a blog? It was so much more.

* * *.

No one had answered at Katie's duplex, and Mike had knocked hard enough to bring out the neighbors to investigate. He parked along Main Street and walked down to the salon where he knew she worked. She'd better be in there, because he would tear up this entire town looking for her before the day was over if he had to. He'd already gone to Aiden about the Facebook page, which his friend had known nothing about, but agreed to get to the bottom of it and have it removed.

A sign hung over the door, with the word *Lovely* written in a loopy script. He'd never been inside the salon obviously, but his sister, Erin, talked about how great it was. He opened the glass door and a tall middle-aged redhead—definitely not her real color—sat behind a black lacquered counter. She looked like a hairdresser, whatever that meant, and her face was a little too taut for Mother Nature. Her smile made him squirm. "Need of a haircut, honey?"

He ignored her question and scanned the room. For a Thursday evening the place was strangely busy; about three stylists worked and one woman waited in a chair by the front window. Pop music played over the sound system. They even had a soda machine, some fancy coffee machine, and cookies—a lot more offerings than Bert's Barbershop at the end of the road. Shit, they were lucky Bert made it to work, as old as he was. The injustices of the male experience never ceased to amaze him.

Finally he spotted Katie in the back; she was getting her nails done by some other blonde, their heads tucked in tight in an engrossing conversation. He could only imagine what they were gossiping about, and his jaw ticked at the sight of her. As soon as a hair dryer quieted he spoke, loud enough to let her know he meant business. "Katie."

She jumped and turned to look over her shoulder, as did every other woman in the room. For a moment he felt awkward, but when he looked back into her wide eyes, he let that go. She'd hurt Anne, humiliated her, and in turn hurt him. She deserved this to be a spectacle. "Come outside."

Her mouth dropped open, and the woman behind the front counter stood up. "I'm sorry, but do you—"

He put up a hand to silence her, every eye on him. "This is between her and me." When Katie didn't move, he lowered his head and leveled her with the most serious look he could muster and then pointed at her. "Now."

She huffed and gave him her most irritated face, but she stood and made her way to the front, high heels clicking and wet fingers spread. She nodded to the front door. "Do you mind?"

He shook his head in irritation and pushed it open for her. When they were both standing on the sidewalk, he got right down to business. "What the hell is wrong with you? You didn't need to take your hate for me out on Anne."

Her mouth dropped open. "What the hell are you talking about?"

That really pissed him off. "Katie, don't fuck with me. You know full well what you did, and why."

Her eyes were furious and she glanced into the salon. Several women immediately made themselves busy. He knew they could hear. It was just glass, after all, and these old buildings on Main Street, while charming, were far from soundproof.

"You have the biggest ego, Mike Everett. I didn't do anything to Anne. I have no idea what you're talking about."

He wanted to hit something. She looked like she was being honest, but she had a motive. "So you're telling me that you didn't post on Anne's blog linking to the video and the pictures of us at Smokey's."

Her head jerked back in shock. "No! Why would I do that? I mean, you really hurt my feelings, but I wouldn't post my rejection on the Internet for the entire world to see. I haven't even been on Facebook in a couple of days and the only person—" Katie gasped and covered her mouth carefully with her hot-pink nails. "Oh no!"

"What?"

Without explanation she grabbed the front door and stomped back into the salon. "Where the hell is she?" Katie pointed to the front desk. The redhead had vanished, and the stylist at the first station pointed to the back.

Katie took off and Mike followed her into a storage room and then through an exit into the alley. The redheaded woman turned hard, her eyes frantic. She was sucking on a cigarette like it was her last.

"What the hell is wrong with you, Annette?" Katie yelled. "How could you do this?"

Annette dropped her cigarette onto the ground and stomped at it with a black high heel. She took her time speaking, so Mike stepped in. "Are you responsible for that video of Anne on the Internet?"

She put her hands on her hips and stared back at him. "Yes, got a problem with it?"

Katie's hands went to her face. "Oh my God!"

"Why would you do that?" Mike interjected. He was so confused he didn't know what to think. Why in the world would this stranger do something to mess up Anne's life, or his?

"It just started out as good fun. The girls and I saw Anne drunk at the bar. It was ironic, she's so squeaky clean, and I didn't mean her any harm. But then he started seeing her and I knew it hurt you. So my motherly instincts kicked in. Sheila and I talked about it and then next thing I know we were on Smokey's Facebook page." She dropped her arms and sighed before she turned to Mike. "It was stupid, I'll give you that, but maybe you should think before you drag a woman's emotions through the wringer."

Mike was speechless. Who called their mother by her first name, and what kind of mother harassed strangers on Facebook? He turned to Katie, who looked like she wanted to crawl under the Dumpster. "This is your mom?"

Katie closed her eyes and nodded her head, turning to her parent. "Do you realize what you've done? You made it seem like I posted that!"

Annette squirmed. "I shouldn't have done it, okay? I'm sorry."

Mike had never felt so annoyed and simultaneously outraged at a woman, but this one was testing every honorable bone in his body. If Anne hadn't been hurt in the process he might have been amused at their relationship, but right now amused was the last thing he was feeling. "Annette, you're going to fix this. I don't know how, but you better think of something and you better do it yesterday. Do you understand me? Anne is hurting over your *mistake*, and just so you know, I didn't intentionally put your daughter through the damn *wringer*."

Her eyes widened and then anger attempted to furrow at her overinjected brow. "You have a lot of ne—"

"*Mother*," Katie screamed, and that shut the woman up immediately. "You have to fix this, not only for Anne, but for me."

Annette pursed her lips and stepped up to Mike. She smelled like hairspray and cigarettes. He stared straight into her eyes, making sure she knew how furious he was as she spoke. "I'll tell Sheila to take it all down . . . for my daughter, not for you, young man."

"I don't care who you do it for, just do it. And make a retraction comment," he added.

"Fine." She poked him in the chest with a pointy fingernail. "But you ought to be careful next time, so you don't let a good thing slip through your fingers."

He narrowed his eyes at her. "I had a good thing, until you interfered."

With a huff she went back into the salon.

"Your mother is a real piece of work. What the hell?" He turned and quit talking. The sun was setting, the building casting a deep shadow that covered Katie, but it didn't hide the pitiful look of her standing there with her head hung and eyes downcast. A quiet sniff pulled at the gallant part of his brain. *Shit.* He'd come into her work like an angry bull looking for something to ram into, which wasn't like him. Another reason he knew his feelings for Anne were unprecedented.

He took a deep breath and blew it out as he stepped toward Katie. "I'm sorry this happened, Katie. I have a feeling you've experienced drama with her before?"

She gave a weak laugh. "You have no idea."

"Why the hell do you work together?"

She looked up at him. "It's a dysfunctional relationship at best, but she's all I have. There aren't many choices in Preston."

He nodded. Family loyalty was something he could understand. His parents weren't perfect, but he would give up anything to have them back. "What she did is really messed up, Katie."

"I know, and I'm sorry. I'll make sure she does what she said."

He hesitated to say anything, but she looked so emotionally fragile, and at one time he'd been into her. Not for anything serious, but she was a nice girl and she liked him enough to tell her mom about it. "Katie, I'm sorry if I hurt you. Truly."

Her lips quirked and she finally met his eyes. "No biggie."

"You're beautiful, and you're right, I flirted with you. I did like you, it's just . . . I really like Anne. It might even be more than like. I'm not sure where I am with her or what I'm feeling, but she's important to me, she's the most important thing in my life right now, and you deserve someone who wants you like that."

Silence surrounded them. Even he was shocked at what he'd just revealed. Finally Katie sighed and smiled. "Wow, she's pretty damn lucky I guess."

"Yeah, well, I'm not sure if she'd agree right now. This has kind of screwed things up between us."

"I am sorry. I mean, I'm a little hurt and jealous, but I never would have done that. I hope you're right and I do find someone to want me like that."

"You will, Katie, but I'm going to be honest with you and I don't think you're gonna like it."

Her eyes narrowed. "What?"

"I think you need to take it easy on the alcohol. I'd hate to see you in trouble . . . or do something you regret." He was prepared for her to lash out at that. Nobody liked to be told they had a problem, but instead she shocked him when she sucked in a breath and gave him a tight smile.

"Thanks, I'll remember that."

After they parted he cut down the alley and around the front, not wanting to go back through the salon. When he got to his car he called Derek and made plans to meet up at the bar so he could wallow. He wasn't sure what hurt more, that Anne had shunned him, or that he probably deserved it. It was because of him that she'd been publicly humiliated, and that made him feel like shit.

He just hoped that she could forgive him because he couldn't stop thinking that they were meant to be together.

Twenty-Four

The big sweet sixteen party day came and Anne sipped at her third cup of coffee. It wasn't even noon. Claire was with Lindsey since Anne's mother had come down with a cold and needed to rest, and it was just as well. Anne had leaned on her mother a lot this week—probably too much.

She'd arrived early at the event space to make sure everything was running smoothly and work on the last-minute details, one of which was to pot pink geraniums in eight galvanized metal buckets to sit around the cement patio in back. She was now done and admiring her work. They looked lovely and would complement the Mustang nicely once it was parked.

After sweeping the excess dirt into the grass, she gathered her trash and coffee mug and walked back into the main room. It looked beautiful, rustic and elegant, but she couldn't linger long; there was still plenty of work to be done before the party started that evening.

She let her eyes skim over the room and mentally processed what was finished and what still needed to be done. One corner of the barn had been blocked off and converted into a makeshift kitchen for the catering staff, she still needed to make a call to the rental company to find out why they were missing sixteen folding chairs, and she was short two extension cords.

She walked over to the table she was currently using as her work space and picked up her master checklist. She'd only looked at it a hundred times already today. Checking off the flower pots, she exhaled a sigh of relief as she saw the band pull up in their van. They'd set up now and then come back this evening to perform. The DJ would be there at four, the caterer arrived at three, and Callie was bringing the cake and pastries in about two hours. Thankfully, Callie and Eric both planned to stay the evening with her to help, which Anne greatly appreciated.

She was also thankful that they'd planned to have Mike drive the Mustang over during the mocktail hour. While everyone was mingling in the garden he could cut around the other side of the house and park the car behind the barn on its brand-new custom parking spot. She planned to be very busy doing anything during that time.

The last four days had been a blur, but despite her exhaustion at the end of each day, the nights had been restless and lonely. She'd tried desperately not to think about him, but obviously it wasn't possible to be too busy for your heart not to ache. Even when she wasn't actively thinking of Mike, sadness shadowed her.

High heels clicked against the old stone floor of the barn, and Anne turned to find Jill Monser striding in her direction. "These high heels are kind of a pain in that grass, but—oh, Anne. It's worth it, everything is gorgeous. You were so right about the chandeliers. You're brilliant."

Anne smiled. She'd taken around two dozen vintage light fixtures, some ornate, some with crystals, all different sizes, and spray-painted them a hot-pink lacquer to match the centerpieces. They now hung in various lengths from the barn rafters. It hadn't been easy to run the temporary cords and wiring, but with the Monsers' money she'd found someone willing to do the job.

"I'm so happy you like it," Anne said. "It is the showpiece, if I do say so myself."

"Absolutely. I can't wait for Jessica to see it, she'll be thrilled."

"Did her dress get altered in time?" Anne inquired, but she already knew the answer had to be yes or Jill wouldn't be in such a good mood.

"Yes, thank God, although as expensive as it all was, we almost should have just bought her new boobs." Jill laughed. Anne wasn't sure how to react, so she just smiled.

"Well, I hope Jessica is happy with this evening. I know it will be beautiful."

Jill grabbed Anne's hands and looked into her eyes. "I'm delighted with your work, Anne. I can't wait for everyone to get here this evening. It isn't every day a mother gets to watch her daughter's dreams come true, and I thank you for giving me that."

Anne felt tears threaten. Having her own daughter, she could certainly understand Jill's sentiments, even though she knew they were on completely different levels. "That means a lot, Jill, truly. Tonight will be wonderful for Jessica, I know it."

"Thank you." Jill gave her hands a squeeze and let go of her as she tilted her head to the side. "And I must say how refreshing it was to see Annette Williams post an apology to you this morning, as insincere as it might have been. Who would have suspected a grown woman to act in such a childish way? I've gone to her salon nearly fifteen years, but no longer, and I'll make sure everyone I know does the same."

Anne let out a deep breath as she watched Jill retreat, touching the centerpieces as she did. Anne had no idea who Annette Williams was, but obviously she must be the video poster. How odd; she thought it had been Katie. Now she wondered what the hell was going on.

She pulled her phone from her pocket and clicked onto the blog. The most recent post was from that morning, a review of a fellow blogger's new decorating book. Anne had quite a few blogger friends, all of whom had rallied around her during the week's drama, sending her encouraging emails and linking to her blog in a show of support.

She skimmed through the fifty or so comments that had been made so far and didn't see anything. She paused for a moment to think, and then clicked on the *My Perfect Little Life* Facebook page, and there it was. A woman named Annette Williams had posted late last night.

I've been instructed to apologize to Anne for my actions, but I don't regret my intentions. No mother likes to witness their child's heart take a beating, but I shouldn't have been cruel to Anne. It's not her fault she's dating a heartbreaker. I've removed the video.

There were already over a thousand likes and 345 comments. The photos of Mike with Katie had also been deleted. She clicked on Annette's profile picture and gasped. She was immediately reminded of that night at Smokey's when she'd had a shot at the bar with some women who claimed to be fans of hers. Annette had been there; Anne wouldn't forget that head of red hair or that laugh. Well, you just never knew about some people.

Anne closed her laptop. She couldn't indulge in the comments right now, and she wasn't even sure if she should. The only way to get over it was to move forward. Obviously it was Katie's mother, and Anne almost respected her for what she'd done. Still, that was a really lame apology.

Mike was a heartbreaker all right. He'd explained what happened and she actually believed him, and his story had now been proven true, but even so, it still hurt, *she* still hurt. She began thinking of the possibilities, of the future, but before she got too carried away Anne shook her head; she couldn't let her thoughts go there. She had a job to do, a party to make special, and if she'd learned anything it was that she could weather almost any storm.

"Have you seen Facebook?" Callie breezed through the barn doors with her arms full of pink boxes.

"You're really early, and yes, I just saw it. Strange, isn't it?"

Callie set her items on the dessert table, which was ready for her to fill with goodies. Various pink and black milk-glass stands and silver trays stood empty and waiting. "Very. Annette comes into the bakery at least once a week, I wouldn't have thought she'd do that to us. I always wondered if she held a grudge that I go to the city to get my hair done."

Anne smiled. "I doubt it. She was just acting as a woman scorned, or mother of a scorned woman. I guess I can sort of respect that."

"I didn't even think that it could have been Katie. She's sweet, comes in for coffee a lot, but according to Eric she's quite a party girl." Callie carefully arranged pink-frosted mini cupcakes on the trays.

"Yeah, that doesn't surprise me. She looked like something that would prance around the Playboy Mansion." And that was the shocker. Had Mike really been able to resist that kind of woman? How could she ever compete against Katie, who was pert, young, and overtly sexy?

Anne Edmond was none of those things. In fact, she specialized in the complete opposite of that. She was all crafty-mom and coordinating sweater sets. There was no way she was Mike's type for anything more than a novelty fling. It hadn't even worked for her husband and the father of her child; Scott had even gone as far as to call her "Boring Suzy-Homemaker" once. Sexy was a language she didn't speak.

"Anne, your internal thoughts are screaming at me right now and I want you to stop it. Why don't you see how hot you are? Mike wanted you bad, and I'm sure he still does. Are you going to let Annette get away with breaking you up?"

"He hasn't tried to talk to me since Wednesday."

"Anne, he's a dude. You tell them to take a hike, they're gonna do it. Boys are never thinking what we assume they are." Callie tweaked the cake stands once more before she went out to her car. "But don't throw this wisdom back in my face next time I'm crazy over some man. I'm only a genius when it comes to other people's problems."

Anne laughed as her best friend left the building to retrieve more goodies. Callie was right, Anne had told Mike to back off, and he'd listened. And hadn't she meant it? Yes and no. Deep down she'd wanted him to prove that he would be there no matter what. Accept and love her, all of her, and that meant also loving her sweater sets and her blog persona.

The next few hours were a crazy mix of final touches and vendors coming and going. This party was on par with a wedding, and that meant the details were incredibly important. Anne looked over the garden and the outdoor bar once more. One end for the teenagers and one for the adults. Giant oak barrels were filled with ice and colored bottles of soda and beer. Servers were ready with trays of wine and a specialty pink mocktail made with pomegranate juice and ginger ale served in martini glasses and garnished with a lime twist. Anne knew the teenage girls would love them.

Thirty minutes later when the first few cars began to arrive, Anne's stomach twisted into knots. Everything was ready, the band was playing some light jazz in the garden, but she had an overwhelming need to walk back through the barn and the main house to check each detail once more. Nothing was forgotten, down to the pink soap and lotion in the restroom. Conveniently the main house had a nice-sized restroom that could be easily accessed off the garden.

The barn was gorgeous with the chandeliers on and the lanterns being lit. She couldn't help but think of all

of the amazing parties and weddings she could plan in
this space. On one side of the room Callie's three-tiered
cake was beautiful. After the Mustang was revealed,
they would top it with the tiny fondant replica. It was a
sixteen-year-old girl's fantasy, and Anne was really proud
of what she'd accomplished with this job.

The sound of revelry growing louder in the garden
distracted Anne and made her smile. This party was going to be a hit. It was still empty in the main party room
except for the catering staff prepping the food table and
putting out water glasses, but everything was coming
together and then some.

The large barn doors in back were still open a crack,
and Anne glanced out to the empty patio. Mike was
set to arrive in the next ten minutes. The plan was to
have the partygoers come inside from the garden after
cocktails, which would happen in about half an hour, and
then Jessica would have a formal introduction on her
father's arm. At that point, the back doors would be
opened and she would be able to see the car sitting
outside against a beautiful backdrop of wheat field and
early-evening blue sky. It would be a magical surprise.

If Anne was going to make herself scarce, now was
the time to do it, but something was keeping her feet
planted in place, looking out back toward the empty
cement pad littered with pink geraniums.

As hard as she'd tried to avoid thinking about Mike
the past few days, she missed him, and her desire to get
even a peek of him almost won out. In the end she knew
it would only cause sadness, and she needed to keep herself together this evening.

"I just got a call from Mike," Dan Monser said, entering the barn from the front. Anne turned toward him, hoping her expression didn't give her panic away. "He's just now pulling into the drive and should be heading through the yard on the far side of the house as we planned."

"Great, the flower pots are moved and ready for him to back his trailer right up to the cement. Will you direct him, or shall I?" What was she doing asking that question? She had no intention of seeing him tonight.

"No, no. I'll do it. I have his final payment."

"Perfect. I'll leave it to the two of you." She wasn't sure if she was relieved or disappointed, which was ridiculous. "I've marked the ideal parking spot with pink duct tape on the concrete right out the center doors."

"Fantastic."

Anne gave him a wink and turned toward the kitchen. It was better if she didn't see Mike at all; she'd best get away before it was awkward.

"Oh, and Anne," Dan said. She turned to face him. "I want to thank you. I was furious when the country club canceled on us. I never dreamed I could still give Jessica the party she wanted, but you've done it. It's amazing, even better than it would have been because it's totally her. Thank you."

"You're so very welcome. I'm honored."

With a smile he turned and walked outside. Anne heard the telltale rumble of an old beefed-up engine. Her heart nearly stopped at the sound, and she forced her feet to move. She cut right through the festivities in the garden and directly in to the main house. The owners, Joanne and Pete, were enjoying a lavish evening away in the city, on the Monsers' dime of course.

Anne rushed into a second bathroom and stood in front of the mirror. Her little black dress was adorned with a pink belt to match the party. It was almost sad that she actually felt pretty tonight. Too bad there would be no one to appreciate it. Two deep breaths later she tried to collect herself.

She jumped when her hip vibrated and she pulled her cell phone out of the pocket in her dress. It was Lindsey, who was babysitting Claire at Anne's house.

"Lindsey, hey, is Claire okay?"

"Anne, I'm so sorry to bother you tonight, but Marie's apartment complex called. She was just taken into the emergency room. I'm not sure what's wrong, but they wanted you to know."

Anne's stomach dropped. She glanced in the mirror and her face had gone pale. "Oh God. They didn't say *anything*?"

"Just that she's stable, but—"

"Never mind, it doesn't matter, thank you."

She disconnected, ran from the bathroom out into the garden, and found Callie refilling the pink sodas in a bucket. Her grin was wide until she saw Anne.

"What's wrong?" Callie asked.

"It's my mother, she was taken to the hospital. I need to go, but I can't leave the party."

"Yes, you can. Eric and I've got this, Anne. Go."

She nodded. Without another thought she headed back to the barn to grab her purse, then hightailed to the far side of the house where she'd parked her car.

Mike was relieved to receive Dan's approval of the finished Mustang. He knew it looked amazing, but hearing a client's praises was the ultimate reward. He stood by while Dan inspected the new V8 in awe.

"As usual, your work is flawless, Mike. I'm really happy with this. I may have to borrow my daughter's car," Dan said with a chuckle.

"I don't know, Dan, I think the color would make me hesitate to be caught behind the wheel."

"Very true, but damn, she's gonna love it," Dan said as he lowered the hood carefully.

Mike was pleased with the money Dan had added onto the final balance, an extra three thousand just for the rush and inconvenience. He folded the check and put it in his back pocket as something caught his eye from the side of the house. There were no mistaking Anne's curves in that black dress as she ran to her car.

"Excuse me, Dan." Mike didn't wait for a response before he took off after her. She was in heels, and the pitted yard slowed her. "Anne."

She froze but didn't immediately turn. Her body looked amazing in this dress, her trim waist accentuated with a bow, and the bottom skirt hugged her hips and rear so nicely he wanted to groan. Her hair was pulled into a low knot at the nape of her neck. She was like a sexy June Cleaver, and he wanted to touch her so bad it hurt.

"Anne, look at me." He kept walking until they were only a car length away from each other. She turned slowly, barely meeting his gaze.

"Hi, Mike, I'm kind of in a hurry."

And that was when he noticed her eyes were red and her skin pale; even her hands shook. He immediately went to her and grabbed both of them, holding them in his own. "Anne, what's wrong?"

She didn't pull away; for that he was grateful. "My mother was taken to the hospital. I have to go to her."

Shit. "Let me take you."

Her eyes widened as she looked up into his eyes, finally. "Oh no, I'll drive myself."

"No way, Anne—"

She pulled her hands from his grip. "I want to go alone."

"It doesn't have to mean anything, we don't even have to talk, but I *am* driving you to the hospital."

The worry and fear he saw in her eyes made his chest ache. She swallowed, and her shoulders visibly relaxed. He prayed that was a sign she was about to give in, because he'd pick her up and carry her to the hospital if he had to in order to keep her from driving while she was this upset.

"Okay," she whispered with a slight nod and handed him her keys.

He grabbed her hand again and walked her around to the passenger side before he quickly went to the driver's side. Carefully he maneuvered through the packed makeshift parking lot and pulled her car out onto the highway. He had an overwhelming urge to ask for her hand once more, just to hold some part of her, like all the times they'd done before, but he didn't. He let her have her space. For now at least.

Twenty-Five

St. Agnes Hospital was only fifteen minutes away, but with the tension humming between them it felt like an eternity. Anne had already called and verified that her mother was in fact okay, but she was being monitored for a few different concerns, all of which were related to her diabetes and her kidneys.

Relaxing slightly, Anne remained quiet in the seat next to Mike. A few times she'd glanced at him from the corner of her eye. He looked amazing, his strong arm resting on the console between them in her car. If only she could go back in time, relive those few days of bliss they'd shared. But now things had been said that she couldn't take back. She had cast doubt and insecurity into the relationship, and she feared it couldn't be undone.

He dropped her off at the emergency room entrance, telling her to go on ahead, that he'd find her inside. Right away she discovered that Marie had already been moved to a regular room on the second floor, so Anne rushed to the elevator, hoping that was a good sign. They directed her to the end of the hall and she fought the urge to run, panic overtaking her. Right before she could burst into the room, she heard her mother laugh, the sound pulling her up short. Anne gently pushed the heavy door open, and a handsome young doctor looked her way.

"This must be your daughter, Marie. You were right, she is lovely." He said then put his hand out. She didn't miss the way his blue scrubs hugged his firm biceps. "Hello, I'm Dr. Nelson."

Anne took his hand with a small tilt of her lips and then instinctively swiped under her eyes, fearing some of her earlier tears had streaked her mascara. When she turned toward her mother she found her looking surprisingly alert, but frail tucked into the hospital blanket and linked to an IV and monitor. Anne still sighed with relief upon seeing her mother's smiling face. She went to her and grabbed her hand.

"Mom, you scared me to death. What's happened?"

"Sweetie, you shouldn't have rushed over here. I'm fine, just some swelling and my heart was beating a little too fast."

"But—"

"Now, Marie," Dr. Nelson interrupted. "You are fine, but this isn't anything to brush off. Your blood pressure was extremely high, your blood sugar too low, and the swelling in your ankles would have been enough to let me know you're not taking care of yourself."

"*Mom*," Anne said breathlessly. She turned to the doctor. "This is my fault, I've been too busy to check in properly, and I've asked her to help watch Claire too much this week. Oh, Mom, I'm so sorry."

"Anne, don't you dare apologize to me. It's my job to help you."

"Marie," Dr. Nelson said, "I'm sure Anne wants you healthy more than anything, and at your age, with your recent health concerns, you really need to consider this a serious warning. I've just spoken with Dr. Timmons, and she informed me that the two of you have already discussed the likelihood of dialysis."

Anne sighed. "Do you hear that, Mom? This is serious. No more coffee and I'm going to start doing the cooking on Monday night. No salt, no sugar, no carbs! You got it?"

"And no fun!" Marie said.

Anne felt tears start to roll down her face—from relief or fear she wasn't sure, no doubt a mixture of both. She wasn't ready to lose her mother so soon, and definitely not when it could possibly be avoided with some lifestyle changes.

"She'll do whatever she has to do, Dr. Nelson. We need her to be healthy," Anne said.

"I know she will, she loves you and her granddaughter too much. She just needed to get this out of her system. Right, Marie?" he asked, his words more a demand than a question.

Marie nodded. "I hear ya, but I only agree because you're rather handsome."

Anne rolled her eyes and followed the doctor into the hall to have a few words. He gave her a little reassurance that her mother still had many happy years ahead of her, even on dialysis, but it was going to take some work on Marie's part. Anne assured him that she would do what she could to help her mother.

"We're keeping her overnight just to make sure the edema goes down and her levels all come back to normal. Unchecked, this could have quickly become dangerous. The fact that she alerted someone shows me that she knows that, she's just struggling with it, which is normal. No one wants to accept that they're getting older and their body is failing them. I'm sending in a nutritionist tomorrow morning, and Dr. Timmons will come by before we release her."

"Thank you, Dr. Nelson, for everything. My mother needs to be pushed around a little bit," Anne said.

He hesitated a moment, a nervous grin on his face. "I hope this didn't pull you away from . . . a date . . . or anything?"

His words surprised her and she bit at her lip, completely unsure of what to say. "No, actually, I was working. I plan parties and tonight's was a rather fancy sweet sixteen."

"Ah, so that explains why you look so beautiful."

A blush traveled up Anne's cheeks. Dr. Nelson was certainly handsome . . . and a doctor. How much more perfect could it be, and yet he wasn't the one for her at all, despite how flattering his flirting was. "Well thank you, Dr. Nelson, that's very sweet."

"Please, call me Gabe."

"Oh well . . . ." She tucked her hands into the pockets of her dress. So they weren't only for cell phones, but awkward moments as well. "Thank you, *Gabe*, for taking care of my mother."

He grinned at her, but it cooled a little as a warm arm wrapped around her waist and pulled her into a firm chest. Her step faltered slightly in her high heels but she managed to regain her composure quickly, pasting an embarrassed smile back on her face.

"Everything okay here? I assume you were discussing your mother?" Mike said in a calm voice, but she knew better. There was a definite edge to his tone. Gabe Nelson's sheepish grin told her that he caught it, too.

"Of course, I'm sure Anne is eager to fill you in." He looked at Anne once again and added, "I'm sure I'll see you again when Marie checks out tomorrow."

She swore she felt Mike's grip on her waist tighten. She should have been annoyed with him, but instead she felt only comforted and safe. Her traitorous body loved the feel of his arm wrapped around her and the possession she felt in his grasp. He really had no right to stake the claim he just had, but she was helpless to correct him.

When the good doctor was back at the nurses' station, she turned around in his arms. "Mike! What was that for?"

"I was telling him to back the hell off. Trust me, that could have gotten a lot uglier."

"You had no right to do that. He's just my mother's doctor, it was nothing."

"Really, Anne? You're not that naive. You're also not for him."

For a moment she was speechless; then she reluctantly untangled herself from Mike's arms and sighed. He was right, she wasn't that naive, and she also wasn't immune to his touch or his possessive streak. She needed to remember why they were here and stop thinking about how happy she was that he was here with her. "It appears my mother is fine, but they're going to keep her overnight for monitoring."

Mike let out a deep breath. "Well, that's a relief."

"Yes, it is. But now I'm torn. She'll tell me to go back to the party, and while I'd love to, I hate to leave her here all alone."

"You should stay. I'll go back to the party, tell Eric and Callie what's going on and see if they need any help."

"No, no. You don't need to do that. They really can handle it. But you should go. I'll have one of them come get me."

"Anne, I'll come back and get you in a couple of hours. You just relax and keep your mom company. In the meantime I'm going back to make myself useful. I don't know how, but I'll do whatever your friends tell me to do."

She stared at him, and he grabbed her hand. She let him hold it. "Why would you do that?"

"Anne, you need to start catching on. I'll do anything for you."

She had no words to respond with. The air was yanked from her lungs and she nearly passed out when he pulled her into his body and placed a kiss on the top of her head. He looked into her eyes before he spoke. "And stay away from that doctor."

And then he headed for the elevator.

In a daze she walked back into Marie's room. Anne noticed she was frantically turning the TV volume back up. "Handsome doctor, isn't he?" Marie asked before Anne could make it all the way in.

"Gracious, Mom," Anne said with a sigh. She sat down in the chair next to the hospital bed. "But you're right, he's not bad to look at."

"But you felt nothing when he flirted, did you?"

"How did you know he flirted with me?"

"Well, you just told me, and I assumed he would after the way he looked at you when you walked in." Marie flipped the TV off and turned to Anne. "I don't think you see how beautiful you are, Anne, which is what makes you all the more wonderful for it."

"Thank you, Mom." Anne grabbed her mother's hand and squeezed. "But enough about me and men. I still need you, so please let's do this right from now on."

"Uh-uh. You're avoiding the conversation at hand. I especially enjoyed what came after the flirting with the hot doctor. Mike's voice carries wonderfully, all deep and sexy."

Anne groaned. "Oh my goodness, Mother."

Marie gave her a small smile. "That man is in love with you. Why are you making him suffer?"

"There are things you don't understand, Mom." Anne fiddled with her bracelets. She couldn't believe they were going to have this talk.

"You're right, there *are* lots of things I will never understand, like why my husband had to die so long before me, or why I can't eat chocolate cake every day. But all those unfair things aside, one thing is for sure. If I died tomorrow it would be with my heart full of happiness that I had the most wonderful daughter and granddaughter and I married the love of my life. Could you say the same?"

Anne sighed. She most definitely hadn't married the love of her life, and just the thought that her mother was that content with her own life brought tears to Anne's eyes. "That kind of talk is so morbid. You certainly can't be ready to die."

"Oh heavens no. My point is that at this very moment I have no regrets."

Anne nodded in understanding, but she wasn't satisfied. She wouldn't be happy until her mother was home and taking care of herself. And this conversation was over.

"Do you know it crushed your father that we couldn't have children? He was certain that marrying him was a horrible mistake because it killed him that he couldn't give me every single thing that I wanted."

Anne's eyes went wide. "Oh Mom, you never told me that. I thought it was you that couldn't have children."

A wistful expression crossed Marie's face. "That's what I told everyone. I was trying to protect your father's pride. We found out later that it was probably those damn chemicals he loaded onto the planes during the war that did it, and probably caused his cancer, too, but that's neither here nor there."

Anne was shocked. She had known her father was a Vietnam vet, but this news made her outraged, and incredibly sad. She missed Wade Harris so much. Every time she thought about how much he would love Claire, she felt a deep emptiness inside her heart.

"What I'm trying to get at, Anne, is that your father spent his whole life trying to make sure I was happy, and he was always so worried that he wasn't the best husband for me because he couldn't give me all that I wanted. Therefore I spent my whole life showing him that I loved him no matter what. He was the perfect husband for me whether he thought so or not. You can't overthink if you're the right person for someone; sometimes you just have to just trust fate. And each other. So

Wade's swimmers were no good, oh well, we ended up with you."

Anne laughed and swiped at her eyes. "You're right, I keep trying to convince myself that Mike will realize we're not good together. But he doesn't seem to agree."

"Anne, I think there's a good chance he never will have that realization. He sees you exactly the way I do, and you're perfect."

Tears ran down Anne's cheeks. "All I ever wanted was to make you proud of me."

"Oh, Anne. I'm always proud of you. Even when I see you dance on the Internet."

"Oh no!" Anne groaned and covered her face with her hands. "You weren't supposed to see that, Mom!"

Marie laughed. "You know how the girls love Facebook, but that's beside the point. Now look at me."

Anne dropped her hands, and almost felt relief knowing that her mother had seen the video and could laugh about it.

"Anne, what will make me even more proud is if you start living for yourself. The only thing I want you to worry about is you and Claire. And obviously that Mike, too, because I think he would make you girls very happy."

Anne smiled. "Maybe."

"Maybe my eye, I saw that young man with no shirt on."

"That's not the only thing that matters," Anne said with a laugh. Her blush was probably bright pink at this point.

"No, sweetie, it's not." Her mother patted Anne's hand as her eyes fluttered close. "But it's sure a nice bonus."

*   *   *

Almost two hours passed before Anne stood up from the chair, desperately needing to stretch her limbs. She had flipped through the channels on the TV while her mother slept peacefully, thinking of how lucky she was to have her mom in her life.

She peeked into the hall, used the restroom, and then checked in at the nurses' station where they all assured Anne that Marie's blood pressure was coming down slowly but surely and that they'd be in soon to check her legs. Anne pulled out her cell phone in the hallway. She had one message from Callie.

CALLIE: Everything here is great, don't worry
   about us. :)

Anne sighed. She had known she could count on Callie and Eric; otherwise she would have been a wreck here at the hospital. She wondered what they had put Mike to work doing. Or maybe he had just decided to take her car back and go home. No, surely not, not after telling her he would do anything for her. She called Lindsey to check on Claire and update her on Marie and then made her way back to her mother's room. A woman was adjusting the bed and prepping her for dinner. Anne smiled and lifted the lid off the tray. "Mmmm, grilled fish and green beans, looks yummy, Mom."

"I'm sure it will be." Marie sounded unconvinced but thanked the woman and opened up a package of crackers. "Shouldn't you be getting back to your party?"

"I don't mind being here with you."

"And I love you here, but this was a big night for you if I recall. You should go. Come back in the morning."

It was tempting. She hated not being there, seeing it all through, but she knew Callie and Eric could handle it. "I don't know . . ."

"Anne, I'm not dying, at least not this evening, unless this fish kills me, but I doubt it." Marie winked. "Now tell Mike to come back and get you. That way you can tell me all about it tomorrow."

After a little more arguing she sent Mike a message; twenty minutes later he texted her that he was at the outpatient door waiting. Anne kissed her mother and made her way down to the first floor. On the drive back they didn't really speak beyond her telling him a little more about Marie's condition. She wasn't sure where things stood. She'd told him she needed space, yet tonight had felt right, especially when he'd stormed into the hospital and played the caveman in front of the flirty doctor. Why did she want to smile when she thought about it?

Her thoughts settled back on the party, and panic began to set in when she realized all the things she'd failed to photograph for the blog. By the time they pulled into the farm it was nearly dark, and at this hour dinner would be over and they would be on to dancing. Mike drove her car through the grass and parked off to the side of the barn doors so she didn't have to walk far. She could hear the music when she got out.

"Anne, you're back. How's Marie?" Callie and Eric stood outside the side door each holding a little plate of leftover food. The lights from inside put off enough of a glow that she could see them when she walked up.

"She's fine. Thank you, guys, for taking care of things while I was gone."

"Of course," Eric said. "You had it planned and arranged down to the letter. It all pretty much happened on its own. And the food is amazing." He held out a bacon-wrapped water chestnut and she let him drop it into her mouth.

"Hmmm, that is delicious." Anne covered her mouth with her hand as she chewed. "I'm so relieved to have it all over with? Did Jessica love the car?"

"Oh Lord, you should have seen that girl." Eric's eyes went wide and Callie laughed. "She nearly peed herself. Mike here knows how to give the ladies what they want. I'm jealous."

Anne couldn't help laughing when Eric gave Mike a pouty face.

"Cool it, man," Mike said, but his tone was all teasing.

"I wish I could have seen her reaction. Hopefully the photographer caught it. I wished I would have told you where my camera was so you could get photos."

"No need, Mike barely left the photographer's side when he got back. Was insisting she shoot this and that, the cake, the car, even the centerpiece candles."

Anne turned and looked up at Mike. He had his hands shoved into his pockets and appeared to be a little embarrassed when he met her gaze.

"Thank you," she said quietly.

"You're welcome." His eyes flickered over her face, and he took a deep breath. "Well, I'm gonna run, I think. Unless you need anything else."

She wanted to protest, tell him to stay. But she didn't,

because he'd already done too much for her. "No, please. Go home and relax, you earned it. Thanks for everything tonight."

Eric and Callie had been quiet as church mice, which Anne knew would normally be impossible for the two of them except for the fact that they hadn't wanted to miss a thing. When Mike walked back to the truck and trailer and shut the door, Anne let out a long breath.

"He is so damn whipped, Anne," Eric said. "And why didn't you go kiss him good night?"

"I don't know, things are . . . weird, and he's not whipped," she said. But the thought that Eric might be a little bit right made her feel giddy. Was it possible that this man really felt that strongly for her?

"It's true, Anne. You should have seen him with that photographer. He made sure the poor girl took a ridiculous amount of photos of every detail from the food to the chandeliers you painted. It was the cutest thing. He even took your notebook out and made sure every food on your catering order was present. He about made Eric and me nutty, but it was so sweet."

"He also looked really hot doing it. The teenage girls couldn't keep their eyes off him," Eric said as he popped the last of his crab cake into his mouth.

"I just don't know what to think."

"Come on, Anne!" Callie yelled. "That man's in love with you. You should forgive him. He deserves it, especially after tonight."

"There's really nothing to forgive, I know he didn't do anything wrong. I'm just being stupid. I don't know, I'm worried."

"It's scary to love someone." Eric said.

"Pssh, you're in love with someone new every other week." Callie interjected.

"That's not love, it's lust. I just call it love so I don't sound so promiscuous."

Anne laughed and walked into the barn, leaving a giggling Callie and Eric outside. She made her way through the room. The dance music was loud and the lights were low, but it was breathtakingly beautiful. The scent of a delicious meal lingered, but the tables were mostly empty as the catering crew cleared them of dishes. The DJ had lit up the full dance floor with some flashing colored lights, and everyone seemed to be having a great time. Many of the adults lingered outside on the back patio near the Mustang so Anne made her way out. Jill Monser caught sight of her instantly.

"Oh, Anne, I heard about your mother. How is she?"

"She's fine. Thank you so much for your concern." Anne had been a little worried about how Jill would handle her abrupt departure, but she seemed to be okay. "I hope tonight has been a success?"

"Tonight has been absolutely fabulous. I can't even believe how perfect everything was, and Jessica has had a ball."

Anne smiled and felt the pleasure roll through her body at Jill's words. "I'm so happy to hear it."

Jill walked Anne around to several other women, who poured praises onto her for the evening's festivities. Even Dan Monser came by and told her how impressed he was once again.

At ten they opened the s'mores bar outside and the

teenagers all circled around a large fire pit; by eleven the kids were pilling into their cars and heading out to heaven knew where. While the party waned, Anne, Callie, and Eric had been able to get almost everything cleaned up.

"Well, the catering was fast. They were cleaned up and out by ten thirty," Callie said. "I managed to nab the box of fancy dark chocolate, though. Anne, excellent call on the s'mores made with imported chocolate and homemade graham crackers. Ridiculous."

"Uh-huh, so ridiculous that's your third one," Eric said.

"Shut your mouth, I'm already dreaming up s'mores cupcakes. Ooh, or s'mores brownies."

"S'mores cheesecake!" Eric said wide-eyed.

"Oh yes! We're so good."

"You're so *crazy*, both of you." Anne rolled up the last string of lights. She'd come back tomorrow when the man returned to take down the chandeliers. "But thank you guys, seriously. You're too good to me."

"You're welcome. But now, why don't I go to your house and relieve Lindsey so you can go to Mike's?"

"Callie . . ."

"You know you want to, Anne."

"A little, but it's late. I'm also physically and emotionally exhausted. I'll call him tomorrow."

After they all loaded Anne's car and said good-bye, she headed for home and told Lindsey how the evening had gone.

"I'm so glad Marie's okay. I wasn't sure what to do when they called," Lindsey said.

"Well, you absolutely did the right thing calling me. Everything worked out just fine." Anne hugged her friend and told her good night.

She took a hot shower and put on her favorite pajamas before she sank into her soft bed. It was nearly one in the morning, but for some reason she was now wide awake. She clicked her lamp on and stared at the painting above her dresser. Never before had she felt alone in this bed, but tonight someone was missing.

Twenty-Six

With the pressure of the Mustang reno behind him, Mike could finally get on to his next project. He didn't usually work this late, especially not on a Saturday, but he'd already tried and failed at sleep. He'd even talked on the phone with his sister, something he rarely did, but he'd needed to talk to someone. Erin had encouraged him not to give up on Anne, which had been well-meaning but unnecessary advice because there was no way he was letting her go. Now two cups of coffee down and he almost had both quarter panels on the '71 Skylark welded and ready for sanding.

He lifted himself off the floor, removed his mask, and stretched his back. The ridiculous thing was that he couldn't stop wishing that he'd just stayed with Anne at the party. Helped her or, shit, just stood there and watched her. But he'd gone because he'd done all he could. He didn't want to push her. Yet.

Surprisingly, he'd enjoyed helping at the Monser party. He certainly wouldn't be making a habit of attending fancy events, but knowing that he was helping Anne made it feel special. He'd noticed details in a way he never would have before he began reading her blog, and because he was a guy for God's sake. He'd loved it because she did. It was important to her and she was important to him. He'd wanted to do everything in his power to make sure her party was the success she'd planned and make sure she'd have the most beautiful photos for her blog.

He'd even sneaked the photographer an extra hundred bucks to get Anne some photos within the week for her to post. The poor girl had assured him that she would do it for free, but he wanted to be sure it happened swiftly and he felt bad for dogging her steps most of the night.

The only thing about tonight that had him on edge was the way he'd felt when he'd seen that damn doctor flirt with Anne. He'd instantly seen red; never in his life had he felt such jealousy. There was no doubt that he hadn't really earned the right to claim her publicly, especially after the past few days, but there had been no reasonable thoughts going through his head. He'd acted completely on instinct. Anne was his; every bone in his body knew it. He wished she would see it, too.

Now here he was alone, wondering what it would take to break down her damn walls. She'd made it clear that they weren't a good idea, and he wondered exactly what was going on in her head. Did she think he was just some playboy who couldn't give her what she wanted? God, he wanted so badly to give her whatever she wanted. That was part of the reason that doctor had really pissed him off. He could never compete with a guy who saved lives and probably made serious bank while doing it.

With a groan he pulled a beer from the fridge and headed through his office toward the bedroom. He'd drink it in bed and hope it made him tired. How pathetic.

He was halfway down the hall when his phone vibrated in his pocket. He pulled it out and looked at the time: one thirty-four. His heart sped up when he saw Anne's name on the screen.

ANNE: If I asked you to come over now, would you?

Holy shit, his heart nearly stopped beating. He set his beer down.

MIKE: You know I would.
MIKE: Don't even bother asking, I'm on my way.

With a wide grin he set his phone down, showered in record time, and was out the door. He drove to Anne's in five minutes and right before he went to knock she opened the door. Just the sight of her standing there, her pajamas wrinkled and her hair up in a bun, made him incredibly happy. She looked wonderful. Perfect.

"Hi," she said quietly. She looked a little unsure, but she'd made the move, so he wasn't going to take any chances. He pushed through the door, closed it quietly behind him, and then filled his arms with warm, soft Anne.

"Hi," he said against her hair as he breathed in the lilac scent of her shampoo.

"Callie and Eric told me in detail how much you did for me tonight. I know I said thank you, but . . . it didn't seem like enough."

"Is that why you asked me to come here, so you could thank me?" He pulled back and looked into her eyes.

"Well, no. I mean—not entirely."

He breathed a deep sigh of relief. "What did I tell you at the hospital, Anne? I meant it when I said I'd do anything to make you happy."

Her eyes widened, and he was afraid she was going to cry. "Thank you. But I need to say something else."

"Okay." His heart sped up and he caressed her face in his palms, their bodies close. "Say it."

"I'm afraid." She blinked and stared into his eyes. "I love that you call me Perfect, and . . . well I'm just scared that you'll figure out that I'm not. I try to live this ideal life, be a good mother. I even tried to be a good wife and it was a failure. And my blog, it's more than just a silly little blog for my business. It's very important to me, I know I said that before, but . . . it's really *part of me*."

He bit back a laugh, his thumb brushing her bottom lip. He wasn't letting her off this easy; she needed a little goading. "So you like to write about things, okay."

"No, you don't understand." Her hands left his side and latched onto to his forearms. "I may not truly be *perfect*, but helping others try to be the best they can be . . . well, it makes me happy. It seems to have struck a chord because I have a lot of readers. I get at least fifty fan emails a week and usually around five thousand hits before noon. I make money from my blog, enough to pay my mortgage."

He forced a serious face and wrapped his hands

around her waist. He felt a little guilty making her struggle through this explanation when he knew the reality all too well, almost. The fact that she made such a good living blogging did surprise him. She was just so damn sweet when she spoke about it. "Soooo, what you're telling me is that you're kind of a big deal."

She gave him a shy look, and he kept a tight hold on her so she couldn't turn away. She started to lower her eyes. "Uh, uh, uh, Anne. Is that what you're saying?"

"Not exactly, it's more about the community, the teaching, and the sharing."

He leveled her with a hard stare.

"Okay, yes. My *blog* is kind of a big deal. Happy?"

He grinned, loving the way she wrapped her hands around his neck. He wondered if it was even a conscious decision. He hoped it was instinct.

"The truth is, I'm incredibly proud of the site, it's done well. Callie, Lindsey, and I do a good job and I have to admit that I devote a good chunk of time to maintaining it. I've even been invited to speak at a conference this fall. I can't give it up, Mike."

He chuckled. "Anne, who in the world would want you to give it up?"

"Well . . . Scott did. We didn't have the best marriage, obviously. We began to grow apart after Claire was born. I don't know why, it was my fault just as much as it was his. But then I started my site and I just spent so much time on it. He was jealous, made me feel guilty and said I only cared about my online image and not being a true wife to him. He may have been right a little."

"Anne, the guy's an ass if he blames a website for the end of your relationship."

"He used it as an excuse, but my insecurity about it has remained. Not to mention the fact that I am a mother, and I'm older than you, and although you make me feel sexy I don't know why you would—"

He cut her off with a hard kiss on the lips. The taste of her after days without was so delicious. He pulled back and looked into her eyes. "Anne, listen to me. I don't call you Perfect because I see you that way all the time. I don't care if you can plan a fancy party, or get a million blog hits a day. I don't care if you make a complete fool of yourself or a bad decision, as long as you make the decision to be mine. I call you Perfect because you're perfect for me."

Anne scrunched her nose and bit her bottom lip. Damn, he loved that. "You sure? Because sometimes I skip showers or feed Claire corn dogs twice in one day."

"You're gonna have to do a lot worse than that, babe." Mike's body warmed as Anne melted into him. He took the opportunity to maneuver her over to the couch. He sat and pulled her down to straddle his lap.

Without a second thought he kissed her, the slickness of her lips making him instantly hard. "God I've missed you, Anne."

He ran his lips across her jaw and down her neck as one hand came up and cupped her right breast, which was free under her pajama top. "Every night I've gone to bed missing the feel of you, and the taste of you."

She whimpered as he shoved the fabric over her head and instantly pressed his lips to the hard peak of her nipple. He sucked at and fondled her breasts, her moving slowly on top of him until the movements of her center against his dick nearly made him come from the fric-

tion. Sensing what she was doing to him, Anne moved off his lap and lay down on the couch, pulling him on top of her.

"I need you inside me, Mike."

"Here? Shouldn't we—"

She silenced him with a deep kiss and pushed her hands between them, her fingers reaching the fly of his jeans.

"Uncle Mike, what are you doing here?" A tiny voice came from the stairs. Mike froze, leaning down to conceal Anne. A small squeak came from below him, and Anne tucked her head into his shoulder next to the back of the couch.

"Don't. Get. Up," he heard Anne whisper beneath him. And he wouldn't, because although the lights were off, the living room wasn't in darkness. Anne's pale breasts would be completely visible. He almost laughed at the absurdity of the situation.

"Uhhh, hi, Claire. What are you doing up this late?"

"I'm thirsty, why were you kissing my Mommy like that?"

He cleared his throat. "Well . . . I was kissing your mommy like that because I love her." Anne didn't move a muscle below the length of his body. He hadn't really given much thought to his answer; it had just come out. But he knew it was true. Absolutely 100 percent true.

Claire stared at him for a moment, then finally appeared satisfied with his answer and spoke again, moonlight catching the whites in her eyes "Okay. Will you come tuck me in and sing 'Twinkle Twinkle'?"

"Of course I will. Now run and get into bed, and I'll be right up with a drink."

Claire grinned and ran up the stairs. Mike adjusted his arms and looked down into Anne's face. She looked so beautiful there, the moonlight from the window highlighting her messy hair sprawled across the couch cushion, and her lips glistening from their kiss.

"Why did you say that?" she asked in a whisper.

"Why do you think, Anne? I'm in love with you. I love Claire, and I love us."

A tear instantly ran down her face and into the upholstery. "Are you sure?" she asked, her voice full of emotion.

"Yes, I'm absolutely sure, and I have another confession, Perfect."

Her eyes widened. "What?"

"Since they day I met you"—he leaned down and spoke against her jaw—"I've probably accounted for at least five of those blog hits before noon. I happen to be a huge fan of yours."

She shoved at his chest and he lifted up, laughing at her shocked expression. "Oh my gosh, why didn't you tell me? Really that long?"

He could see her mind racing, and he couldn't help but be amused. He shrugged. "Since the day of your party. I liked seeing that side of you. I love how everyone adores you, how funny you are, and creative. I just kept waiting for you to tell me how famous you are."

"How embarrassing. Now I'm trying to think of all the silly things I must have said." She bit at her bottom lip for a moment, then met his eyes as she spoke. "I know this sounds ridiculous, but as public as it is, in some ways it's still very personal. I know people in town read it,

but we don't usually discuss it. I guess I feel free to really be myself."

"I think you're pretty good at being yourself in real life. In fact, the real-life Anne seems just as smart, funny, and witty as online Anne. I should know, I'm in love with her, remember?"

She smiled and cupped his jaw with her hands. Her skin was warm and held her familiar scent. He'd missed it so much. "Thank you," she said quietly. "Although I can't imagine what would have made you want to read it. It's not very guy-friendly."

"You, Perfect. You made me want to read it. I'll admit the content is not my thing. I don't bake, I don't make crafty shit, and I certainly don't need to know how to make party decorations out of toilet paper rolls. But if I did, your blog would be the one I read. And I also just love hearing you talk about all that stuff. I want you to talk about the blog with me from now on."

"Really?"

"As long as this blog is what makes you happy, then it makes me happy."

A shiver ran down her spine. She nodded and leaned in to kiss him once more. "Thank you."

"Uncllleee Miiiikkkeee," Claire's voice called from upstairs.

He leaned his head against hers with a groan and then stood up and adjusted himself. "Is this what I have to look forward to?"

Anne laughed. "You have no idea, mister. Just you wait. You head up, I'll bring a drink."

He began to walk toward the stairs, and Anne quickly grabbed her shirt and stood up. "Mike, wait."

He turned back to her and in two strides she had her hands on his face and her lips on his mouth. She kissed him hard, her tongue tangling with his until she felt his whole body respond. "Anne, not if I'm gon—"

She silenced him with a finger on his lips. "I love you, too, Mike."

Epilogue

The past three months with Mike had been the happiest of Anne's life. She would have been content for him never to leave her side, but after that first interruption with Claire, he insisted that he only stay the night when she was away with her father—which, while frustrating, made Anne love him even more. The bonus was that the nights apart made the ones together even sweeter, and waking up in his arms—as she had on this Saturday morning—was still her favorite treat.

After coffee and breakfast they'd met Bailey and her family, Scott, Claire, and Scott's girlfriend Dana at a gymnastics tournament where Claire and Bailey had both earned trophies . . . along with every other girl in their division. They were only six, after all. Now they were all having ice cream at the Carey Darey. The pleasure of Scott's discomfort around Mike never got old, and Anne wasn't sure if Dana's constant staring at him made Anne smug or annoyed. A little of both, but she didn't need to worry, Mike was definitely hers and continued to show her his devotion constantly.

"Well, I'm ready for a nap," Erin said. She turned to her husband. "You're on daddy duty for the rest of the day, champ."

Mike looked at Anne and raised an eyebrow. His sister and her husband had the oddest relationship, but Anne liked them both and Erin had welcomed Anne and Claire like family. They all stood up and said their good-byes, then Mike, Anne, and Claire made their way to the Camaro. Scott had asked Anne if he could cut his weekend a little short because he had a business trip, and she'd been gracious enough to say yes.

"Mind a little drive through the country?" Mike asked when they got into the car. He slipped his hand into hers on the center console just like he did nearly every time they drove together. She wondered if she would ever get tired of his touch.

"No, that would be fun." It was a beautiful September day, the air warm and the breeze light.

He drove through town, pulled out onto the two lane highway, and cruised for a while. Eventually he pulled into the farm lot where the Monser party had taken place. She glanced over at him, and he shrugged.

"What are you doing?"

"I have no idea," he said in a teasing voice. "Get out of the car."

"Get out, Mommy," Claire said from the back. Since it was a two-door, Claire had to wait. She shoved violently on Anne's seat with her little hands. "Hurry!"

"Hold on, Claire, goodness." Anne popped the seat forward, and Claire scrambled out of the backseat.

Mike came around to her side of the car and took her hand. "Come on, babe, no need to worry."

"I'm not worried, I'm just confused."

He laughed. The three of them walked through the gravel lot and into the garden behind the house. Claire ran ahead and found a swing hanging from a high branch; the tree had to have been nearly a hundred years old. It was truly the most beautiful setting.

"Michael Everett, what are we doing here? Did you tell Joanne and Pete we were coming?"

"Yes, I have in fact spoken with Joanne and Pete. Did you know that last week they moved into the same complex your mom lives in?"

Anne turned to him. "No, Mom didn't tell me that. That's too bad, they loved it here."

"They did, yes, but it was just too much to care for at their age." He stopped them in the middle of the garden and turned her body toward his. The autumn mums had just begun to bloom, and a few bees buzzed around their heads. Anne looked up into Mike's face. Every time she did so she couldn't get over how handsome he was, and how lucky she was to have him. "Joanne and Pete felt a lot better about leaving once I assured them that we would love it just as much as they did."

Anne cocked her head to the side, then her mouth dropped open. "What? What are you saying, Mike? Did you buy this place?" It surprised her how much she loved the idea.

"I did, I bought it for us, you and me, and Claire. Please say you're happy."

Anne knew her smile told him exactly what he wanted to hear when his eyes lit up, and his grin matched her own. "Are you serious?" She was almost embarrassed

about how shrill her words came out, but Mike's laugh made her forget that.

"I'm serious, babe. You can plan all the parties you want here, and I've already had Derek come out and look at the house. He's going to design a complete renovation for us, however you want it. I told him you're the boss."

"Oh I'm sure he loved that," she teased.

"Who cares what he loves. The only thing that matters is that I love *you*."

"Oh gosh, Mike." She was breathless, and so happy she could explode. "I love you so much."

He smiled and gave Anne a quick kiss before he called Claire over. "Claire, it's time for you to do your job." He pulled a camera out of his pocket and handed it to Claire.

"Is Mommy happy?" Claire asked. Anne's daughter appeared to be completely unfazed by the proceedings.

Anne gasped. "Did you plan this with my daughter?"

"I have no idea what you're talking about." He knelt down on one knee and pulled a box from his other pocket. "Now let's make this official. You ready, Claire?"

Anne's heart pounded as she stared in disbelief into Mike's smiling face. She glanced over at Claire, who was holding the camera up to her face, ready to shoot. "What's that for?"

Mike ignored Anne's question and grabbed her hand before sliding a ring on her finger. "Joanne assured me next spring this garden will be full of blooming lilac bushes. So Anne, I've decided this would be the most perfect place for me to marry you. What do you say?"

"Oh my gosh." Her chest constricted and tears rolled

down her cheeks. She heard the snap of the camera and Claire's small giggles.

"Say yes, Mommy!"

"Yes. Of course. Yes, yes, yes, but why is Claire taking pictures?"

"Why do you think?" He looked incredulous and squeezed her fingers. "You've got to blog this as soon as we get home."

Anne's Breaking the Silence
Triple-Chocolate Brownies

½ teaspoon baking powder
½ teaspoon salt
1 cup flour
½ cup cocoa powder
3 eggs
1½ cups sugar
1 cup (2 sticks) salted butter
1 cup 60% dark chocolate chips
1½ teaspoons vanilla extract
½ cup mini semisweet chocolate chips
½ cup chopped pecans

Preheat the oven to 350°F.

Mix the baking powder, salt, flour, and cocoa powder and set aside. In a mixing bowl, lightly beat the eggs; add in the sugar.

In a double boiler (or microwave if you're careful not to overcook), heat the butter and 60% chocolate chips until they're melted but not hot. (Check their temp before the next step.) Stir in the vanilla, and then stir the chocolate-butter mixture into the egg-sugar mixture. Gently mix in the dry ingredients until fully blended, but be careful not to overmix.

Pour the batter into a lightly greased 9 x13 pan. Drop the pan on the counter a couple of times to remove any air bubbles. (We want these suckers dense and fudgy!) Sprinkle with mini chips and pecans and then bake for about 20 to 24 minutes or until a knife

comes out clean. Careful not to overbake. Let cool and then serve to the hot man in your life!

Don't miss the next book in this
romantic and crafty series

Win Me Over

Coming Fall 2015 from St. Martin's Paperbacks

And look for Nicole's e-original holiday romance

Blame It on the Mistletoe

Available Now!